BAD MEN

Julie Mae Cohen is the darker side of Julie Cohen, an award-winning author whose novels have sold over a million copies worldwide. A former teacher, she's currently an Associate Lecturer in Creative Writing at the University of Reading and a Vice President of the Romantic Novelists' Association. She grew up in Maine and now lives in the U.K. with her family and a terrier of dubious origin.

Julie Mae Cohen

BAD MEN

ZAFFRE

First published in the UK in 2023 by
ZAFFRE
An imprint of Bonnier Books UK
4th Floor, Victoria House, Bloomsbury Square, London, WC1B 4DA
Owned by Bonnier Books
Sveavägen 56, Stockholm, Sweden

A CIP catalogue record for this book is
available from the British Library.

Hardback ISBN: 9-781-80418-216-1
Trade paperback ISBN: 9-781-80418-217-8

Also available as an ebook and an audiobook

1 3 5 7 9 10 8 6 4 2

Typeset by IDSUK (Data Connection) Ltd
Printed and bound in Great Britain by Clays Ltd, Elcograf S.p.A.

Zaffre is an imprint of Bonnier Books UK
www.bonnierbooks.co.uk

For you. Yes, you. You know who you are.

'It's easier for people to imagine a dead woman than a woman prepared to kill.'

– Alia Trabucco Zerán, *When Women Kill*
(trans. Sophie Hughes)

Prologue
Newport, Rhode Island,
seventeen years ago

WE'RE PLAYING SUSIE'S FAVOURITE GAME, the one where I own a shop and she plays the part of all of her cuddly toys coming in, in turn, to buy various items from her bedroom, and I pretend that I don't want to sell any of them to her.

'Oh no, sir,' I say in mock affront. 'I couldn't *possibly* sell you a pair of *socks*, we have no socks in this shop to sell, you must be mistaken and want the sock shop next door, they have plenty of socks there.'

'But there are some socks right there,' her toy sheep says in a deep voice, nodding its toy head to the open drawer that is right near my head.

'Those socks aren't for sale,' I say. 'Not at any price.'

'But I need socks, and this is a shop.' Her lisp makes this sentence adorable.

'These are special socks, on no account to be sold ever, and always to stay in our collection of precious items to be preserved for future generations.'

Susie giggles. She tugs on one of her blonde plaits, which I did for her specially this morning because she asked to look like Heidi out of her new book. The left one is still pristine,

1

but the right one is already coming undone because she plays with it.

'Saffy,' she chides me, 'you have to sell Mr Sheep what he wants.'

She breaks the fourth wall like this all the time when we're pretending. She likes to boss me around and tell me I'm doing it wrong. Susie has her own rules for every game, and unlike most games that I see going on around me all the time – the games played by adults – I can't work out exactly what her rules are or predict how they'll change. This is one of the reasons I love playing with her so much. She's never boring.

'Well, the sheep should ask for something that I'm allowed to sell him, Susie-san.'

This is my pet name for my sister. Harold pays for us to have Japanese lessons, like he pays for everything else.

'If I can't have the special socks,' says Susie in her Mr Sheep voice, 'then give me the socks that you're wearing.'

'These socks?' I stretch out my feet in indignation and wiggle my toes. 'These are my socks. My feet will get cold without them.'

'I demand your socks, and I demand them now.'

'How much will you give me for them?'

Susie furrows her brow, thinking.

'Five hundred dollars,' she says at last.

'I couldn't possibly give them to you for less than five hundred dollars and fifty cents.'

'Five hundred dollars and eighteen cents.'

'Sold.' I peel off my socks, which are pink and have Hello Kitty on the top of them. They're much too young for my age and they're too small for my feet, which have grown two sizes this summer. I flatten them carefully so they are as crease-free as I can make them and roll them up into the shape of a chocolate-covered Swiss roll. 'Just don't do what you did last time, Mr Sheep, and tell me you haven't got the money.'

I reach out my hand, twiddling the fingers in the universal sign for 'give me cash'.

'Miss Susan?' Meg appears at the door. 'Your father wants you to come and swim with him.'

My hand freezes. Absolutely still, with fingers coiled like snakes in the air.

'OK,' says Susie. She gets up, leaving Mr Sheep on the carpet. Her carpet is light blue, like the sky, and it has a pattern of white clouds on it. I asked for it when they were decorating her room so every day she could feel as if she were walking on air. I wanted one of us to be light and happy.

'No,' I say.

'I like swimming,' says Susie.

She does. She's good at swimming. I taught her myself when Harold wasn't at home. The pool isn't a bad place. It isn't the pool's fault. Settings have no meaning in themselves; it's the things that happen there that have meaning.

'But you've had a cold,' I say. 'It's not a good idea. You might get sick again.'

Message delivered, Meg has melted away. Since our mother died, they often melt away, the servants. They do their best not to see what's in front of them.

'But Daddy—'

'I'll tell Harold you've got the sniffles. You can watch *The Little Mermaid*. I'll go swimming with him instead.'

3

'You always go swimming with Daddy.' She pokes out her bottom lip, so my only recourse is to tickle her until she laughs. She has a child's pot belly under her pink T-shirt and when she laughs she shows gaps where her front teeth should be. She's only six.

Only six.

But I was five when I started swimming with Harold.

'You and I will go swimming later,' I tell her. 'We'll play Marco Polo.'

'Promise.'

'As long as Mr Sheep pays up, it is a binding and sincere promise.'

I go to the television in the corner and find the DVD. Susan settles on her beanbag and I press play. I lean over and kiss my sister on her parting, that perfect parting I made in her hair this morning, the innocent white skin.

Then I go to my room down the silent carpeted corridor and I put on my bathing suit.

I always put on my bathing suit, even though I know it's useless. It's part of the game he plays, the game he has forced me into playing, the game where I know all the rules as well as every freckle on my wrist, the shape of every one of my fingernails.

Sometimes he swims, afterwards. Lately, the last few times, I've taken to swimming, too. A strong crawl, up and down the length of the pool, again and again and again. I show him that I know what I'm doing. I show him that I can control my breathing and my body, that I'm powerful in the water.

Is that why he's asked for Susan today, instead of me?

There's no one to be seen as I walk down the glossy main staircase, my hand smoothing the polished banister. No one

4

alive, anyway. His ancestors look down at me from their gilded frames on the walls. About half of them look like him; the other half don't, which is a mercy, as our mother used to say. The staid and stuffy portrait near the bottom of the stairs is wearing some sort of ruff and a wig. He was a judge and he has the same pale blue eyes as Harold. They're painted so that they follow you. The trick is that the irises don't touch the bottom lids; my art tutor showed me that once. I drew a dozen faces over and over whose eyes followed you, and put them up on the wall of the schoolroom. They didn't protect me.

I could have gone away to boarding school back in England if I'd asked, but I wanted to stay with my sister. I knew this day would happen.

My bare feet make a whispering sound on the Persian carpet and then slap on the flagstones. I've walked this route so many times that there should be a path carved in the floor. Harold hates staying in New York in the summer. He likes sea air, his yacht and his outdoor pool, his own little aquatic domain.

The pool is shielded from the house by a tall hedge. When I round it, Harold is already in the water. He's in the corner in the deep end, the end closest to me, his arms propped up on the sides of the pool by the diving board, his legs kicking free in the water.

Harold Lyon is a handsome man. I've heard this since I was a young girl, when my mother married him, though I can't see it myself. He has sandy hair which hasn't started to recede like it has on some of his ancestors in the portraits, and pale eyes with lashes so blond that they're almost white. He does plenty of exercise, which keeps his body fit and strong. His chest is covered with freckles and a mat of sandy hair in the middle of it which I know is crisp and springy, not like the hair on his head.

My mother loved him. This is alien to me, but I try to think about it objectively, so it doesn't hurt so much.

He turns to look when he hears footsteps, and frowns when he sees that it's me.

'I asked Meg to send your sister,' he says.

'You're not having Susie.'

I stand about half a metre from the pool, near the corner where he is, my toes curling on the concrete. It's cold outside today; by rights it's not a swimming day at all. My skin is all gooseflesh. Underneath my bikini top, my nipples are hard and sticking out like miniature breasts. That's all I've got; although I'm tall for my age and my feet are big, I haven't started to develop any of what the magazines call 'curves'. I haven't even started to menstruate yet, although the books that I've been given tell me that soon, I'll be on the uncertain and frightening path to adulthood.

Maybe that's why he doesn't want me anymore. Maybe it's not the swimming or anything that I've done at all, or at least nothing that I've done on purpose. Maybe it's just nature. The course that our lives are supposed to run.

It's September, and the leaves have started to turn yellow on the trees. Harold owns all of the trees, as far as the eye can see from all of the windows of the house.

'What do you mean?' he says to me. 'I just want to swim.'

He's got a smirk on his face as he says it. He's the one I've learned this particular game from: how to say one thing and mean totally another. How to tell lies and make everyone else pretend to believe them too.

'You're not going to do it to her,' I tell him. 'You can keep doing it to me. I'll even pretend to like it if that's what you want. But you can't touch her.'

'I don't know what you're talking about.'

'She calls you Daddy. At least I never did that.'

'Well, I'm her father.'

'You're not her real father.'

Harold frowns. 'Seraphina, stop being difficult. Go and get your sister.'

'No.'

He turns around all the way now and his face is ugly with anger and thwarted desire.

I have to stop my teeth from chattering. I have to remind myself that I shouldn't feel any shame. I'm doing this for my sister. No one can see me. No one can hear anything. If they could, this would have stopped a long time ago.

Or maybe it wouldn't have. Harold is a powerful man, and we're just little girls.

Harold frowns harder than ever. He half-rises from the pool. It used to be that he coaxed and flattered me. It used to be that he promised me anything. I have a room full of toys I've never played with and cupboards full of chocolate I didn't want to taste.

'Stop being so pathetic,' he says. 'Stop trying to be a woman. It's grotesque. You're all hide and bone. Why would anyone want you? You're an ugly girl and you're going to be an ugly woman.'

I hear his voice saying other things, the things he said to me before. The way his voice echoes against the tiles of the pool when you're in the water with him. *My girl, my pretty girl, my secret girl.*

I imagine him saying these things to my baby sister who hasn't learned the game yet. Susie, who thinks she can break the fourth wall and shape what will happen. Who's so innocent and happy, and doesn't know how to lock the most important parts of herself away.

I jump. Crouch on all fours and launch myself, over the concrete, to land on him. I want him to shut up. I want him to stop. My fingers are outstretched to claw his face. They miss his eyes and my nails graze his cheek instead, but I've taken him by surprise and his head snaps back. I hear his teeth clack together as the side of his head strikes the diving board.

A wet smack of hair and skull.

His body, which is stronger than mine, has always been stronger and bigger, goes limp and my weight bears him down into the water. I'm on top of him and his head is under water.

He's not unconscious. I know this somehow. Maybe I've spent so long reading him that I know every mood and every breath. But he's surprised, and I'm on top of him. I can get my legs on his shoulders and close my thighs around his head and push down. I can hold onto the side of the pool and use all the strength I've found from doing the front crawl, up and down and up. Trying to show him that I am powerful and I am growing.

Harold struggles. He claws at my thighs in a version of what he used to do to me. He even snags his fingers in my bikini bottom. The back of his head pushes against the place on me that he always touched with so much authority and ownership, as if he'd gained the rights to it when he married my mother.

The air bubbles from his lungs and mouth like a fart.

I giggle to the cold air. With him pushing against me, helpless, I see all at once what adulthood might mean to me. What
I'll become with my first blood, with the swelling of my body
into a womanly shape. I'll be able to change the rules. I'll have
the power to make things right.

This . . . is going to be *wonderful*.

Harold stops struggling long before I would've expected. I
keep him there for a while anyway, limp between my legs. I
gaze at the evergreen yew hedge, remembering how I used to
make magic potions in a jar out of pool water and the red yew
berries, squishing them with a stick until the brown seeds
floated free and the water was the colour of blood.

They're poison berries, my mother told me. *Don't drink that
water after you've put them in it*. Mum didn't know that her
husband and his swimming pool would be much more dangerous
than any berries. She died too early and I found her in her
bed, still beautiful but choked with pills, and my stepfather
told me it was her fault.

Clinging onto the side of the pool, I keep him under the
water until the power leaves me and I begin to shiver from
the cold, even though my blood is singing. Then I unclench
my legs, which have started to cramp. Harold floats free. They
said he had handsome shoulders, a full head of handsome
hair. His hair and shoulders are lax in the water. His hands
bob like limp jellyfish. He looks like a discarded and forgotten
doll.

I grab him by the waistband of his shorts and haul him to
the side of the pool. I try to pull him up the ladder, but he's
heavy when he's not in the water, so I leave him there, floating
face down. He always loved the water. It all seems perfect.

I watch him for a minute. My breathing is steady and I'm smiling, because I'm picturing Susie in her room watching *The Little Mermaid* and singing along to 'Part of Your World' and hoping one day her prince will find her and she'll be happy ever after.

Now she'll be safe.

I just have to keep myself safe, too. So I push my happiness down and lock it away. I close my eyes and I heave in a breath as hard as I can, and another one, and another, with my hair dripping water onto the concrete.

I scream.

Then I run for the house as fast as I can, because I've just gone for a swim and found my stepfather drowned in the pool, and now, at last, I'm the one who's choosing what's going to happen.

I'm twelve years old. I've got so much to look forward to.

1

London, now

MY NAME IS SAFFY HUNTLEY-OLIVER, and I kill bad men.

Of course, that's a secret. To the outside world, I'm something entirely different. I'm a former model, and apparently a 'socialite', though that makes me sound more sociable than I am. I have a degree in Art History from Durham, as is practically compulsory for women in my social class. I got a second-class degree, which was quite hard work – not because the degree was difficult, but because I was savvy enough not to want a first class. No one trusts a clever woman. I sit on the board of three charities – one for feeding hungry children, one for protecting abused women, and one for the rehabilitation of mistreated donkeys (I was sort of sweet-talked into that one). I'm a vegetarian and the only run-ins I have ever had with the law were two speeding tickets I got at the age of twenty-two and twenty-four. Fortunately, the second one was caught on a speed camera, so no one was able to see what I had in the boot of my car.

Killing bad men is my private hobby, my passion project, the thing that makes me tick. It's my own humble attempt at smashing the patriarchy. I started at the age of twelve, sort of

11

by mistake, and I've got progressively better at it with more practice. As a hobby, it's not as Instagrammable as baking, but at least it's better for your thighs.

You might never have heard of me, but you've probably heard of some of my victims. There are a lot of bad men in the news. Murderers, rapists, paedophiles, stalkers, liars, wife beaters, embezzlers, cheaters, misogynists, mansplainers.

Just joking about the last one. I don't have *that* much spare time.

Obviously, I have to keep my hobby a secret, but I'm not ashamed of it. Why should I be ashamed of something that's fun and which makes the world a better place? Is Cher ashamed of her plastic surgery? Is Dolly Parton ashamed of her wigs?

No, what I'm ashamed of is something else. Something less illegal but more messy. Less explicable but more mundane.

I've got a crush.

* * *

'How does it feel to catch a killer?'

Jonathan Desrosiers sits on the theatre stage in a blue chair. He's slender, clean-shaven, wearing a pair of jeans and a white button-down shirt. His hair is dark and thick, and looks as if it'd be curly if he allowed it to grow a little. He's got high cheekbones and behind his glasses his eyes are green. I'm in the seventh row, not close enough to see his eye colour, but I know it because of the photograph on the back of his latest book, *Without Mercy*.

I've got it bad.

The cover of *Without Mercy* is projected onto the screen at the back of the stage. Jonathan's sitting in front of it along with

12

the festival interviewer, a pretty young woman who looks as if she's just come out of school. She's wearing a floral dress and glasses that are too big for her face, and an air of innocence that's out of step with her apparent obsession with Jonathan's work. In fact, I'd say that a good proportion of the audience at this book event are women between the ages of twenty and fifty. It seems to be the top demographic for true crime these days. Maybe because we're all so pissed off with the world.

'How does it feel to catch a killer?' Jonathan repeats the question, and I bite the inside of my lip. I first 'met' Jonathan Desrosiers via his podcast, *Stone Cold Killers*, and when I say 'met', I mean 'lay in my bed listening to his incredibly sexy voice discussing murder while I writhed on the sheets'. That was two months ago, and I've been bingeing episodes ever since.

'How I feel doesn't really matter,' Jonathan says. 'The important thing is that Timothy Bachelor was caught and brought to justice, while Efraín Santander was exonerated. And Lianne's family were able to finally get some peace.'

'Yes, of course. But how did you *feel?*'

'Well. Let's be clear about this. I wasn't there when Timothy Bachelor was arrested. I wasn't there when he confessed. Those moments weren't mine. They belonged to the very fine law enforcement officers who took a dangerous killer off the streets—'

'They never would have caught him if not for you,' interrupts the interviewer. 'They'd arrested completely the wrong man, and it looked as if they were happy with their choice. It was only your work that got them to look at Bachelor in the first place.'

A murmur of assent in the audience. They all love him as much as I do. I almost hate them for it.

'That credit belongs to my friend DCI Harrison, who actually gave me a chance, listened to the evidence I'd collected, and decided to present it to his team.'

'He was a friend of your father's, yes? From his days in the Met?'

'Right, and he's the real professional. It's one thing solving a crime from your armchair, but it doesn't do any good if you can't arrest anybody. The police did all of the dangerous stuff while I stayed safe and sound in my studio, making podcasts. And of course—' Jon leans forward in his chair, and the interviewer onstage leans forward too, and so do I, because his voice has dropped and I don't want to miss a single word – 'I never would have got anywhere if not for the very brave actions of Lianne Murray's family. They gave me so much of their time, many, many hours of conversation, going over and over the most terrible night of their lives in more detail than anyone could ever ask for. They opened their homes and their hearts to me, even though they didn't have to. They knew they could never get Lianne back, but they would do anything to bring her killer to justice.'

I remember the episode in his podcast when he visited the scene of Lianne Murray's murder with her sister and her mother. The way Jonathan was quiet, and respectful, and let the women talk about their murdered loved one. He really cared about them, and he really cared about Lianne, an innocent nineteen-year-old girl whose life had been cut short by a bad man.

'The Murrays' lives haven't been easy since,' he continues. 'Marcia has stage four cancer. Dorothy sits in Lianne's untouched bedroom every night and talks with her daughter. While Timothy Bachelor, the man who killed their loved one with a tyre iron, is sitting pretty in prison, studying law. They got justice, but they'll never get Lianne back.'

I know from the internet that Jonathan donated the royalties of his book to the Murray family, though he's not mentioning it now. Jonathan's a good guy.

'But you still haven't answered my question,' says the interviewer. 'A young woman was brutally murdered while she was out running. The police arrested the wrong person. And a relatively unknown true crime podcaster saw something was wrong, and worked and kept working, gathering evidence, conducting interviews, until he found the true killer and persuaded the police to investigate him. It's because of you that Timothy Bachelor was caught, convicted and put in prison. Because of you. And it's made you into the most popular true crime author in the country. You've solved half a dozen cold cases since. But it all started with Lianne Murray, and her killer Timothy Bachelor. How does it make you feel, to know that you've made the world a better place?'

Jonathan Desrosiers takes an audible breath. He looks out over the audience, and for a moment it's as if he's looking straight at me. But I'm wearing a hat and a frankly terrible turtleneck, and I know he wouldn't notice me even if he did see me.

'It feels great,' he says.

We have so much in common. It's a pity he's married.

And also, incidentally, that he catches killers. But nobody's perfect, right?

2

H IS PUBLISHER PROVIDED STACKS AND stacks of
books, a box full of Sharpies, and a young and eager
man from PR to pass him each hardback opened
to the title page and affixed with a Post-it note with the name
of the person for the dedication. It was up to Jon to pass a few
friendly words with each person who came up to his table, to
listen to them talking about their favourite episode of his
podcast, *Stone Cold Killers*, or their suggestions for new cold
cases he could try to solve for the podcast, or about the book
they were writing or wanted to write, or the podcast they
wanted to make someday when their work wasn't so busy. There
was always one person who said they were a victim of crime
and they wanted Jon's help to set up a fundraising campaign
(he told them to email him via his website) and one person
who wanted to talk to him about the typo on page 216 of his
last book (he told them to email his publisher). There were
several people who, blessedly, only wanted him to sign a book
and didn't want him to speak with them at all.

And then there was Simon.

'Hi Jonathan,' he said, sidling up to the table. He was wearing
his usual beige jacket, his usual blue jumper with the blue shirt

underneath, his hair carefully combed over his bald spot. His fingernails were buffed, his skin shaved and pink, his glasses reflecting the banner behind him. 'You did a great job tonight.'

'Thanks, Simon,' he said, accepting the book from the PR. 'Wow, it seems like I just saw you.'

'Nottingham, last week. You were wearing the same shoes.'

'You're very detail-oriented, aren't you.'

'That's what they say at work! I guess that's something you and I have in common.'

He glanced at the book. 'Is this one for you, too? You've already got five at least.'

'Just put the date on it next to your signature. I like to have a record. Remember, it's spelled Simon Simons, but it's pronounced—'

'Simon Simmons. I remember.' He signed it like he signed every book.

> *To Simon Simons:*
> *Happy clue-hunting!*
> *Best wishes,*
> *Jonathan Desrosiers.*

He added the date, closed the book and gave it to him. Simon held it with both hands in front of him and gave no indication of intending to move along and let the next person in line have their book.

'I really liked what you said about how murder is about circumstances instead of destiny,' Simon said. 'I mean you're totally right, any one of us could be murderers given the right situation. I've often thought about it. My neighbour—'

'The one with the cats?'

'You remembered! That's so kind of you, Jonathan. Yes, the one with the cats. Do you know I counted again yesterday and I swear to God there are fifteen now. You should see how many cat food tins are in his recycling and he doesn't even wash them out properly. I think there's something wrong with him. I wish you could see him and give me your opinion.'

Jon caught the eye of the person standing behind Simon in line and gave them an apologetic look.

'The fact that he has a lot of cats is probably a good sign, actually,' Jon said. 'There's a certain empathy required to be a pet owner, that clashes with the personality required to be a stone-cold killer.'

'Ah, well, you would think so, but then there's Dennis Nilsen and Bleep, and Harold Shipman had—'

'Well, it's true that everyone's different,' said Jon.

'Do *you* have any pets, Jonathan?'

'It happens that I don't. Simon, this is fascinating, but I think there are people waiting?'

'Oh sure, sure, of course.' But he didn't make a move. 'Listen, Jonathan, I realise this is maybe a little cheeky, but I find this discussion fascinating too. Maybe you'd like to join me for a drink after you've finished here? There's the Red Lion on the corner. I think I owe you a drink after all this time.'

Oh, Simon. His hands were tight on the book, his cheeks pinker than usual, as if he'd been psyching himself up to ask this for a long time.

'I'm sorry,' Jon said. 'I can't tonight.'

'Oh,' said Simon. 'Do you have plans with Amy?'

'Yes,' Jon lied. 'Thanks for asking, though.' He reached for the next book, and smiled invitingly at the woman behind Simon, who stepped forward.

'Oh, OK,' said Simon. 'Well, thanks for the book. I guess I'll see you next month in Oxford. I almost didn't get a ticket because I had a concert that night but I managed to find a replacement to fill in for me.'

'You're very welcome,' he said, already glancing down at the name on the next Post-it.

* * *

The car dropped him off outside his house in Shepherd's Bush just after midnight, after a sojourn in a pub other than the Red Lion. Jon noticed with a little surprise that the lights in the living room were still on. He fumbled with his keys and let himself in.

'Babe?' he called, bending to take off his shoes. 'Sorry I'm late. I didn't expect you to still be up. I've been spending the evening watching the PR guy and the interviewer hook up with each other.' He hung up his jacket, on the second attempt. Maybe that last pint of beer had been one too many.

'I feel dried up and ancient,' he added. 'Think you can help me with that?'

Jon went into the living room, expecting to see the television on, an open bottle of wine on the coffee table, his wife in her pyjamas under a cosy blanket.

Amy stood, fully dressed, next to two suitcases.

'I was waiting for you to get home,' she said. 'I didn't want to have to leave you a note.'

He couldn't breathe for a minute, and then all the words rushed out of him at once. 'Amy? What are you doing? Where are you going? I thought we sorted this out.'

'*You* thought we sorted this out. So you never bothered to ask me what I thought.'

'Where are you going?'

'That is literally none of your business anymore. The house is still in my name, but I don't want to make you homeless, so I'll go elsewhere until you can find somewhere else to live.' She shouldered her handbag. Jon instinctively moved sideways, to block the door.

'But you've been – you've seemed happier lately,' he said.

'News flash. I haven't been happier. I've been just as miserable and lonely with you as I've been for months. Years.'

'Because I've been working?'

'Because you've been obsessed, Jon! You don't just go to work, you live and breathe it!'

He held up his hands. 'Hold on a minute, that's not fair.'

'It is fair! It's not like we need the money right now. You're doing well, I'm doing well, we could both take some time off and enjoy life. But you're always in that studio, bent over that computer, or off who knows where talking to people who are miserable, and they make you miserable too, and then I'm miserable. It's a house full of misery.'

'It's *not* fair, because I'm not doing this for money. I'm doing it to help people.'

'If you want to help people, Jon, volunteer for a charity. Run a marathon. Go build a school somewhere. Why don't you do something like that instead?'

'I – I can't.'

'No, you won't. Because your whole life is about murder.'

'Amy, you're being—'

'I'm not being anything. I'm fed up with it!' She gestured to the bookcases, stuffed with true crime and forensic titles. The notebooks scattered over the side tables. The twenty-odd copies of Jon's latest book shoved into a corner. 'You only think about dead people. It wasn't always this way, but it is now. Everything here is murder, murder, murder! And I need *life* in my life.'

She picked up her bags. They looked heavy. As if she were going away forever.

'Amy, please don't go. Let's talk about it.'

'The time for that passed long ago. Get out of my way.'

He didn't move. 'I don't just think about my job. I think about you. All the time, Ames. If you only knew—'

'You've got a funny way of showing it.' Her jaw was set.

'Please. We can make this work. I'll change. I'll do anything.'

'Jon, I don't think that you will ever change.'

Her voice was so sad as she said it that he stepped aside and let her walk past him.

'I love you,' he said to her back.

'I'm sorry,' she said. She opened the front door and walked out into the night.

3

THE NEXT MORNING, HE WOKE up alone and with his eyelids stuck together. He stumbled to the bathroom and splashed his face with cold water, noticing the empty space where Amy's toothbrush used to be, the cleared shelf that had used to hold her collection of serums and moisturisers. 'Why do you need so many bottles and tubes of gunk to put on your face?' he had used to tease her, every time a new bottle or tube or pot had appeared. 'To look beautiful,' she'd always responded, but this morning he knew why the bottles and tubes and pots really existed: to be witnesses of Amy's presence, to be evidence that she was in his life, settled into every nook and cranny of the house.

He went back to bed. His head pounded and his mouth was dry. The glass on the bedside table still had some whisky in it. Funny how 'a nightcap in bed' seemed so sexy when you were with another person, and so pathetic when you were drinking yourself into oblivion because your wife had left you.

'She left,' he croaked aloud to the ceiling. 'She's gone.'

He was supposed to be detail-oriented. He prided himself on it; he'd built a career on it. But he'd been oblivious to the fact that his wife – the only person he'd ever really loved – was planning to leave him.

He'd run after her last night, out onto the street in front of their house, pleading with her until she'd got into a waiting taxi and driven away. She must have called the taxi before he'd returned home. It was so deliberate, so final – like the clearing of her potions in the bathroom, the careful excision of her half of the clothes in their shared wardrobe, her favourite books from the shelves. Her wedding and engagement rings sat on the kitchen counter.

It wasn't spontaneous. It was surgical.

Jon fumbled for his phone on the bedside table next to the whisky glass. Maybe she'd called or texted. Maybe she'd changed her mind. Maybe there was a penitent message: *Baby, I'm sorry, I made a mistake. Can we talk?*

'Please let there be a message,' he whispered, though he didn't believe in God so he wasn't sure who he was praying to. Maybe to Amy.

There was no message. Just the record of all the calls he'd made to her last night, all the texts he'd sent. None of the calls were answered, and none of the messages were read.

It was a clear message in its own way. She didn't want to hear from him, and if he kept on trying, he would not only seem desperate, but he would deliberately be going against her wishes.

He called her again anyway. A recorded voice told him to leave a message. He didn't recall all the messages he must have left last night, especially after the first few glasses of whisky, but at the risk of being repetitive, he left one anyway: 'Amy, please. Let's talk.'

Then, because he had no pride left, he called her mother.

'Oh Jonny, I'm so sorry,' Monica said as soon as she picked up. 'I can't tell you anything. Are you OK? Do you have enough to eat?'

'I didn't know she was so unhappy,' Jon said down the phone to his mother-in-law, who had always liked him. 'Did you know?'

'Well …'

'You did?'

'It's been pretty obvious, Jonny.'

'What did she say?'

'She said that you've been working all hours, more than ever.'

'Yes, but I'd planned—' He stopped. Because had he really planned to spend more time with her? Or had that been an empty promise, like all of the other empty promises to put his marriage above his career? He hadn't booked any flights, or made any dinner reservations. Somehow he'd expected the romance to take care of itself, without any effort from him.

'Jonny,' Monica said, gently, 'you understand why that's such a problem for her. Her father lived with us for years, without really being there.'

'Tell her I'll move out as soon as I can find somewhere,' he said, and ended the call. Then he threw his phone against the wall, as if all of this was the phone's fault, and not his.

* * *

It was a choice of finishing off the bottle of whisky, or going for a run. He sniffed underneath his arms and made a face. His dad used to smell like this – whisky and sweat. When he was young, he used to find it comforting. Now he knew what it meant, and he hated it.

He pulled on joggers and a T-shirt from the dirty laundry basket. Movement might help him figure out what he was going to do. Then a bacon sandwich, then a couple of ibuprofen, then he'd sit down and figure out how to solve this. It was a puzzle, right? The puzzle of his marriage. He was good at solving puzzles.

He was good at solving puzzles, except for this one. This one only had one answer, and it was that she'd left and it was his fault.

In the kitchen, he avoided looking at the rings on the counter as he put a pod in the Nespresso machine. Amy had given him the machine as a present. 'If you're going to drink coffee at home,' she'd said, 'you should at least have decent stuff, not instant.'

Was this what it was going to be like? Was he going to be reminded every time he made coffee that his marriage was over?

Get a new coffee machine, he told himself. But he knew, with a writer's keen sense of the inevitability of things, he wouldn't get a new one. It hurt to look at the machine, and remember how delighted Amy had been to give it to him. It would keep on hurting. But he would keep on using the machine, because the pain meant it had all been real, and how fucked up was that?

He stood at the kitchen counter to drink the coffee. It was short, black, and bitter with self-loathing.

Then, head slightly better, he found his trainers under the kitchen stool where he'd kicked them last time, pulled them on, spent ten minutes searching for his door key, and then finally opened the front door to go for his run.

There was a black bin bag on his doorstep. It was full and had been tied with a knot at the top.

'What the fuck,' he said, glancing up and down the street, as if he would be able to tell what someone who'd just dumped their rubbish on his doorstep would look like. Of course he couldn't. There were a few people around, doing normal things like going to work or walking the dog, but none of them looked like fly-tippers. It could be one of the neighbours' rubbish. Though that seemed unlikely, as Bridie, who lived next door, had given both him and Amy incredibly detailed instructions about bin days and recycling and composting and the proper receptacles to use when they had moved in, and she periodically repeated those instructions, just in case they'd forgotten.

Had he committed some rubbish crime, and this was Bridie's passive-aggressive way of reminding him? But Jon didn't use black bags, and Bridie was waging a war against plastic, which she also told Jon in great detail about when their paths crossed. This bag wasn't even your standard flimsy plastic, but thick heavy-duty stuff that you'd use for garden waste. So . . .

His head throbbed, and he considered leaving the bag where it was and running around it, but then he'd just have to deal with it when he got back, all sweaty and thirsty, and by then some fun-loving passer-by or curious dog might have decided to split it open and scatter the contents all over his front step.

He sighed and hoisted the bag up by the knot so he could drop it into the council-and-Bridie-approved black bins in the front area. He grunted; it was ridiculously heavy. More heavy than normal old rubbish, as if someone was disposing of a load of bricks. The plastic bag strained with the weight. Jon hauled it down their front steps and into the bin by the front gate. It landed inside with a thump.

'Good morning, Jonathan,' said Bridie. He looked up; she was standing on her front steps, ostensibly checking the post.

'Did you see anyone leaving rubbish at my front door?' he asked her.

'No, I can't say that I did. I did hear you outside last night, though. Seemed like some sort of altercation. Is everything all right?' She squinted at him through her old-lady spectacles.

'Fine,' he said. 'Yes, all good.' He rubbed his forehead and caught a whiff of a strong chemical scent, like a perfume. It was familiar – not something Amy used – masculine, more of an aftershave. For some reason it brought up a strong memory of blue wool.

'Doors slamming, cars coming and going,' Bridie added.

'Well,' he said, 'we do live in a city, after all. I'll catch you later, Bridie.' He turned and began jogging down the street before suddenly realising that the bin bag could have been full of Amy's things, or even his things – stuff she'd packed by mistake and was returning.

He stopped at the corner and stood there behind a postbox until Bridie had gone back inside her house. Then he quickly went back to the bin.

The bag sat on top of other bags of household waste: food wrappers, coffee grounds, old socks, toothpaste tubes. The remnants of things that he and Amy had bought when they had still been together, and had discarded without a thought, and now were so much rubbish. Like their marriage.

He tugged at the knot. It was tight enough that he had to use his fingernails to open it, and it took him long enough that he felt ridiculous leaning into a bin. He was about to give it up for a bad deal when it suddenly came loose, and he opened the bag.

The first thing he saw inside was a bundle of dark, wet-looking material.

The second thing he saw inside was a human foot.

4

'IT'S THE BIN BAG KILLER, isn't it?'

As the past few hours had proved, Jon wasn't the best judge of human character, unless that character belonged to a ruthless killer. But he had no trouble interpreting the expression on DI Atherton's face. The man loathed him.

'The remains were in a bin bag,' said Atherton. 'But that doesn't necessarily mean a serial killer is involved. Not every murder is a high-profile type thing, though you wouldn't know it from listening to your podcast. Sometimes bodies are just found in bin bags because bin bags are cheap, don't leak, and are convenient for disposal.'

They were sitting on plastic chairs in the police station. Jon had been told that his statement would be taken there, so that his house could be examined for forensic evidence. He was acutely aware of the half-empty wardrobe, the cleared drawers, the two rings on the kitchen counter.

'You listen to my podcast?' Jon asked.

'No,' said Atherton. 'I think it's a puerile piece of sensationalism, if you want to know. Same with your books. Pure garbage.'

'That's a point. Another reason why killers could use bin bags for their victims is that they literally think of their victims as garbage.'

'I think that people like you love to grandstand on the fact that you've stumbled across some leads. You like to make the law enforcement professionals look bad.'

'I always give credit to the Met. As DCI Harrison knew.'

'DCI Harrison has retired. And meanwhile you're making murder look glamorous and exciting, when those of us on the ground know that it's anything but.'

'But this *is* the Bin Bag Killer, isn't it?'

Atherton sighed.

'It's the sixth body disposed of this way in London in the past eight months,' Jon insisted. 'When was the first one? Last October, wasn't it? And another in December, another in February, and another two in April. All of the victims are white men, and all of them were found dismembered in various bin bags. No one's found their heads yet. This absolutely fits the pattern.'

'You know a lot about it. Care to tell me how?'

'Just what's been in the press. As far as I know, the bags have all been found in alleys and on waste ground. None of them were found on people's doorsteps.'

'Now, isn't that odd?'

'Is it?'

'Let's go through it again, how you found the remains.'

'Do you mind if I record this conversation?' Jon asked for at least the sixth time.

'You may not.'

'Maybe we can talk later, for the record.'

'That's not happening.' Atherton leaned back in his chair. 'Let's go through it again.'

Jonathan did not want to go through it again.

He had interviewed plenty of witnesses to crimes, and victims of crimes, and the families of victims. He'd seen the trauma and despair. Let's be honest: he'd *exploited* the trauma and despair. Ordinary people, when touched by violence, could react in a thousand different ways. They could dissociate, or relive the moment. They could cry, or be stony-faced, or eerily flippant. But the common denominator was always pain.

He preferred being on the other side of the microphone, the one who asked the questions rather than answering them. It was much safer to ask and to analyse, rather than to feel and be afraid.

'Have you seen a dead body before, Desrosiers?'

He thought about how pale the flesh in the bag had been. Bluish. Every dark hair on the leg had stood out. The toenails had been carefully trimmed, which meant that the victim had taken a shower before he died, a shower or a bath, and stood in the bathroom with a pair of clippers, undignified but meticulous. It was such a normal thing to do, trim your toenails. Never imagining that your severed foot would be found in a rubbish bag by a stranger.

'No,' Jon said. 'Never before, not in real life. Only in photographs.'

'Stays with you, doesn't it?'

It was with him now. 'Do you know who the victim was?' Jon asked.

'I'm asking the questions. Tell me again what happened.'

Some people cried. Some people became manic, or distant. Some people couldn't say the words at all. Some people included lots and lots of detail, extraneous detail, even random detail, as if they wanted to bury the horror in trivia. Some people's words were stark. He remembered Deven Michaels, the young man who'd found Lianne Murray's body, who could only repeat the same thing, again and again: 'There was so much blood.'

'Can I have a glass of water?' Jon asked. Atherton grunted and got up.

Jon knew he was stalling, because despite being obsessed with crime, despite being steeped in every little detail of the disasters that happened to other people, he didn't want to talk about what had happened to him. Not waking up, desperate and lonely, mouth sour with booze and the knowledge that he'd destroyed his marriage. Not finding a bin bag full of body parts right on his own doorstep, as a twisted and incredibly apt metaphor for what his life had become. And certainly not rummaging in the bin: the sight of a human foot, pale and terrifying, the jumble of flesh, the scent of rotten food and blood and—

'Blue wool,' he said aloud.

'Pardon?' Atherton was back, with a plastic cup of water.

'Nothing. Just – something reminded me of something. There was a scent on the bag, that made me think of blue wool. Soft wool.'

'How can a scent be blue and woolly?'

'I don't know. It's . . .' Jon shrugged, and took a sip of water. Atherton sat heavily back in his chair.

'Listen, Desrosiers, I met your father. He was a legend. But you – I don't like you.'

'I gathered.'

'I think you're a vulture. I think you feast on other people's misfortune.'

'I've solved cases, DI Atherton. I've helped grieving families.' The line slipped out of his mouth. Did he even believe it anymore?

'And you've got rich off it too, haven't you?'

'OK,' Jon said. 'Since you want, let's go through it again. I woke up at about eight, and I didn't hear anything outside, but my bedroom is at the back of the house, so I wouldn't necessarily hear anything anyway. I haven't got CCTV or an alarm system installed, but my front door was locked.'

'And the night before? What happened then?'

'I was in Bloomsbury at a speaking event, and then we went to the Marquis Cornwallis in Marchmont Street. That's me, and my publicist Todd, and Rachel, who worked at the venue. I got back at about quarter to midnight in an Addison Lee. I don't remember the driver's name but it will be on my publisher's account. I had a conversation with my wife, Amy, until about midnight, maybe ten past. She took a minicab after that.'

'Where did she go?'

'I don't know.'

'Did she come back?'

'No.'

'Did a flit, did she?' Atherton smirked. Jon didn't answer. 'What did you do after she left?'

'I had a couple of drinks and went to bed.'

'Alone?'

'I just told you, my wife had left.'

'Do you have any evidence that you were home alone, doing nothing?'

'My neighbour Bridie heard my wife leave. The houses have thin walls, and she's probably not above peering through windows.'

'Is this the neighbour who saw you throw the bag into the bin?'

'Yes.'

'So you found the bag on your doorstep at what time?'

'I'd say it was about eight forty-five.'

'And why did you put it in the bin?'

'Because I thought someone was fly-tipping. And I didn't want it on my doorstep.'

'Why did you look in the bag after you'd put it in the bin?'

'Because it occurred to me a few minutes later that it might not be garbage, but something else.'

'Like a body?'

'No, like … oh, I don't know, some of my belongings. I'd had an argument with my wife the night before.'

'Oh, an argument is it now?'

Jon ground his teeth and said nothing.

'Have you found anything like this on your doorstep before?'

'A cut-up murder victim? No.'

'Have you found anything unusual at all?'

He thought about it. 'No, I don't think so. Occasionally I get some literature from the more off-the-wall side of the political spectrum.'

'Nothing strange from your fans? They're all just as obsessed with murder as you are.'

'I don't give out my address to fans.'

'Everyone's online these days. You'd be surprised how easy it is to find someone's home address.'

'I try to be careful with online security. But yeah ... it's possible.'

'Do you have any enemies that you know of?'

'Timothy Bachelor. But he's in jail.'

'Oh yes. Thanks to you.' Atherton's voice dripped with sarcasm. 'The great podcast detective. I bet the first thing you thought when you found the body was how great it would be for your listener numbers.'

'No, the first thing I thought about was calling the police. The victim is the important person here. My podcast can wait.'

'You are most definitely not discussing this in public, at all,' commanded Atherton. 'It's an ongoing case and I'm not having you fuck it up.'

'Though maybe the Bin Bag Killer *wants* me to talk about it,' said Jon. 'And that's why he dumped his victim at my house this time – he wants more recognition. Do you think—' He winced. 'Do you think he's one of my listeners?'

'Here's the thing, Jonathan. If you glamorise murder, sooner or later it's going to turn up on your doorstep.' Atherton closed his notebook.

'Speaking of which, can I go back home now?'

'We'll let you know when we're finished. I'd book a hotel for the next few nights. Or maybe find out where your wife is.' Atherton smirked. 'We'll want to speak with her too, by the way. And also: don't leave the country.'

'Wait. Do you think *I'm* a suspect? You think I've been leaving dead men in bin bags all around London since Christmas?'

'It's way too early in the investigation to rule anything out.'

'. . . Which means that up till this point, you haven't had any good leads at all.'

'Where were you on 22 October, by the way? And 15 December? 17 February? And 11 and 20 April?'

'I don't know offhand. I'd have to look in my diary.'

Atherton stood. 'Just don't leave town. We'll be in touch.'

But Jon couldn't go quite yet. 'DI Atherton? I'm aware that you don't like me. But will you do me a favour?'

'That depends.'

'When you identify the victim and find his family, can you please tell them that I'm sorry? Tell them—' He swallowed hard. 'Tell them I said that their loved one didn't deserve to end up that way. Tell them that I hope they can find some peace.'

Atherton snorted. He stood up and held open the door for Jon.

'Well,' he said. 'Aren't you a good guy.'

* * *

He didn't go to a hotel. Instead he walked quickly down the road, as far away as he could get from the interview room and its smells of bad coffee, plastic and farts. He'd always had a sensitive nose; as a child he'd recoiled at the scent of burning food, strong perfume, sweat. His father used to tease him about it: 'You'll never make it as a detective if you can't stand the scent of blood.'

But it wasn't the scent of blood that had kept Jon away from the Met.

He turned the corner and leaned against the wall of a Wetherspoons, breathing hard. When he closed his eyes, he saw the foot again.

Someone had done this six times. That added up to a dozen feet, all severed from their bodies. How did you do that? Kill a human being and then butcher them like meat?

Jon retched. The remains of his morning coffee spattered on the pavement. A passer-by made a detour around him, but otherwise didn't glance in his direction.

That was how murderers did it. You had to see your victim as something less than human. Garbage, no more than flesh. In London, no one looked anyone else in the face. Everyone averted their eyes on the Underground; they never talked to their neighbours if they could help it. This whole city was a collection of individuals, all little islands unto themselves, all so disconnected and lonely that other people became disposable and without souls. Passing shadows. Spare meat.

It was a wonder more people weren't murdered.

He pulled out his phone and rang Amy for the two-dozenth time that morning. Again, she didn't answer, so he tried her mother.

Monica answered on a sigh. 'Jonny, I'm sorry, but I told you that—'

'Is she with you?'

'She asked me not to—'

'I just need to know that she's safe, Monica. I need to know she's all right. Someone left a dead body on my doorstep last night. I need to know that Amy is safe.'

His voice broke on the last word.

'What? Oh my God. Yes, yes, she's fine. She's here. She's OK.'

'OK. Don't open the door to any strangers, all right? Or answer any phone calls where you don't recognise the number. And tell Amy not to go home for a while. If she was going to.'

'Are *you*—'

He hung up and immediately turned into the pub.

This early in the day, it was half-full. Several of his fellow patrons looked as if they'd been drinking since the morning. Jon ordered a pint and a Jameson chaser. 'You look like how I feel, mate,' said the barman, which Jon didn't take as a good sign. When he picked up his glass, he saw his hand was shaking.

He stood at the bar and drank the whisky first, but it did nothing to remove the remembered scent from his nose, the taste from his mouth. Gulping his pint didn't help either. But they made him feel that he was at least doing something, if only to live up to the cliché of a man who'd been left by his wife and then gone on a bender. He signalled the barman for another two drinks.

A group of lads came into the pub and approached the bar, boisterously elbowing each other out of the way and yelling out their drinks orders above the sound of their own banter. Jon stood at the bar beside them, waiting for his own drinks. As a boy he'd been intimidated by young men like this: loud and sporty, wearing tribal football colours in red and white, fuelled by lager and with an edge of violence to their laughter. They reminded him of his father.

A skinny lad with gelled hair and acne slapped his friend on the shoulder and Jon thought: *blue wool*.

Wait.

He caught the skinny one by the wrist. 'What's that scent you're wearing?'

The lad pulled his arm away from him, but Jon held on. 'What the hell is wrong with you?'

'Nothing,' said Jon. 'Sorry. I just need to know – what are you wearing? Is it some sort of cologne, or body spray?'

'Who's your boyfriend?' said one of the lad's friends, and he scowled.

'Listen,' Jon said, in a low voice. 'I have had the worst day of my entire life, and trust me when I say you do not want to know why I'm asking you this question. Just tell me: what's your cologne?'

'How the fuck should I know? My brother bought it for me from the States. It's called Axe or something.'

Axe. Blue wool. But not any wool: cashmere.

He let go of the lad, who stepped back quickly, as if Jon had frightened him. The group jeered, but he didn't hear them, as he abandoned his second round of drinks and headed for the door.

He knew who the Bin Bag Killer was.

5

THE SECOND BAD MAN WAS the first one I killed on purpose. Sure, I wanted to kill Harold – subconsciously, I'd probably wanted to maim him from the minute he married my mother, and to murder him as soon as he laid a finger on me. But I can't really say that I hatched a plan or anything. It was more spur of the moment, in self-defence. He was a paedophile, and there was a handy pool.

But the second one … that one, I thought about it before I did it.

Not for long, to be honest. I definitely thought more about my prom dress. *That*, I'd been imagining for years. When I killed Mr Scheeler, I'd only been thinking about it for two days.

It started late one night. I was in my sophomore year at an all-girls' boarding school in Massachusetts, and while I liked the academics and the sports, Susie was hundreds of miles away, at a boarding prep school in New York State. We only got to see each other during school vacations, which we spent in Harold's Upper West Side apartment, or Harold's beach house in the Hamptons, according to the seasons, along with a succession of paid guardians who were selected by the lawyers who administered our father's and mother's and stepfather's trust funds for us until we reached majority. This wasn't too unusual – a lot of the girls I was at school with hardly ever saw their parents, even if they were still alive. Anyway, going to boarding school and spending vacations with strangers was definitely better than living with Harold.

I missed Susie, though. Even though I knew she loved her school, especially the sports teams and dance lessons, and I knew that she was safe and happy there, I felt every empty, lonely mile stretching between us. Which was why I was up after lights out, under my blankets with a flashlight, writing Susie a letter on daisy stationery, which was her favourite, and pink ink, which was also her favourite. Until the pen started leaking all over my hands.

Sighing, I turned off my flashlight, got up and made my quiet way past my snoring room-mate and down the hall to the bathroom. The house mother had gone to bed hours before and all the lights were off, but like all the other students, I was very used to groping my way down a dark hall, past other rooms containing snoring girls. You'd think that with what my stepfather's estate was paying for tuition, we'd get private bathrooms, but the school leaders evidently were of the opinion that sharing facilities would keep us rich kids humble or grounded, or something like that. In my experience it mostly meant that the shy kids developed bowel problems from holding it all in until the dorms were deserted, and the kids with eating disorders or body dysmorphia became even more miserable. Take a bunch of teenage girls and give them zero privacy without other gossiping and prying teenage girls seeing every single thing they do, and it's an ideal breeding ground for paranoia and narcissism. But hey, what do I know? I was just a kid, and possibly a budding sociopath.

I could tell there was someone in the bathroom before I got in there because the light was shining underneath the door. The lights were on movement sensors, which meant that you could never sneak into the room without anyone knowing, or conversely that sometimes when you were doing your makeup or having a shit in peaceful solitude, the lights would suddenly go off, plunging you into darkness and ruining your eyeliner game.

Also, I could hear someone crying.

I opened the door stealthily, using my hip rather than my ink-stained hands, and listened. When you hear someone crying in the girls' bathroom you have basically three options: ask if the person is OK and run the risk of getting tangled up in some puerile teenage drama; ignore it and potentially miss out on some top-class gossip; or eavesdrop and hope to get all the dirt and none of the hassle. In this case, I struck gold, because I'd only been standing there for five or six seconds when I realised that there were two girls in there, one crying and one whispering.

'Are you going to tell anyone?' the whispering one whispered.

'No,' the sobbing one sobbed. 'No one will believe me!'

'They might believe you.'

'Then they'll know it was me! He'll get fired and everyone will blame me! Everyone loves Mr Scheeler.'

'Everyone knows you're his favourite.'

I perked up at this, because it gave me two bits of vital information. Mr Scheeler coached the softball team, which I was on (first base, because I was really good at the quick catches). Everyone did, in fact, love Mr Scheeler. He was a former minor league baseball player who'd coached our team to the top of the state. He had a big belly, a booming laugh, a penchant for terrible puns, and he carried a genuinely signed by Babe Ruth wooden baseball bat with him everywhere. I'm not kidding – the Babe Bat had its own seat on the team bus. In anyone else, this would be incredibly cringey, but something about Mr Scheeler managed to make his obsession look quirky and fun. In addition to coaching the softball team and teaching computer science, he also directed the annual senior play, where the senior class dressed up as various teachers and staff. The senior who played Mr Scheeler always got to carry his Babe Ruth bat, which was the only time that it ever left his side.

I also knew who was crying: it was Neve Owens, because Neve Owens was our star pitcher and also the senior most likely to act as Mr Scheeler in the play.

I pressed my ear closer to the ajar door.

'Maybe it was a mistake,' said the other girl.

'He had his hand *in my bra*,' said Neve.

'Are you sure? Maybe he didn't mean to.'

'Even if he did, I can't tell anyone. And you're not allowed to tell anyone either. My life would be miserable. They'd all say it was my fault. Promise you won't tell!'

'Are you going to quit the team?'

'I have to. I can't look at him anymore.'

This was enough. I scooted away from the bathroom door and back to my room, where I cleaned my inky hands with some tissue. Then I climbed back into bed, with visions of killing Mr Scheeler dancing in my head.

You may think that a bit of overheard gossip is a slender basis for killing a much-loved softball coach, especially one who'd got us to the top of the state rankings, and who had personally increased my batting average from 400 to 450. But in my defence, paedophilia was a touchy spot for me, and with good reason. I knew, beyond a shadow of a doubt, that no one ever put their hand inside someone's bra 'by mistake'. How many teenagers had Mr Scheeler groped, or worse? Neve was right: no one would ever want to believe it about him. Added to which, Neve Owen had the best right arm on the entire East Coast. She couldn't quit. Our team might never have won all those games without Mr Scheeler, but we definitely wouldn't go on to win the championship without Neve.

Also, in my opinion at least, my plan was foolproof.

Of course, I was wrong, but again in my defence, I was only fifteen, and I'd already gotten away with murder once. I thought I was invincible.

* * *

My foolproof plan came into effect just two days later, at the softball team pizza and bowling night. We had these twice a season and they were just another reason for Mr Scheeler's popularity; at a boarding school, no matter how exclusive and venerable, everyone loves the excuse to get off campus for a night, away from the house mothers and most of the teachers, and into a place where you might even see a few boys to flirt with. No matter that the local bowling alley was a maelstrom of orange and turquoise Formica, the land that the 70s forgot.

Neve didn't come. Rumour had it that she was sick. Only I, and her as-yet-unidentified bathroom confidante, knew the real reason.

And Mr Scheeler, of course. The slimy paedo bastard.

The pizza party went without incident. It was in the second half of the evening, when we moved over to the bowling lanes, that I engaged the first part of my plan. While everyone was changing into their Febreze-reeking rented bowling shoes, I slipped away to the restrooms. It seemed fitting that this scheme, that had begun for me in a bathroom, would continue in another one.

I snuck into the men's room, took out the two slices of pepperoni pizza that I had hidden in my handbag, and shoved them into the only toilet. The men's room stank, much worse than the women's room, which wasn't all too clean either. I had to hold my breath as I threw half a roll of toilet paper into the bowl along with the pizza. To be extra safe, I used the frankly disgusting toilet brush to push the blockage right down into the pipes, and added a wad of paper towels. I flushed the toilet again and again. The pizza and toilet paper stuck right where they were supposed to, and I was gratified to see the water level rising and rising in the toilet bowl. When I left the men's room, it was already overflowing onto the floor.

I washed my hands and checked my hair in the women's room, and then made a detour to the front desk. 'Sorry?' I said to the bored-looking and acne-ridden clerk sitting on a stool next to all the abandoned shoes. 'I think I saw water coming from underneath the door of the men's toilets?'

The clerk sighed and got up. I guess a stinky toilet was even less appealing to him than cubicles full of stinky shoes. I still wonder if he'd have been more cheerful about it, if he'd known he was assisting in the removal of a child molester from the world. By the time I'd laced up my bowling shoes and joined my team at their lane, I could see him heading towards the men's room with a mop, bucket, and OUT OF ORDER sign.

The next part of the plan was merely a matter of waiting. The beauty of this was that I got nearly a whole game of bowling under my belt before I had to do anything. The other beautiful thing was that Mr Scheeler was walking himself right into my trap, without even knowing.

You see, Mr Scheeler's Babe Ruth bat was not his only eccentricity. The man also put away gallons of Gatorade. He usually had at least one sixteen-ounce bottle with him, and on a night like this, he'd bring three or four. He preferred the blue kind. He always said he owed his professional baseball career to Gatorade and its special electrolyte formula. Sort of like Popeye with spinach.

So all I had to do was to keep one eye on the pins, and another on Mr Scheeler's liquid consumption.

Sure enough, within about half an hour, Mr Scheeler got up from the turquoise bench where he'd been watching the bowling, and wandered, with his Babe Ruth baseball bat, to the men's room. I watched him out of the corner of my eye as I bowled, which meant that I missed my final 7–2 split, sending my ball straight through without hitting a single pin and losing the game to Paige Wheeler. That was OK; I had bigger prey in mind.

'Anybody want a Diet Coke?' I asked. Naturally everyone raised their hand. On my way to the snack bar, I passed Mr Scheeler coming the other way, from the direction of the men's room.

'Staying hydrated, Seraphina?' he asked me, with a wink.

'Certainly am, Mr Scheeler!'

'Keep up the good work! You'll beat Paige next game.'

I watched as he headed for the front door of the bowling alley. Then I quickly nipped round the corner behind the bathrooms and went out the fire exit, propping it ajar with a brick. I paused to put on the latex gloves I'd stashed in my pocket (contraband, from a dorm-mate who dyed her hair against the school rules).

The parking lot was lit only from the glowing sign of the bowling alley. I crept round the side of the school bus that had taken us here, and saw Mr Scheeler heading for the far side of the parking lot, into the shadows. Of course a well-respected teacher at an exclusive private girls' school wouldn't want to be seen taking a leak in public. I'd been counting on that.

That's something you can always predict about men: they think they're bulletproof. Imagine a lone woman heading straight for the darkest part of a public area on a dark night so that she could relieve herself. No; a woman would be clutching her keys between her fingers as a makeshift weapon, staying within a few feet of the door, dancing around clenching her pelvic floor muscles and frantically searching her mind for places with well-lit public restrooms within a bladder's-reach distance. Most women would literally rather wet themselves than pull their underwear down in public, because we've all heard what happens to women like that.

But a man goes blithely into the shadows, all by himself, and flops out his dick into plain air. Because what could possibly happen to a big, strong man like him?

I followed him, keeping to the shadows myself. A top tip for those of you considering committing murder at a bowling alley: wear your own shoes, if possible, because those bowling shoes have slippery soles and are a lot noisier than sneakers.

But fortunately, Mr Scheeler had no suspicions, and of course, as I said, he thought he was bulletproof. Even before I got close enough to see him clearly, I could hear him humming under his breath, and I could hear the stream of his piss hitting the grass by the side of the parking lot.

He was facing away from me. The Babe bat was propped up against the fender of a nearby car. This was something else I was counting on: that Mr Scheeler would be one of those men who believed he was so manly that he needed both of his hands to pee.

I grabbed the Babe bat and while Mr Scheeler was still peeing (because of thirty-two ounces of blue Gatorade), I swung it as hard as I could at his head.

Anyone who has played softball, if they're lucky, knows the satisfying sound and feel of getting a good hit. It's different than when you hit a baseball. A baseball makes a sharp crack. But a softball is bigger and, yes, a little softer, and it makes more of a *thwack* sound. I'd say that Mr Scheeler's head wasn't all that dissimilar. Of course Mr Scheeler was standing still, while a softball would have been pitched at me, so there's the whole inertia thing to consider, and also the fact that Mr Scheeler's hair and his baseball cap probably gave him a little padding. And also, his head was attached to his body. So I couldn't exactly bat it over the fence.

However, Mr Scheeler did keel over heavily to the side, and his head made a similar sound when it hit the asphalt, and blood started pooling around him. So there was that.

Home run.

The only thing I hadn't planned was the fact that his penis would be dangling out of his fly when I killed him, which made finding his wallet much more unpleasant. Fortunately I had the gloves, which were basically hand condoms. I removed the cash and dropped the emptied wallet on his inert body, along with the Babe bat. A random mugger wouldn't know the value of such an item.

Then I stuffed the cash and my gloves back in my cross-body bag, slipped back inside the building, checked my hair again, and bought everyone on my team a Diet Coke.

I beat Paige Wheeler by thirty points, and nobody even noticed that Mr Scheeler was missing until an hour later, when it was time to get back on the bus.

Thinking back on this whole thing, I can see I made a lot of mistakes. For example, if there had been CCTV in the parking lot, I would have been caught immediately. I didn't even think to check. Also, we weren't exactly in a high-crime area, and it was only sheer luck that the police believed it was a brutal mugging. I don't know if anyone was ever arrested for it, but the rumour mill said it had been a group of crazed druggies. It was foolish to base the whole thing on the predictability of Mr Scheeler's bladder. If the bored clerk had been better at unclogging toilets, or if my teacher had been slightly less hydrated, the whole plan would have gone to . . . well, piss.

But call it beginner's luck, whatever – our boob-groping ball coach was gone, smashed with his own Babe bat. Neve didn't quit the team. The school got a new all-weather sports field named in Thad T. Scheeler's memory (I might have convinced my trustees to contribute a significant sum, 'for my favourite coach'). And while our team didn't win States – the murder put a damper on our enthusiasm for a little while – we did come second.

If you ask me, that's not a bad result.

6

J ON HAD FIRST MET CYRIL Walker in a pub in Lavender
Hill, and he had noticed two things about him then:
he wore a blue cashmere jumper and way too much body
spray. He'd made a note of these facts at the time, along
with Walker's bitten fingernails and the tattoo that peeped
out from under the sleeve of his jumper. These little details
could be useful when you were writing about people. It
helped to humanise them for the listener – especially as
Walker wasn't the sort of person who you'd normally associate
with cashmere.

Cyril Walker was a builder. He was divorced, didn't have any
kids, and lived alone in a terraced house in Clapham. 'It's a
wreck,' he'd said to Jon during that first meeting. 'I never have
time to do work on my own house. Typical builder.' He drove
a white van and when he hit forty years old, he'd decided to
give up smoking and take up jogging.

This was why Jon had met him.

Cyril had first got in contact with Jon via his podcast, in an
anonymous email from a burner account. *I've been listening to
you, and I think you're right*, he'd written. *That Spanish man isn't
guilty of killing Lianne Murray. I've seen his photo in the papers,*

*and he looks nothing like the man I saw on Clapham Common that
night with blood all over his hands.*

It had taken a week of constant emailing for Jon to persuade
his anonymous tipster to meet him in person, and even then,
he was surprised when Cyril turned up. His anonymous
emailer's prose style was well chosen, but Cyril Walker was a
big bloke with a shaved head and workman's hands, reeking of
body spray and South London rough charm.

'I don't like the filth,' he told Jon over a couple of pints of
Stella. 'They put my brother away for a burglary he didn't
commit back in 2000. Stitched him up, and he was never the
same since. He's addicted to drugs, been sleeping on the streets
on and off. I don't trust the cops, and I knew as soon as I saw
a photo of that Santander in the papers that they were doing
the same to him. That's why I had to say something, right?'

According to Cyril, he'd been jogging on Clapham Common
on the same day that Lianne was attacked. The weather was
terrible, and there was hardly anyone around, which was why
he said he noticed the man walking swiftly in the opposite
direction to him. The man had his hands shoved in his pockets
and he had a bright crimson streak of blood on his forehead.

'Could you recognise him if you saw him again?' Jon asked.

'Sure thing. His face, but also his jacket. It was from the
2016 H&M/Balmain collaboration.'

Jon blinked. 'H&M what?'

Cyril looked a little abashed. 'I'm a bit of a fashionista, to
be honest, mate. I don't look like it, and I can't afford to buy
much, but I like browsing eBay, you know? This jumper is a
Burberry, look.' He twisted his body around so that Jon could
see the label on the back of his jumper. Sure enough: it was

Burberry. 'Anyway,' Cyril continued, 'I'd been on the lookout for this same jacket for months now. It sold out in, like, twenty-four hours when it was in the shops and usually they charge an arm and a leg for stuff like that, but sometimes you can find someone who doesn't know what they've got.'

'Had you seen this guy in the park before?'

'No. And I haven't seen him since. And I've been looking for him, believe me. But when I heard they'd banged that fellow up, I knew I had to say something to someone. I mean – getting away with murder is one thing, but letting someone else take the blame . . .' Cyril had shaken his head, and downed his pint, and Jon had bought him another.

Cyril was good company. And his tip was good, too – from the description, Jon was able to track down Bachelor. In the end, Jon did convince Cyril to speak to the police, but only so that an innocent man would be spared. Cyril had come to the celebrations at Jon's house when Efraín Santander was freed; he'd shaken Santander by the hand. Efraín told Jon later that Cyril had slipped him nearly two hundred quid in cash, 'to help you get back on your feet'.

That same night, after the party, Amy had put her cold feet on his warm legs in bed and murmured, 'That Cyril is a nice guy, but boy he needs to lay off on the Lynx.'

'Axe,' said Jon, half-drunk on champagne. 'Axe Stellar, to be precise. It's a special edition not made in the UK. He told me all about it.' And then he'd pulled Amy on top of him and stopped thinking about Cyril, and he hadn't thought about him much after that either, except when he'd found a bin bag on his porch reeking of the exact same type of body spray that Cyril wore.

It was a wonder it had taken him so long to put it together. But he had, inside that Wetherspoons.

He thought of going straight back into the police station, telling them of his hunch. But DI Atherton hated him, and Jon knew what he'd say. 'You want us to investigate someone because they've got terrible taste in deodorant?'

So Jon got a cab. And that was how he found himself in the scrubby garden at the back of Cyril Walker's house, breaking through the rotten bathroom window that Cyril hadn't bothered to replace yet.

He realised, as he pulled himself through the window, that he was scared shitless: heart pounding, palms sweaty. He noticed it with an almost professional detachment. He scrambled through anyway and stood in the bath. Jon had never broken into a house before, let alone the house of someone who had helped him solve one murder and might be guilty of another. Or, to be precise, another six at least.

The bathroom was cold. As in lots of these Victorian terraces, it had been built onto the back of the kitchen, like an afterthought. Someone, presumably Cyril, had started to remove the 70s-style pink tiles on the wall. Jon listened, even though Cyril hadn't answered when he'd knocked at the front door. Hearing nothing, he stepped out of the bath.

The scent of Axe was overwhelming, and now that Jon was actually in Cyril's house, it was almost impossible for him to be certain that the scent he remembered was the same as the one he smelled now. Anyway, it was definitely Axe Stellar: there were three cans of it on the shelf by the sink and another, presumably empty, in the bin. Jonathan opened the medicine cabinet and saw two more.

Well, he'd confirmed that Cyril did, indeed, use too much cheap (but niche) body spray.

Jon gritted his teeth and, as quietly as he could, he sneaked out of the bathroom and into the kitchen. What was he looking for? Bin bags? A saw? Wouldn't these be the things that a builder would have in his house anyway?

And yet . . . the fear had turned into that tickle down deep, between his stomach and his lungs. The itch, the feeling he got sometimes when he was on the verge of figuring something out. When he'd almost solved the puzzle, put the pieces together, found the exact bit of evidence he needed to prove someone was innocent or guilty.

Or it could be panic because he'd left a police station after being questioned about one crime and promptly committed another.

This was ridiculous. Tens of thousands of people wore this body spray. That didn't mean that any of them were murderers. Cyril Walker was a witness in a case, that was all. He listened to Jon's podcast. He was a good bloke who rarely finished a tiling job in his own house.

Right. He'd have a quick check round, now that he was here. But then he'd let himself out and get back to solving the real problems in his life. After he'd had several more drinks.

His feet stuck on the linoleum kitchen floor, making little tacky sounds as he moved. The built-in units were fake wood, probably from the 80s. An empty dish with a smeared butter knife and crumbs on it sat on the counter next to a tea-stained mug. Another mystery solved: what did Cyril Walker eat for breakfast? He snorted and opened a few kitchen drawers, looking for offensive knives. They were mostly full of takeaway menus, though one had bin bags in it. As far as he could tell, they were normal bin bags, but he ripped one off the roll and put it in his pocket to examine more closely later.

Unlike everything else in the kitchen, the fridge-freezer was new: a big American-style model with a roomy freezer on top. It hummed quietly in what sounded like self-satisfaction. Jon opened the fridge, glanced at the bottle of milk and cans of beer, then opened the freezer.

Lined up on the shelf, like misshapen cartons of ice cream, were five human heads.

Jon could not move or make a sound. He took in every detail, powerless not to look, not to let this sear into his memory forever. Their skin was blue-tinged grey, their cheeks hollow, their features slack and chapped. Ice crystals clustered on their eyebrows and in their hair, on the scruff of beard on their chins and lips. Blood stood out on their necks in frozen maroon droplets. All of them had their eyes closed, except for the man on the right. One of his eyes was half-open, exposing the white of an eyeball. Jon knew that if he touched it, it would be solid like rock, and horribly cold. It would stick to the damp, living warmth of his finger, and when he tried to pull his hand back, the severed head would come with it, and fall against his chest with the weight of an unconscious drunk, cold lips drooling onto his shirt.

He reached his hand out anyway.

'What are you doing here, Jonathan?'

For a moment he thought the voice was coming from one of the heads. But then he knew, because of Axe, Axe body spray, and the pleasant voice of the man that he thought had been a friend. He half-turned, hand still outstretched, and Cyril stood in the entrance to the kitchen. Jon must have missed finding where the offensive knives were kept because Cyril had one in his hand, a long butcher's knife, blade pointed at Jon.

'You had to know, didn't you?' Cyril sounded sad. 'You always have to know. You just couldn't let it lie.'

'Don't hurt me.' His voice was strange, not his own, a breathless croak.

'I wish I didn't have to, mate. You are really not my type at all.'

Cyril lunged at him. Jon, without thinking, jumped aside and swept his arm forward. His fingertips caught on something cold and rigid, and a dark, round shape flew out of the freezer. At the same time that he heard a sickening thud, he felt sharp fire in his chest. It was so quick it was impossible to tell whether it was coming from outside him or from inside, from his own heart.

'What are you doing to them?' Cyril cried and he turned away from Jon, bent over, oh God he was retrieving the head from the floor, cradling it in his hands like a baby. Jon took his chance and bolted for the entrance behind Cyril.

He heard Cyril scrabbling behind him as he ran through the shadowed house. It was a small house, but every inch seemed a mile: through the dining room with newspapers piled high on the table, into a narrow corridor leading to the front door. The floorboards were bare, the small window in the door an impossible distance away.

There was something hot on the back of his neck and he heard breath loud in his ears. His own breath, or Cyril's? He reached for the door and the fire in his chest turned to searing, terrible pain. He screamed and scrabbled for the doorknob. His hands were too wet to get purchase. Blood. His.

'Please please please,' he whimpered. The knife was going to strike again. It would stab him in the back this time, through his lungs, through his heart, it would stab him again and again until he was dead and then Cyril would cut off his limbs, one by one, and put them in bin bags to leave somewhere in the city and his head would sit in the freezer, in a row, next to the others. Blackness, blankness, nothing else, forever.

Cyril thundered up behind him as the door swung open, into the afternoon street. Jon stumbled out of it, blinded by panic and light. New pain slashed across his shoulder and the back of his neck. Somehow he ran out into the street, waving his hands, in front of a bus. Cyril behind him with a bloody knife in hand, Jon hammering with his fists now on the bus's wide windscreen, leaving red smears on the glass. The last thing he saw before he passed out was the shocked face of the driver behind the windscreen: a man who has witnessed a nightmare come to life.

7

*In a twist of fate, Bin Bag Killer Cyril Walker's crimes were
solved by the very same journalist who had interviewed him
for a podcast about murder.*

'WHAT ARE YOU SMILING ABOUT?' Susie asks.
I glance up from my phone at my sister, who looks happy to be distracted from her fresh fruit salad with non-fat yoghurt and chia seeds. We're at our usual brunch place, which is in Chelsea, exactly halfway between my house and her flat. This healthy food is new for Susie. Our waiter actually did a double take when she ordered it for brunch instead of her usual double-chocolate waffles.

'Nothing,' I say, and turn my phone face-down. Even though the photograph of Jonathan that goes along with the article is adorable. He's standing in a garden, smiling at someone off-camera, and his hair has been ruffled by a breeze. It's an old photo; his hair is a little longer than it was when I saw him at his reading earlier in the week. And right now, he's in hospital, because according to the media, Cyril Walker stabbed him before he could escape.

For some reason, I find this unbelievably sexy.

'Oh my God,' says Susie. 'I knew it.'

'You knew what?'

'You're on Tinder, aren't you?'

I screw up my face. 'I'm on what?'

'Tinder. Hinge. One of those dating apps. Or are you on the hook-up one, what's it called?'

'I have no idea and don't want to,' I tell her. 'I was just reading the news.'

'No you weren't. You had that look on your face. I know what you're thinking.'

I must pause here and explain that Susie does not know about my little hobby. She has always accepted the official explanation of what happened to Harold, and so far, she hasn't known any of my other victims. She and I are very close, as in six-years-ago-I-moved-to-London-to-distance-myself-from-a-crime-scene-and-she-followed-me-three-weeks-later close. But even close siblings need a modicum of privacy from each other. Though it's slightly worrying that she's decided that she can tell what I'm thinking just from the expressions on my face. Do I have a 'planning a murder' expression? Is it different from my 'I must remember to buy light bulbs' expression?

'What am I thinking?' I ask.

'That you just saw a pic of someone who you fancy like mad. Who is it?'

'Oh.' I shrug. 'Just someone on the news.' I close the app.

'Who is it? Let me see.'

'No. I'm not going to sit here while you mock my taste in men, again.'

'I can't help it if you have shitty taste in men.' She picks up her own phone and taps and swipes. 'Now . . . this is cute.' She holds up a photo of Chris Hemsworth and licks her lips. 'Don't you think he looks like Finlay?'

'No,' I say. Actually he does a little, especially in the jaw, but Finlay is a jerk and I'm not going to encourage her crush. And suddenly a mystery is solved: Finlay is the reason for Susie's health kick. Last week she told me that he'd mentioned that his last girlfriend was skinnier than she is.

'You're perfect,' I tell her. 'Just the way you are.'

'I know.' My sister reaches for my phone. 'What's your passcode?'

'What are you trying to do?' I ask.

'I'm downloading Hinge.'

'What's Hinge?'

'It's a dating app.'

'No. Just . . . no.' I grab my phone from her. She pouts.

'If you're fancying men from the news, you need to go on a date. You've literally been a hermit for the past year.'

'No, I haven't. There was Tom, and then there was Ridwan.'

'That was before Christmas! And also, both of them were so boring.'

'What can I say? I like boring men.'

'Nobody likes boring men, Saffy.'

'Well . . . I don't find them boring.'

I'm lying. They were boring.

It has been a dry patch lately, when it comes to men. The thing is, Susie is right: I always end up with boring men.

Because I like good men, and good men are boring. Is this the central tragic paradox of my life?

This might sound overly philosophical, but I'm about to turn thirty. These milestones get a girl to wondering. Maybe my huge crush on Jonathan Desrosiers is some sort of weird biological clock.

'You like boring men, because you're afraid of falling in love,' Susie persists.

'Love, for a heterosexual woman, is a collection of lies and compromises.'

'But they're *wonderful* lies and compromises.'

'I'm not going on dating sites.' I put my phone in my jacket pocket. 'Unless you do, too.'

Susie smiles like the cat who's got the cream. 'I don't need a dating site. Finlay's taking me to Paris next weekend.'

'Is he taking you to Paris, or is he going to Paris for a tech-bro conference and he's said you can tag along?'

'He's *taking me to Paris*.' She points at my eggs Florentine. 'Are you going to finish that?'

'Only if you don't sign me up to any dating sites.'

She pouts again, and I push my eggs over to her. I can never resist my sister.

'I'm not going to be at the mercy of a computer algorithm,' I tell her, as she tucks in. 'I can find my own men for myself.'

Except later, after brunch, when I ring the hospital pretending to be Mrs Jonathan Desrosiers, I'm told that he's discharged himself. And though I wait for a new podcast to drop – a murder podcast to end all murder podcasts, an absolute gift for Jonathan Desrosiers, an actual first-hand account of how he found a serial killer and got stabbed for his trouble – nothing happens.

For days.

And then weeks.

No podcast, no interviews, no television appearances. Nothing. Jonathan Desrosiers has been handed the biggest story in his career. And instead of making the most of it . . . he's disappeared.

8

Scotland, three months later

THE FIRST TWO TIMES EDIE rang, Jon ignored it. He moved the phone to the other side of the cabin, where there was no reception. Then went out for a walk around the loch, batting away black flies, and didn't return until he was all chewed up and itching.

Unfortunately, the third time, he was drunk and he picked up.

'I'm beginning to think you're avoiding me,' his agent said, in her gravelly two-packs-a-day voice.

'Don't take it personally,' said Jon. 'I'm avoiding everyone.'

'I'm well, thanks for asking. How are you? The Highlands treating you well?'

'It's not too bad. Aside from the nights. Even then it's OK sometimes, if I don't sleep. There are a lot of stars up here. You can forget that people even exist.'

'You're still having nightmares?'

The answer to that was so obvious that Jon didn't bother to answer. He'd been having nightmares since the minute he'd opened Cyril's freezer.

'I had Louise on the phone today asking about the second book in the contract,' Edie said.

Louise was his editor. Or had been. 'I'm not writing that book.'

'It doesn't have to be about the Bin Bag Killer. It can be about anything. Any other case. Although obviously, they'd prefer it if it *were* about the Bin—'

'I'm done with books.'

'You could base it on the transcripts of your podcasts.'

'I'm done with the podcasts, too. All of it. I'm finished with crime and murder and killers. They've cost me my marriage and my peace of mind. I've had enough for a lifetime.'

'I'm sorry to hear that. If so, the publishers are going to want their money back.'

'I don't care.'

'Do you have the money?'

'I don't know.'

Edie sighed. 'When I signed you, you were such a courteous and enthusiastic young man. You were excited about life, and passionate about justice. You wanted to change the world, for the better. What happened to that Jonathan I used to know?'

'He found a dismembered body and five severed heads on the same day that his wife left him.' Jon reached for the Ben Nevis and poured himself another measure. 'None of this is new, Edie, and you could have done it by email.'

'You never answer your email, either. But you're right. I didn't ring to talk about the next book.'

'That sounds . . . ominous.'

'Have you opened any of your mail lately? I don't mean email, I mean real mail.'

'No.'

'You might want to open this latest batch.'

'I think you're using "want" in quite a loose sense, Edie.' He took a deep drink.

'Tell me the truth, Jonathan: are you drunk? I don't blame you if you are, even though it's only two o'clock in the afternoon, but I just like to know what I'm dealing with here.'

'I'm all right. I'm fine.' And because he liked Edie – he liked her quite a lot, in fact – he added: 'This is a good place for me to be.'

'You spend all your time talking to sheep.'

'There are also salmon.'

'Are the nightmares very bad?'

The eyes. The sunken cheeks. The waxwork skin. The ice crystals clinging to eyelashes and blue tips of noses.

'I can only sleep when I'm drunk,' Jon told her.

His father had used to say the same thing.

'You should come back to London, Jonathan. You've got friends here.'

'Amy and I had friends. Together. I haven't got any.'

'You've got me. And you shouldn't be alone. I've got a spare room with your name on it. You can stay with Marj and me for as long as you like. Just say the word.'

'I'll come back for the trial, if they need me to testify. But my life is here, now.'

Gently, Edie said, 'I'm not sure it *is* a life, Jonny.'

The kicker was, she was right.

'Listen,' she said. 'I'll ring again tomorrow, after you've collected your post. And you really need to collect it, and read it. I made some promises. We'll talk more then. Please pick up. Or you could call me, whenever.'

'Goodbye, Edie,' said Jon. 'Look after yourself.'

Jon put down the phone and went outside with the bottle to try to find some wildlife to look at.

Edie was right. This was unsustainable. But what other choice did he have? Whenever he thought about writing or broadcasting, he saw the heads of those five men, and the body of the sixth, tossed aside like rubbish. He thought about how he had swept one of the heads out of the freezer: the noise it made as it hit the floor. He thought about what DI Atherton had said to him: *You are a vulture. If you glamorise murder, sooner or later it's going to turn up on your doorstep.*

But that was the only thing he was good at. He was a failure at everything else.

Just like his dad.

* * *

The following afternoon, he picked up two weeks' worth of post in the village. The woman behind the counter, clearly not having learned her lesson from the previous times, tried to engage him in conversation. 'Rain again tomorrow,' she said, handing over the bundle of envelopes. 'Is your roof holding up out there? It must be miserable when it's wet.'

When it was wet, the rain dripped through the slates and ran down the wall of the kitchen. He had a plastic bucket permanently next to the sofa and a saucepan at the end of his bed to catch the drips. Last week he'd found a mushroom growing in the bathroom, poking a soft head up like a finger in the gap between the wall and the vinyl flooring. But the water streamed down the outside of the windows and made the air grey, made the loch a sheet of iron. Jonathan liked the lack of colour. He found it soothing: blankness was better than what he saw at night with his eyes closed. And the smell of damp was strong enough to drive memories of other smells away.

'I'll tell that Callum Morris for you when I see him,' the post office woman continued. 'He's the world's worst landlord, I hear, won't do any repairs unless he's shamed into it.'

Jonathan shrugged and didn't answer.

In the shop nearby – beans, bacon, eggs, bread, milk, coffee, two packets of paracetamol – he paused, out of habit, near the newspapers. He skimmed the headlines. Politics, wars, scandals. Then he realised that he was looking for news about murders, and felt sick.

On second thoughts, he picked up another bottle of whisky too.

*   *   *

His battered Land Rover was parked outside. He sat in it, heating full on, to go through his post. He remembered the post he used to get in London, the thick thud of it every day. People said that no one wrote anymore, but he got plenty through his door: gas bills, electricity bills, broadband bills, postcards from friends, invitations to weddings and christenings, fundraising pleas, letters from Amy's mother, fan mail via Edie and his publisher, junk mail, catalogues. Amy liked furniture catalogues; she liked to refurnish their house in her imagination once a month, at least. If Amy got to it first, she would sort it into piles of his, hers, and theirs. In the early days, if it was something for them both she would open it first and stick it up on their refrigerator with colourful magnets, the plastic ones shaped like food, so he would see it when he paused his work and went to the fridge for something to eat. She hadn't done that for a very long time.

Today he had one A4 envelope and two large Jiffy bags. None of them were from his friends; those that were left of his friends had tended to try to ring him until they gave up. They might have sent him emails, too, but he wouldn't know; the cottage didn't have an internet connection and he'd deleted all the apps from his phone.

He knew what the first envelope contained, and he barely glanced at it before putting it to one side, on the passenger seat. He felt it sitting there, waiting for him.

The two Jiffy bags were addressed to him in Edie's familiar handwriting. One had a postmark from two weeks ago, and one was postmarked two days ago. He ripped the older one open. It contained the royalty statement which currently comprised his only income, and which he would donate directly to Victim Support Services. It also contained his credit card bill and his bank statement, both of which he'd had forwarded to his agent. He didn't need to open them to know the large figure of debt on the first and the small figure of credit on the second, but something made him open and look anyway. Maybe it was force of habit, or maybe it was the last dregs of his feelings of responsibility, that he ought to be the sort of person who paid bills and worried about the money running out.

There were also a dozen pieces of fan mail. He browsed them without interest. Four of them were requests for him to investigate a cold case – three murders and one case of arson. One of them contained lots of yellowed news clippings. Back in the day, it would have made his Spidey senses start tingling.

It would have sent him straight to his study to pore over every detail, and ignore his lonely wife.

There were also two familiar light blue envelopes, with Jon's name and Edie's address written in careful capital letters. They were both from Simon Simons, who had been writing to Jon like clockwork for years now. He stuffed everything except for the royalty statement back in the envelope, and opened the second large Jiffy bag.

This was the one Edie had rung him about. It contained another letter from Simon, four pieces of fan mail, and a white envelope with a yellow Post-it stuck to the front.

Jonny, read this one. Please. E.

He put the envelope with the Post-it on top of the royalty statement and the other envelope, the one he hadn't opened yet. Then he scooped up everything else into his arms: fan mail, bank statements, cold cases with newspaper clippings. He got out of the Land Rover and shoved the whole mess of paper into a nearby bin, pushing it down so the sheets wouldn't blow away in the gathering wind.

Back at the cottage, he made himself a strong coffee and tipped whisky into it. He swallowed two paracetamol and then made himself sit down at the scarred table and look at his post. Jonathan considered the two unopened envelopes for some time, knowing he wasn't going to like either of them.

Finally, he swore and opened the A4 envelope from Amy's lawyer. For a split second, he had an irrational hope, but he hardly had to glance at the contents to confirm what it was. He pushed it aside and opened the second one, the one Edie was going to call him about. It had only a single piece of paper inside. As he read it, noise escaped him: low and ragged and shocking in the quiet of the room. To his ears, it sounded like the growl of some desperate animal.

Jon jumped to his feet, tipping the wooden chair over onto its back on the floor. He grabbed the letters and the bottle of whisky and, shoving them both under his arm, he slammed the door open and went outside, into the lowering storm.

9

H<small>E'S LOST WEIGHT SINCE THE</small> last time I saw him, but that doesn't stop me from recognising him as soon as he walks out of the post office. He looks like hell. He's too skinny for his clothes and his hair is all rumpled, as if he hasn't combed it in weeks. He's got a ragged, scruffy beard and epic dark circles under his eyes.

He's utterly, breathtakingly beautiful.

He doesn't glance in my direction as he passes by my BMW and goes into the small shop. I shouldn't risk it – I've seen enough for now – but I slip out of my car and follow him inside. He moves through the aisles with a fierce concentration, picking out items and throwing them into his basket as if he's angry at them. I don't think much of his diet. No wonder he's skinny.

I hardly have to worry about him spotting me; he looks neither right nor left until he hesitates by the rack of papers and stares at the headlines. I risk walking behind him. His hair has grown and it curls over his jacket collar; he's wearing muddy boots. When I breathe in, he smells of woodsmoke and damp. I stop by the magazines, pretending to browse strategies for losing weight and the must-have denim this season, and I get another waft of his scent as he passes. I close my eyes for a moment and picture him cross-legged on the floor, feeding wood into the fire, surrounded by shadows, the flames flickering in his eyes.

Although he's chosen some of the least expensive food in the shop, he bypasses the cheap booze and adds a bottle of single malt to his basket. He doesn't reply at all to the friendly comments from the boy at the till about the coming storm.

Once he's gone, I buy a bottle of water and a packet of mints. I'm nice to the boy at the till. Then I stroll outside and watch him go to his car, a battered and muddy Land Rover that has 'third-hand' written all over it. I've got plenty of time to go back to my car and drink some of my water because he sits behind the wheel for a while, looking down at something.

I thought I fancied Jonathan Desrosiers before – which is why I've tracked him up here to the asshole of nowhere – but now, somehow, he's on a whole other level. Maybe it's just because I haven't seen him for months, and not since he caught Cyril Walker, but I feel like something has changed about him.

It must be in the way he moves. Maybe it's the way he looks as if he's recovering from a full body blow that he can hardly believe hit him in the first place. Maybe it's because he's obviously angry, but not aggressive. And despite his skinniness, he's strong: there's power in his shoulders and his hands.

Am I turned on by desperation?

'Why are you going up to Scotland?' my sister asked me, when I announced my plans to her. 'Do you actually *feel* like getting rained on?'

'I'm going to see someone,' I told her. Susie immediately pounced.

'Who? Who? Is it a guy? Tell me it's a guy.'

'It might be a guy.'

Susie lolled back on the sofa. 'Is it a Scottish man? Scottish accents are sexy. They sound dangerous.' She pointed at me. 'I want you to go up to Scotland and catch yourself a dangerous, sexy man.'

'I'm just going to help someone out,' I said, but then I winked, and she was satisfied, and didn't threaten me with Hinge anymore.

He gets suddenly out of his car, strides to a bin, and stuffs some papers into it. Then he returns to the Land Rover and drives off. From the sound the car makes, he needs some new bearings. It's certainly not going to be difficult to catch up with him, so I wait a few moments before I casually get out of my own car to toss my water bottle into the bin. It lands on top of a couple of bank statements and some crumpled Jiffy bags, spilling papers. I retrieve all of them.

* * *

When Jonathan Desrosiers pulls off onto a track to the left of the A road, I follow at a distance until it gets too rocky for my low-slung car, and then I pull over and proceed on foot. The Land Rover is parked outside a single-storey, white-washed cottage which badly needs repainting. It's the only building in the vicinity, and looks mostly suitable for goats, not people.

Back on the metalled road I step on the accelerator, pleased not to have to be cautious anymore and to use my car's power. Aside from a few tractors which I pass easily, the traffic is light and I make it to Inverness in less than an hour, with plenty of time to spare. The animal shelter is on the outskirts of town:

a low, ugly building with a chain-link fence around it. As I get out of the car, a chorus of barks starts up from the back.

I give my name to the woman at reception. She's wearing a pinny with pictures of kittens on it, she has her hair in unravelling Princess Leia buns, and she looks hassled. 'I thought you were coming yesterday,' she says accusingly, finding my paperwork in her files, which are scattered all over the desk, along with bottles of antibacterial liquid and boxes of tissues. The reception is foggy with the scent of Dettol.

Yes, so did I, but Jonathan Desrosiers waited till today to pick up his post.

'I got held up. I'm very sorry. I was so disappointed – I had the house all ready, all the food, the bed and everything.' I put on a sheepish expression. 'Does it sound silly that the house felt even more empty last night, because I'd been hoping I wouldn't be on my own?'

That makes her smile. 'Bless you, I know exactly what you mean. It's like once you've made up your mind, you can hardly bear to wait. Well, I've got her all ready in the back.'

'Her?' I say, momentarily confused. 'I thought . . . it was a boy.'

'Ach no, she's a bitch. Is that a problem?'

I smile. 'No, no, not at all. I love a bitch.'

'She's a sweet one, I can tell you. She's been neutered, of course. I'd take her home myself if I didn't have three already.'

'That's a hazard of the job, I imagine,' I say, playing the game. My accent subtly changes to match hers more closely.

'Ach yes. They're all rescue – I've got Jess, she's a chocolate Lab, and Hugo, who's a Staffie – we get a lot of those here, but they've got the sweetest dispositions, Hugo is just a big

78

softie – and last year I got Digger, who's a bit of everything. He's a big ball of energy, but the others put up with him. There's never been a dull moment in my house since I brought them home.'

'I can't wait for her to be mine. I fell in love at first sight.'

'Have you ever had a dog before?'

'Never,' I answer truthfully.

'You must not be able to wait.' She smacks herself on the forehead. 'And here I am blathering when you want to take her home. Wait here, and I'll be right back with her. Do you have a collar and lead?'

I hold them up.

'Brilliant, well, this wee girl will be no trouble to you, she's one of the best-natured dogs I've ever met. I won't be a tick.'

While I wait, I try not to breathe in through my nose, though through my mouth is nearly as bad; I can taste the chemical air freshener and the urine scent it tries to cover up. I peruse the photographs of animals that decorate reception. Nearly a whole wall is covered with snaps of pets with their new owners, along with thank-you letters. The expressions on the pets' faces range from idiotic bliss to glowering ennui, but the expressions on their owners' faces are identical manic happiness.

At last I hear rubber-soled footsteps and the click of claws on tiled floor, and Princess Leia appears with the dog. The animal has short legs and a stumpy body, like a corgi, and a wiry coat, like a terrier, and a snub nose, like a bulldog. It's brown and white with a fluffy, truncated tail. Its face is white but it's got a brown splotch over one eye. One ear sticks up, and the other flops down. In short, it's ugly as hell. I'm not surprised no one has adopted it.

As soon as the dog sees me, its tail starts wagging like mad, and its tongue lolls out of its mouth.

'She remembers you,' says Princess Leia. 'Here, Patch,' she croons to the dog, 'say hello to your new mummy.'

I crouch down to hold out my arms to the dog. 'Hello, darling,' I say, in an imitation of Leia's croon, and to my relief the dog breaks free of the woman's hold and comes scrabbling into my arms. It puts its paws on my knees and licks my face and hair, panting dog breath at me. I laugh and try to hold the dog back, without success, and it lands some more licks on my cheek.

'Now that's a greeting,' says Leia, with satisfaction. 'Utter adoration. Love at first sight. I can tell the two of you are going to live happily ever after.'

At the car, I spread a blanket over my back seat so that the dog won't scratch or shed on the leather upholstery. It jumps into my car of its own accord. I look at the dog, sitting trustingly, panting with its pink tongue hanging out.

The lengths I'll go to engineer a meet-cute.

'I'm sorry,' I tell it.

10

THE WOMAN IN THE POST office hadn't been joking: the clouds rolled in, piling on top of each other in a dark mass over the loch. Jon sat on a rock on the shore and watched the rain advance over the loch in a mathematically precise line. In front of the line, the grey water was mirror-smooth, and behind the line, the water was churned into pits and peaks, rough as a farm track. Before and after.

Before: wife, career, home, a sense of purpose and justice. And then the line drawn, everything changing, the after: blood, body parts, and the documents in his pocket.

Stop seeing every bloody storm as a metaphor, he told himself, and uncorked the Ben Nevis to take another swig.

The wind rippled the grass and heather and the clouds churned in front of him. A palette of greys and browns and dull purple. Soon, he was going to be soaked, but he wasn't yet. He could stay out till the last minute, and race the storm back to the cottage. He raised the bottle to the dark sky in a toast. 'To pathetic fallacy and self-pity,' he said, and then frowned.

There was a figure struggling over the muddy path in the distance. It wore a red jacket and a yellow hat. It was desperate weather for a rambler, especially one on their own. Irritated, he stood up; the path passed straight by where he was standing, and the walker would reach him in ten minutes' time at least.

The walker spotted him and began waving their arms above their head. They picked up their pace to a near run.

Instinct made Jon tuck the bottle inside his coat and hurry to meet the person in distress. It was a woman, he saw as he got closer. Slender in hiker's gear, a light pack on her back, her hair tucked up inside her hat.

'Oh thank God,' she gasped as soon as she was near enough to speak to him. The front of her jacket was smeared with mud, as if she'd been lying down on the path. She had a map in a plastic case around her neck. 'I didn't think I'd find anyone.'

'What's wrong?'

'I was walking along just there' – she turned and pointed along the east bank of the loch – 'and I heard a whimpering sound. So I went to check. There's a hole, an old mine shaft or something, maybe a well. There are lots of them around here.'

Had a child fallen into a well? Without asking any more, he started to run in the direction she'd pointed anyway. The woman ran alongside him, her hands clutching the straps of her backpack.

'This way,' she said, pointing. 'He can't get out, and I couldn't get down there to help him by myself. I couldn't see anyone else, and I can't get signal on my phone. So I came looking for help. That way.' She pointed.

They crossed the rain line, or maybe it was just time for the storm to break, because water poured down from the sky in a sudden sheet. It soaked through Jonathan's jacket in seconds and they were running through puddles and streams in the muddy ground. The woman got in front and led him as the path twisted round rocks that barely looked any different from the rain-filled air. Their boots slipped in mud; the woman nearly toppled over and he reached out his hand to steady her but she caught herself and carried on.

Before he saw the hole he heard the whining – high-pitched and frightened. It was not the whining of a child and he nearly staggered to a halt with the relief of it. But the woman kept going, frantic now through the hammering rain, so he followed.

The hole was wet and slick and steep. Jonathan crouched beside the hiker and peered into it. He saw a flash of white at the bottom, and a sheen of muddy water.

'It's a dog,' he said.

'It must have fallen down there somehow,' said the woman. 'There's a lot of water, too. I hope it hasn't broken its leg.'

'Did you see anyone around who could be its owner?'

'I've been walking around the loch since this morning, and I haven't seen anyone. I just heard it yelling, like I said.'

She had an accent – not quite American, not quite English. She sounded panicked. He assessed the hole: the sides were nearly vertical, but it wasn't too deep. Twelve feet at most. If it was a mine shaft, it had caved in at the bottom. It was narrow, but wide enough for a man. Maybe even a man and a dog.

'Do you have any rope in your pack?' he asked her. She shook her head. 'I'm going to need your jacket, then.'

He'd expected some reticence, but to her credit, he'd no sooner said it than she was pulling off her jacket and giving it to him. Underneath she wore a fleece that looked more or less dry, until she exposed it. He took off his own jacket, considerably less waterproof than hers, and chucked the still mostly full bottle of whisky onto the path. He tied the sleeves of the two jackets together as tightly as he could. He started to pull off his T-shirt, but she put her hand on his arm.

'Take this,' she said. 'It's going to get soaked anyway.' She tugged off her fleece and handed it to him, so he tied that to the others in a chain. He did his T-shirt, too, to be safe. 'You're not going down there?'

'I don't think anyone's going to send a rescue helicopter,' he told her. 'Hold one end. You're going to have to pull.'

Slithering down the shaft was harder than he'd thought: there were roots and rocks in his way. They ripped his trousers and grazed his knees and bare back. He landed in a very confined and dark place, the only light the grey stuff that filtered down from above. There was barely enough room for him and the dog. It was submerged nearly up to its shoulders in water, and shivering. It waved its stubby tail at him.

'Sorry, mate,' he said to the dog. He had to bend at the knees to scoop the dog up under his right arm. It yelped, but didn't bite. Its little body was shivering, its coat sodden with mud. Who knew how long the dog had been in this hole while it filled with brown water.

The jacket chain was long enough to reach his shoulder.

'OK, we're coming up!' he called up to the woman. 'Get ready to pull.'

Only now did it occur to him that the sides of the hole might be too slippery to climb, or that his fellow rescuer might be too weak to pull him up. Or that his injured shoulder might not support him.

He started looking for a foothold anyway.

The roots that had hindered his descent were more useful going up. One arm held the dog, though, so he only had one hand to help him. He got himself and the dog high enough to be out of the standing water and wrapped the T-shirt that was the end of the jacket chain around his right forearm, the arm that hadn't been injured. 'Pull when I say,' he called up. Rainwater poured into his mouth and choked him, so he put his head down and concentrated on finding the next place in the mud to put his hand and foot.

The dog huddled against his side, shaking but silent. He grasped a rock sticking out from the side, pulled himself up with it, and it came free in his hand, sending a cascade of mud that sent him slipping back down several feet, dangling by his forearm from his twisted T-shirt, boots submerged.

'Are you all right?' the woman yelled down.

'Still alive,' he yelled back. She must have found something to tie the jackets to. Lucky she had, or he would have landed on his arse in the water. Which was rising, steadily and almost as quickly as he was climbing.

He swore and licked his lips, tasting mud, and started to look for a foothold all over again.

The dog didn't squirm or protest. It dug its claws into his arm, but not hard enough to break the skin. 'You're a very good dog,' he told it, as he heaved himself upward. He tried to sound soothing. He had no idea if he was.

A root, another stone. The makeshift rope pulling him upward as his hand and boots fought for purchase. The rainwater ran into his face and slicked his hair to his head. His healed stab wound felt as if it were on fire. He felt the cold and the scrapes and the water squelching between his toes as if it were happening to another person. Mostly he felt the warm body against his. Sodden hair, ribs heaving with every pant.

It was the most real, most immediate, thing he'd felt in months.

A few feet from the top, nearly close enough to grab the grass that dangled over the edge of the shaft, Jonathan tilted somehow, the water and mud slippery, and the dog slid from his grasp. The sturdy barrel of its chest was there, and then it was gone. Claws tore at his side, caught in his trousers, and Jonathan grabbed at the creature. He found the scruff of its neck and held on tight to the skin. The dog dangled there by its neck and its hind foot caught in Jonathan's jeans. It didn't even yelp. Jonathan looked down and the water below him was an opaque surface of mud.

'What's happening?' The woman's voice was on the edge of panic.

'I thought I'd lost him, but he doesn't give up that easily.' He hauled the dog up to his chest. 'Hold on, mate.'

The dog licked his cheek.

Blinking the mud from his eyes, he searched for a higher place to plant his foot. 'We're nearly there,' he yelled up. 'Can you reach down and grab the dog?'

'I'd have to let go of you.'

'I'll be all right.'

Arms appeared over the lip of the hole. He heaved the animal upward and it clawed at the muddy side of the shaft, gaining an inch or two until the woman could grab it round its shoulders. The dog was lifted from his grasp.

Jonathan stayed where he was, panting. A thick stream of brown filthy water cascaded down the hole next to his face.

His T-shirt was wrapped around his forearm tightly enough so that his hand tingled. *That water down there might be almost deep enough to drown me by now*, he thought, almost abstractly.

Then a hand reached down and grabbed his.

She pulled, harder than he'd thought she would be able to from her slenderness, and he slithered up and over the edge of the hole into a puddle on the ground.

To his surprise, he lay in the mud and laughed.

11

H E COMES OUT OF THE shaft bare-chested and covered with mud, like a full-grown man born from the earth. I wasn't wrong; there's a lot of strength in those shoulders and arms. He lets go of my hand immediately and lies there in the water, laughing.

I start laughing too. He's transformed, from someone dour and angry, to a joyous (though dirty) man.

'Oh my God,' I gasp. 'Are you OK?'

'Yes. Yes, good. How's the dog?'

The dog is shivering, and it looks like a drowned rat, but it's stopped whining. I reach my hand down to it, and it shies away.

'Why are you laughing?' I ask him.

'I don't know. I guess I'm glad to be alive. It's weird.'

'Well, you've done your good deed for the day.' And looking at the happiness in his face, so have I.

I take my fleece, which is still tied to his jacket and T-shirt, and rub his back with it. It doesn't do much but smear the mud around, and it's a pointless impulse, but he must be cold, and I want to touch him.

He raises his head. His eyes look especially bright under his slicked-down hair, with his face dappled with mud.

'For a few seconds there I didn't think you would make it,' I say.

'Neither did I.' He sits up and pushes away my hands. He's got a long red scar near the top of his collarbone, which is obvious even with all the mud. 'I don't think there's much point in that.'

'Oh. Oh, OK, sorry. I've got – I've got a flask somewhere with tea?'

'We need to get out of the rain.' He stands and picks up the dog. It nestles against his chest as if it's a baby. 'Come on.'

I gather our soaked clothes, and the bottle of whisky he had in his jacket, and hurry along with him. The path has become a stream, but we can't get much wetter anyway. My boots are waterproof enough, but not when rain is running down my legs into them. Thunder rumbles, close by; the daylight's all been blotted away. It takes us a good twenty minutes to reach his cottage, by which time we're both shivering as hard as the dog is. Jonathan pushes the door open with his shoulder. Inside, it's hardly any warmer than outside.

'Fire,' he says, setting the dog on the flagstones and going straight to the woodstove.

'Do you have towels?' I ask. My teeth are chattering.

'On the shelf in the bathroom.' He puts in a log and stands up. 'Actually, look, you do this, I'll get some clothes.'

The dog follows him out of the room; it's been quick enough to transfer its affections from me to him. Smart dog.

I look around his house. It's awful. It's all one living area, kitchen and lounge together, with two doors off it which are presumably bedroom and bathroom. The cooker looks a death trap and there are buckets scattered around to catch the drips coming through the damp-stained ceiling. There's an ugly tartan sofa which has been patched in one arm with silver gaffer tape, an ugly threadbare rug, and an ugly table with two rickety chairs. On it sits a dirty mug and a couple of sheets of paper.

I take off my hat and comb my tangled hair with my fingers while I quickly read the letters on the table. Then I build up the fire with more logs and some kindling. I hear him come back in the room, accompanied by the dog's toenails on the flagstones, but I don't turn around until he says, 'Here.'

He's holding out a towel and some dry clothes. He looks at me and stares, because my long-sleeved white T-shirt is sodden and nearly see-through and it clings to my body.

Yes, this was a good choice of outfit. I smile at him and he immediately averts his eyes.

'You can change into those,' he says, voice rough, and retreats back into his bedroom.

The towel doesn't do much to remove the mud, but I quickly strip and put on Jonathan Desrosiers' clothes: a plain white T-shirt, a brown woollen jumper, tracksuit bottoms, thick socks. Disappointingly, they smell of detergent rather than of him, and I wonder where he does his laundry. I have to roll up the sleeves of the jumper and the bottoms of the trousers, but they're soft and warm. I bring the two chairs near the woodstove and drape my wet clothes on them to dry. Glancing at the closed bedroom door, I look through the pockets of his jacket before I hang it up. Car keys in the hip pocket, and a sodden envelope in the inside pocket. Careful not to tear the wet paper, I take the envelope out of his pocket and open it up.

It's a petition for divorce from Amy Elizabeth Barbour Desrosiers (Petitioner) to Jonathan Michael Desrosiers

(Respondent), on grounds of neglect and estrangement. He hasn't signed it yet.

I hear him saying something in the bedroom, presumably to the dog. I quickly return the document to the envelope and the envelope to the pocket and hang his jacket up on a chair. I'm on the ugly sofa when he comes back in and it's only for a second but when he sees me, he hesitates. Naked emotion crosses his face and I think, *Your ex-wife wore this jumper, didn't she? With the sleeves rolled up just like this? One morning after you made love, walking sleepy and satisfied to the kitchen to make coffee?*

As if to prove my deduction, he goes straight to his jacket and reaches into the inside pocket. He extracts the envelope and places it carefully on the wall shelf above the wood pile.

'Something important?' I ask.

'Not particularly.' He's wearing jeans and a sweatshirt and an ill-at-ease expression. There's still mud on his neck and in his hair. He'll want to take a bath but not while I'm in the house, like an obligation he can't wait to get rid of.

'You were amazing,' I tell him. 'I thought that dog was going to drown down there.'

'Is it your dog?'

'No, I was hiking by the loch and I heard it, like I said.' I consider the dog, which is still covered in mud and is wagging its tail by Jonathan's feet. 'He likes you. He knows you saved his life.'

'It's a girl,' he says, crouching down to scratch the dog behind its mismatched ears. 'She hasn't got a collar; I wonder if she escaped from a house or if she's a stray.'

'I nearly didn't go for a walk today, but I thought I'd be able to get back to my car before the storm hit. I hate to think of what would have happened if I hadn't heard her, and I hadn't found you. With the way it's raining, that hole would have filled with water very quickly.' I shiver. 'I could do with a cup of tea, if that's all right?'

He goes to the kitchen area to put the kettle on. I get the impression he's quite glad to turn his back on me, as if I remind him of something he'd rather not think about. The dog follows him.

'Are you a dog person?' I ask.

'No.'

'Well, this dog seems to think you are.'

He doesn't answer, just takes out two mugs and spoons coffee into both of them. He stares intently at the kettle until it boils, and then pours water into the mugs. When he gives me one, I hold out my hand to shake. 'I'm Saffy.'

'Jon.' He doesn't take my hand, but leans against the kitchen counter to drink his coffee. The wood burner hasn't made much of a dent in the cold in the room yet, and the coffee steams around his face as he sips.

'It's nice to meet you,' I say. 'What do you do, Jon?'

'I'm retired.'

'You're young to be retired. Lucky you. Did you leave your job because you got rich, or because it didn't suit you anymore?' He doesn't reply, so I take another tack. 'You were really heroic out there. You didn't hesitate at all. I bet before you retired, you did something that helped people.'

'It's not important.'

'Maybe not, but I think you've got a natural heroic streak. That's the kind of thing that you can't retire from.'

He snorts.

'Seriously,' I say. 'Most people wouldn't throw themselves into a hole to rescue a dog they've never seen before. They'd want to wait and call someone else to come.' I sip my coffee, which is awful instant stuff, but at least it's hot. 'You're the sort of person who wants to take care of things himself, who wants to make sure it's all right, even if it means running a risk. That's a hero, in my book.'

'I wouldn't say so.'

'Well, that dog loves you, and they say that dogs are great judges of character.' I bend and put down my hand for the dog, who ignores it and presses closer to Jonathan's legs. Which pretty much proves my point that dogs are good judges of character. I wouldn't trust someone who'd adopted me and immediately put me down a well, either.

'It did feel good to save her,' he admits.

I straighten. 'Nice place you've got here,' I lie. 'Do you live on your own?'

'Yes.'

'Maybe you could use a dog to keep you company. If it's a stray.'

He looks surprised at this. 'I thought you were going to take her with you.'

'Oh no, I can't take a dog home.'

'But—'

'I can ring around and see if anyone's lost a dog? Tell them that you've got it?'

'I don't think I can—'

My face falls. 'Should I take her to the shelter, then? After all she's been through, it feels sort of cruel to just stick her in a cage.'

Jonathan looks down at the dog. The dog looks up at him, wagging its tail.

'I suppose . . .'

'I knew you were a hero,' I beam. 'You are a literal knight in shining armour. Can I have your number? I'll make some phone calls and tell people to get in touch with you.'

He frowns. But he finds a pen, writes his number in the margin of the newspaper, rips the strip off, and gives it to me. I retrieve my phone from my waterproof pocket, but there's no signal. I look at him enquiringly.

'It only works in that corner,' he says, pointing to a space between the window and a large bucket. I trot over there obediently and spend the next ten minutes pretending to ring the local police and the animal shelter.

'Nobody's missing a doggy,' I say, finally, putting my unused phone down. 'But they'll ring you if they get any reports.'

'Thanks,' he says, not sounding as if he means it. He glances at the window, where the rain is still chucking down. The desire to get rid of me is clear.

'My car's about two miles from here,' I tell him. 'I was on my way back when I heard the dog. It's no problem; I can walk.'

'Of course not, in this weather. I'll drive you.'

'You're really going beyond the call of duty. A rescue, coffee, warm clothes . . .' I rub the sleeve of his jumper. 'I'll wash them and bring them back to you.'

'There's no need,' he says, going to his jacket and fishing his keys out of his pocket. 'They're old clothes.'

'I insist. I can't repay you for a good deed by nicking your clothes.'

'You can take them to the post office in Fort William, then. I go in there to pick up my post; they'll keep them for me.' He opens the door to the cottage. A blast of cold air and rain comes in. I collect my clothes quickly and follow him out, as does the dog. We're all soaked again in seconds. Jonathan seems confused when the dog appears, waiting to be let into the car, but he opens the door for it and it jumps up into the driver's seat and then hops into the back, leaving muddy footprints on the seat.

I climb into the passenger seat and he starts the Land Rover without any comment. I wasn't wrong about the worn bearings. The windscreen wipers barely increase visibility as he turns the car around and heads down the rutted, muddy track. In parts it's nearly washed out.

I watch his profile as he drives. He's frowning and he looks angry at the road, at the rain, at his worn bearings, at me. When he'd disappeared, I thought maybe he'd given up, but there's still so much fight in him. So much passion.

I can help him rediscover it.

'I'm just a mile or so up here on the left,' I tell him when he reaches the A road. He drives too quickly to be strictly prudent in this weather, and has to brake quite hard when he sees my M5 parked in the lay-by.

'Thank you,' I say to him. 'Thank you again.'

He nods.

'I know you said you're retired,' I continue, 'but sometimes I get funny instincts about people, and you're one of them. I feel that you've still got something inside you to give. I think you can still help people.' His lips tighten, so I add quickly, 'I know it's none of my business, and I don't know you at all, but my instincts are hardly ever wrong. You're a hero, even if you don't want to be.'

I lean forward and kiss him swiftly on the cheek. Damp, woodsmoke, whisky, mud, the warmth of his skin.

Then I open the door and slip out of the car. 'See you again, maybe.'

'I don't think so.'

'You never know,' I reply, and run for my car.

He waits until I'm in it and I've started it. I give him a little wave and he turns the Land Rover around in the road and starts back to where he's come from. I watch the tail lights disappear through the rain, and then I drive off in the opposite direction, feeling fizzy with excitement.

I just love the first heady days of a relationship, don't you?

12

WHEN HE WAS IN HOSPITAL recovering from being stabbed, Amy came to see him. It had been less than forty-eight hours since she'd left him, but when she walked into the room, she almost looked like a stranger.

'You cut your hair,' he croaked from the bed.

'I brought you some grapes,' she said. She put them down on the bedside table and stood there. She was wearing jeans and a jumper and her new haircut was a straight bob with a fringe.

'I miss you so much,' he said, and reached out his hand to her. But she stepped back.

'I'm not staying,' she said. 'I just had to check to make sure you were OK.'

'Yes. I'm fine. Cyril missed all of the major organs. You'd think he'd be better at killing people, after so much practice.'

Amy winced, and he saw he'd messed it up again.

'I'm sorry,' he said. 'I'm sorry for the dark humour. I know it's not funny.'

'That man was in our *house*, Jonny. He was our *guest* at that party you threw for Dorothy and Marcia. And he was a murderer.'

'I know.'

'You brought that type of man into our life. That was you.'

'I know. I'm sorry.'

'I can't live with that. Not anymore.'

'I know I reacted badly the other night. I got angry, and that was wrong. I need to see your point of view, and how lonely you've been. I can change, Amy. This is a wake-up call.'

She shook her head, slowly. 'It's not a wake-up call. It's the opposite of that. You're obsessed, Jonny. You've got a compulsive need to solve puzzles. It's like if you solve enough of them, somehow you'll come to some answer that's going to satisfy you. And I don't know what you're looking to find, and I hope you find it, but it's not going to be with me.'

That was the moment that Jon realised that he hadn't really believed her. He'd been hoping that their marriage wasn't over, that she was just upset, that when she saw that he'd been hurt, that he was a hero, she'd change her mind.

But she wasn't upset now. She was deliberate, and quietly sad, and that was much, much worse.

'Do you want me to call someone for you?' she asked him gently. 'Maybe Edie? Someone who can sit with you, and look after you for a bit?'

'No,' he told her. 'No, I'm better off alone.'

* * *

Now, he sat in his leaky living room, listening to the rain pattering in the various containers, eating bacon sandwiches with a dog. He wasn't much of a cook, but the dog scarfed her sandwich up in about two bites, looked at him hopefully for more, and when she realised he wasn't going to share his sandwich, she curled up next to his feet and went to sleep.

Somehow, he'd saved this dog. And then he'd given his number to a strange and beautiful woman.

'This is the oddest day I've had in months,' he said to the dog, who twitched an ear.

He finished his sandwich, licked brown sauce off his finger, and realised there wasn't anything else to do but ring Edie. So he did.

'Have you come to your senses and realised you have to write this book about Cyril?' she said right away, when she answered. 'Because that book has "Netflix adaptation" written all over it.'

'I'm not writing a book about Cyril.'

'Did you at least look at your post?'

'I did that. Yes.'

'Let's talk about that, but first, let's get this other thing out of the way. I think you should write back to your superfan. He's been ringing the office, too. He sounds concerned about you and obviously he has no life. I think you should throw this poor guy a bone. Tell him you're fine and he should stop harassing your poor overworked agent. Either that, or get a restraining order against him.'

'OK. I'll write to Simon.'

'Good man. OK, so the other thing.'

The other thing was sitting on the coffee table. He reached over and picked it up: a single sheet of A4 with four lines typed on it.

'Atherton hates me,' he said.

'I haven't read DI Atherton's letter, obviously. I just talked to him on the phone, where he told me that since I couldn't share your new phone number or address and since you weren't answering emails, I absolutely must forward his letter to you immediately. He's not exactly a warm and fuzzy person.'

'Atherton thinks I glamorise murder, and I can't say that he's wrong.'

'Why did he write to you?'

'He didn't tell you?'

'No, and I'm dying of curiosity. I thought about steaming the letter open, but I decided that would be unethical agent behaviour. Marj was very disappointed with me.' Marj was Edie's wife and assistant. 'What does it say?'

'He wants me to come down and see him, to "assist with his enquiries".'

A silence, which was unusual with Edie. 'What does that mean?'

'It doesn't mean that he wants to have a drink and swap clues.'

'But surely you gave him a statement already?'

'Yes. But they still haven't identified the sixth victim, and Cyril won't talk about where the head is. Cyril says he'll only speak with me about it. So they want me to talk with him.'

There was a pause.

'This would be so great on Netflix,' Edie said.

'Stop it.'

'Are you going to go?'

Jon sighed. 'If we can find the final victim's head, we'll be doing a service to his family. Right now, they don't know if he's dead or alive.'

'So you have to go.'

'I think I have to. Yes.'

But he didn't want to.

* * *

102

That night, Jon started awake on his sofa. His face was wet, his neck, his hands. For a confused moment he thought it was blood again. For another moment he thought it was coming back: the panic, the fear that came after his physical wounds had healed, that had stopped him from moving for days, that made him hide in damp and shaded rooms, made him afraid to speak or sleep.

Then he heard a soft whimper. He realised he had been asleep. He sat up and next to him, a small dark shape sat up too. He felt a warm, wet tongue lick his cheek and a soft body lean against him.

Heart pounding, he lay back down. The dog lay beside him, its muzzle on his arm. He put his hand on the dog's back and counted its sleeping breaths. He could do this. He could do this. He owed it to the victim's family.

He thought this over and over until he, too, fell asleep.

13

JON DRANK COFFEE OUT OF a plastic cup and regarded the dog at his feet. Actually, to be more accurate, she was *on* his feet, lying across them under the table. Feeling his eyes on her, she blinked up at him and thumped her stubby tail twice.

'I really have no idea,' he told her, and went back to his coffee and staring moodily out of the window as Scotland rapidly ran out. The sun was beginning to poke through the clouds. Despite Jon's predilection for pathetic fallacy, this sight didn't give him much optimism. He wished he'd brought some Ben Nevis to drink instead, so he could forget that he was on his way to London, to meet with a man who had stabbed him. The man who still walked his dreams every night.

At his feet, the dog suddenly stiffened.

'Oh my goodness, you kept her!'

A blonde woman stood in front of him, grinning. She had straight honey-smooth hair, glossy and expensive; sparkling hazel eyes; a perfect complexion. She wore fitted jeans and a white button-down shirt and she was so well groomed that it took Jon a moment to recognise her even though he'd been thinking about her, on and off, for the past two days. The last time he'd seen her, she'd been dishevelled and damp to the skin and wearing his clothes. She was just as beautiful as she had been before.

She didn't wait for him to reply; she stooped down and addressed the dog. 'You're looking very well after your fright, little one! And you've had a bath, haven't you?' She reached out to stroke the dog's head but the animal recoiled, pressing against Jonathan's legs. 'Oh, she's shy. Don't you remember me?'

'She probably associates you with the trauma of being stuck in the well,' Jon said. 'I wouldn't take it personally.'

'But she seems to adore *you*.' The woman – Jon never forgot a name and hers was Saffy, as in 'silly' combined with 'daffy' – slipped into the seat across from his, resting her expensive-looking handbag and a large shopping bag on the table between them. 'I'm so glad you kept her!'

'I didn't exactly keep her. Nobody came forward to claim her. And I couldn't go to London and leave her alone, so.'

'She is totally yours.' Her accent was, again, an odd sort of trans-Atlantic. In an anorak and hiking boots with a map around her neck, she hadn't breathed money, but she did now. Trust-fund private school, rich husband too? He glanced at her hand; no rings. Rich family, then. He remembered her M5 parked by the side of the road.

'What have you named her?' she asked.

'I haven't named her anything.'

'But surely you call her something. You can't just go around saying "Hey you" to a dog.'

'When I have to, I call her Girl.'

The dog lifted her head and thumped her tail again.

'Look, she knows that's what you call her. That is adorable. Absolutely adorable. And you're taking her to London with

106

you, from Scotland. That's commitment if I ever saw it. Some of my ex-boyfriends wouldn't take me further than from Fulham to High Street Ken.'

'I doubt that.' It slipped out before he could stop himself.

She didn't seem to take offence; she laughed. 'I dropped your clothes off at the post office yesterday. Did you get them?'

'No, I haven't had time.'

'Well, they'll be waiting for you when you get back. How long are you in London for?'

'I don't know. It depends.'

She extended her hand over the table. 'Saffy. In case you forgot.'

He touched hers for the briefest of moments. 'I didn't.'

'And I didn't forget that your name is Jon.' She reached for her handbag and started rummaging around in it. He supposed this meant that she was planning to sit across from him for the duration of the journey.

She pulled out a lipstick and unselfconsciously applied it to her lips, without the use of a mirror. Without meaning to, Jon watched her. It was a graceful gesture: a flick of the fingers to twist the lipstick up from its tube, a feather of economical strokes on her lips. She didn't get any in the wrong place. Clearly this was something she had practised a lot.

She pressed her lips together and Jon looked away.

'Let me get you a coffee, Jon. Yours is nearly gone.'

'That's not necessary.'

'It's no bother.'

She started to get up but he got up quickly before she could, impelled by some long-rusty instinct of chivalry. 'I'll do it.'

Saffy smiled up at him. 'Thank you! I'll hold the dog, if you like.' She reached out her hand for the lead but Girl pressed close against his ankles.

'I think she wants to come with me.' And sure enough, the dog trotted happily after him up the aisle of the carriage to the buffet car.

He'd forgotten to ask her how she liked her coffee. He'd given her coffee before, in the cottage, but he'd been too eager to get rid of her to offer her milk or sugar. He filled his pockets with long-life milk and packets of sugar and persuaded Girl back to the seat. He had to bribe her halfway with a biscuit.

'I don't know how you take it,' he said, emptying the milk and sugar on the table next to her coffee. When he sat down again, the dog scooted between his feet and lay down.

'You know how I really like it, is with a shot of whisky. Especially when I'm a bit hung-over.' She gave him a rueful look. 'Is it too early, do you suppose?'

'I don't think the buffet car will sell us spirits before noon.'

'Well.' She bit her lip and looked guilty. 'I might have a bottle in my bag.'

He raised an eyebrow.

'It's a gift,' she said quickly. 'For my housekeeper. But I can replace it when I get to London.' She pulled a bottle of Ben Nevis out of her shopping bag, cracked the seal, and poured a slug into her coffee. 'Can I tempt you?'

He could smell it. 'What the hell.' He pushed his cup towards her, and she topped it up with whisky.

'Here's to a good journey,' she said, raising her cup, and he raised his. They sipped at the same time.

'Railway coffee's a waste of single malt,' he said.

'It definitely makes the coffee more palatable.' She sipped again and put down her cup, smiling. 'Ah, hair of the dog. Just what the doctor ordered.'

'You don't look hung-over.' She was, in fact, the least hung-over woman he had ever seen: her face was fresh-complexioned, her eyes were clear, she didn't have a hair out of place.

'Ugh. I was at the officially worst dinner party ever last night, with the most tedious people. I had to neck the wine just to keep myself from killing someone.'

'In those cases, drinking is a civic duty.'

'I know! And my friend is kind, but she'd invited a selection of single men to meet me, and they were all horrible. What is it about being single, that all your smug married friends want you to stop having fun and tie yourself down to an investment banker with ambitions in politics?' She gave a mock shudder.

'I wouldn't know.'

'Oh! Are you married? I'm sorry. Not all marrieds are smug marrieds; I wasn't calling you smug. It's not in the actual job description.'

'I'm in the process of getting divorced.' The words tasted sour on his tongue. He took a sip of whisky-laced coffee and wished it were stronger.

'I'm sorry again. I seem to be determined to put my foot in my mouth.'

'It's fine.' For a few minutes, they sat in silence, listening to the train.

Or at least, she was probably listening to the train. Jonathan was listening to that stupid hymn that Amy had insisted on in the church: 'All Things Bright and Beautiful'. He wasn't religious, not since he'd been old enough to choose. He associated churches with stultifying Sundays in a slick hard pew, stomach growling from hunger and his father glaring at him whenever he dared to squirm. Religion was something to be endured until you could bolt your Sunday roast and escape to the bench in the back of the garden or a bough of the tallest tree in the park, hiding with a book until darkness fell and Dad would have finished his bottle and be safely asleep and snoring on the sofa.

Standing at the altar, waiting on what was supposed to be the happiest day of his life, he'd heard that hymn. And he was right back there in the church in Putney, collar itching, stomach empty, breathing his father's whisky fumes from the night before.

He'd almost forgotten to look when Amy started walking down the aisle.

Jonathan swallowed and looked out of the window. It was properly sunny out, now; the clouds revealed patches of blue. Dammit.

'I'll trade you more whisky for a look at your newspaper,' said Saffy across from him. He pushed the paper across the table along with his cup, which he was surprised to notice was empty. She poured in a slug, topped up her own, and unfolded his newspaper. 'Hmm. All bad news, as usual.'

'I don't know why I bought it,' he said. 'Habit, I guess.'

'The crossword is good on a Thursday.'

'I don't do crosswords.'

'Do you mind if I do it? I love puzzles, don't you?'

Only the bloody kind. Only the kind that started in pain and ended in more pain.

'Help yourself,' he said.

She took out a pen and filled in a few clues rapidly. He realised he was watching her, and looked away again.

'So what's taking you to London?' she asked, after a little bit. 'Business or pleasure? Oh wait – you said you were retired, didn't you? So it's pleasure?'

'I'm trying to help someone,' he said.

She beamed at him. 'I knew it. You're a proper knight in shining armour.'

'I wouldn't say that. It's well and truly tarnished by now.' She didn't reply, and he realised she was waiting for him to say something, so he asked the expected: 'What about you? Why are you heading to London?'

'Because of my sister and her fucking useless boyfriend.' She put her hand over her mouth. 'Oh no, I'm sorry. I might pretend I've been well brought up, but I have a horribly dirty mouth, especially when I've been drinking.'

Dirty mouth. He glanced at the mark on her cup again, and then away. Thought of the small deft strokes of the colour on her lips. It was the booze that was finding her attractive.

But it was something new. He hadn't had a stirring of sexual interest in anything since Amy left him. He'd tried masturbating to pass the time, but he'd kept getting bored.

'It's all right,' he said. 'I've been known to swear on occasion. What's wrong with your sister's boyfriend?'

'What *isn't* wrong with him, is the question. He split up with her again last night, so this is sort of an emergency rescue mission. He's brilliant but he's unemployed – well, to be accurate, he's a tech bro who created his own start-up and then sold it for shedloads of money. But he hasn't done any work in ages. He sponges off my sister, spends his days smoking weed and filming puerile TikTok videos, and he hooks up with other women every time he gets the chance. Plus, he never wears socks.' Saffy wrinkled her nose.

'Sounds like a bad catch.'

'My sister has terrible taste in men. Of course, she never ceases to give me advice on my love life. Have you got any siblings?'

'Only child. It seems I dodged a bullet.'

Saffy's eyes widened. 'Oh no. No, my sister is the best thing in my life. I don't know where I would be without her. Seriously. I would do anything for her. And that's what life is about, isn't it? Having someone you would do anything for.'

Once upon a time, he would have said he would do anything for Amy. Except he hadn't. He'd left her alone while he wallowed in his own little world of justice and murder. Just like his father had done: giving his best to the Met, and leaving the drunken dregs for his own wife and child.

He shrugged and didn't say anything, and despite her apparently habitual perkiness, Saffy seemed to understand his mood because she lapsed into silence and went back to her crossword.

The carriage was nearly empty, and it was an oddly intimate space. Their knees were inches from each other, and the world was rushing past outside them. He could smell her perfume, or maybe it was the scent of her shampoo: something with sandalwood and rose.

'I'm sorry,' he said. 'I'm not much good for human company these days.'

'Oh, don't worry,' she said. 'It's nice to have someone to share my whisky with. I don't require you to entertain me.'

'That's just as well.'

'Seriously, though, I wouldn't worry if I were you. You should have heard the level of the conversation at that dinner party last night.' She shuddered. 'If I have to hear one more conversation about interest rates and tax havens, I swear I will do something desperate.'

'Do you get bored easily?'

'Very. Apparently it's one of the classic signs of a sociopath.' She winked at him. 'Fortunately I am also very easily amused.'

'I'm … glad I could amuse you.' It sounded strange coming out of his mouth; almost flirtatious.

'Me too.' She held his gaze with her own, and smiled, and he wondered if he could taste her lipstick on his lips from the small contact their cups had made, and he realised he was drunk at the same moment that he realised that the train had stopped at Wigan and a group of people had entered their carriage, chattering loudly and laughing.

He glanced over at them: women, dolled up to the nines, holding bottles of white wine and plastic cups. A hen night or a birthday party on their way to London. When he looked back at Saffy she rolled her eyes slightly. Their intimacy was gone, replaced by another one: the only two sensible people in the carriage.

At his feet, the dog shifted and sighed.

* * *

When the train was slowing to pull into Euston, he stood to take his suitcase down from the overhead shelf. His head swam a bit. They'd slowed down their whisky drinking for the second part of the journey, but by tacit consent she'd kept their cups topped up just enough for them to avoid sliding down into a midday hangover. Though perhaps it was more than that; now that he was on his feet, he could feel the amount they must have drunk. Or the amount he must have drunk, anyway; aside from a slight flush in her cheeks and a brightness in her eyes, Saffy looked almost as perfect as she had when she'd sat across from him as they were leaving Glasgow.

'Where are you off to?' she asked him, standing up herself and replacing the considerably less than full bottle in her shopping bag. 'Have you got a place in London? Or are you staying with friends?'

'No,' he said. 'I guess I'm going to have to find a hotel.'

'A dog-friendly one?'

'Oh. Yeah.' Why hadn't he thought of that? Probably because he'd been preoccupied with Cyril.

He had to pick up Girl to get her to hop off the train. Euston was high ceilings, noise, diesel smells, streams of people. More people than he had seen in a very long time. He heard a whine below him and looked down at Girl: her ears were flat back and her tail tucked low in response to the overwhelming sensation of the city.

'I know,' he told her. 'I know.'

Saffy waited for him on the platform. She had only a small chic overnight case, along with her expensive-looking handbag and shopping bag. She looked as if she usually travelled first class. He wondered if she'd chosen to sit in the cheap seats just to keep talking with him.

'I've just had a genius idea!' she said. 'I'm going straight to my sister's, and I'm going to stay with her for a few days to help nurse her heartbreak. Why don't you and Girl stay in my place?'

'What? No, I couldn't do that.'

'You must! It is the least I owe you, for helping me save Girl, and for lending me your clothes and helping me to my car.' She dug in her handbag and held out a set of keys on a leather tassel key chain. 'Please, use my place while you're in London, for as long as you like.'

'No, Saffy, I can't do that.'

'Of course you can!'

'You don't even know me.'

'Are you kidding me? I know that you're the type of guy who will risk his life to save a dog, and who will drop everything to go down to London to help someone. As long as you promise not to leave your wet towels on the floor, you're the ideal house guest.' She winked at him. 'And if you're worried about *me*, you can google me. Saffy Huntley-Oliver. Just in case you need to know that I'm not an axe murderer.'

'Honestly, it's fine. I'll get a hotel.'

She pressed the keys into his hand. 'You'd be doing me a favour. You could water my plants, if any of them are still alive. Besides, you don't want Girl stuck in a lousy hotel room all day while you're out, do you?'

He looked down at Girl, who looked up at him with haunted and trusting eyes.

'Well,' he said. 'That's very kind. But I'll reimburse you—'

Saffy laughed and dismissed his offer with a wave of her hand. 'Tell you what. You can take me out to dinner.'

He hesitated. Was she flirting? Or was this what she was like with everyone?

'Just dinner,' she said. 'You've got to eat, right? Or do you have a lot of people you need to catch up with, down here?'

'Actually, I don't,' he heard himself saying. 'I don't have any people to catch up with. And it would be nice to buy you dinner.'

She beamed. 'Fabbo. And we can find someplace dog-friendly, if you want to take Girl with us.' She bent to ruffle the dog's ears, and the dog backed quickly between Jonathan's feet, wrapping the lead around his leg. 'You're a shy one, aren't you?' she said to the dog, and then looked back up at Jonathan. 'I've got your number in my phone. I'll text you my address, and we'll sort out the details for dinner. Ciao!'

Before he knew what she was going to do, she'd kissed him briefly on his cheek and was walking off down the platform.

14

I HAVE TO LIE QUITE A bit in my day-to-day life, if only by omission, and I've learned that lies (or omissions) are more believable when they're mixed with truth. So, for example, I didn't tell Jon that I'd read his post and I knew that he would be going to London to talk with the police. I also didn't tell him that I knew that his shitty Land Rover wouldn't survive the journey, and so I'd been watching him to determine which train he took, so I could join him seemingly by chance.

However, I was actually telling the truth about coming to my sister's rescue, because Finlay has shown himself to be a consummate dick. Surprise, surprise.

Susan's halfway through a bottle of Sancerre when I get to her flat in Chelsea. There's a carton of Ben & Jerry's Chunky Monkey leaking on the glass coffee table, two empty tubes of Pringles and the air is a fug of cigarette smoke.

'It's like that horrible scene in *Bridget Jones*,' I tell her, dumping the shopping bags on the armchair, and opening the windows to let the stinky air out. 'You're better than this, Susie-san.'

'I don't care if I look like a cliché,' she says, lying back on the sofa, bottle of wine in hand. At least her pyjamas match. 'I *am* a cliché. Dumped woman. Trodden into the dirt.'

'Resorting to junk food from the corner shop.' I take the bottle from her hand and bring it to the kitchen area of her open-plan mews flat to find another glass. 'You could at least go to Whole Foods and get something that isn't one hundred per cent artificial flavourings.'

'I like artificial flavourings,' says Susan from the sofa. 'And I haven't been able to eat them for the past four months because bloody Finlay was on a bloody macrobiotic high-protein organic diet because of his bloody triathlon next month.'

'Bastard,' I say, and take the bottle of wine to the kitchen. The recycling bin has three empty bottles in it, which considering that Finlay only dumped my sister yesterday, is pretty good going. I make Susan and me a cup of tea and bring them through.

'I want more wine,' she says.

'Later. Drink this, and then I'm going to use that juicer I gave you for Christmas and make you a smoothie full of anti-oxidants. The best revenge is looking good, and if you keep on putting this shit into your body, you're going to have the complexion of a sponge.'

'Oh, that's rubbish, Saffy. You texted me from the train that you'd drunk half the bottle of scotch you bought for Tilly.'

'Yes. But it was in a good cause, and I have other ways of getting revenge.'

'Did you meet your dangerous Scot?'

'It depends. Is dog hair dangerous?'

'You met a dog?'

I curl up next to her on the sofa and watch her drink her tea.

'I met a man with a dog, who is currently staying in my house for a few days. So I'm going to crash in your spare bedroom, and look after you.'

'Is he good-looking?'

'Well, he's not the type that *you* would swipe right on, but . . .' I tap my lips with my finger, thoughtfully. 'There's something about him. And before you ask – no, he's not boring.'

She perks up a little. 'Did you get laid?'

'Susan! No.'

'Too bad. It seems as if at least one of us should be getting laid.' She leans her head against my shoulder, and I stroke her hair. 'I found the texts on his phone, with someone called Ulyana.'

'And you say that *you're* a cliché. Susie-san, he's not worth it.' I kiss her forehead. 'But when we spoke last night you said that he dumped you? Not that you dumped him for being a cheating wank-stain?'

'When I called him on it, he said it was nothing, refused to explain and said that I should trust him, and that he didn't think he could be with someone who was so suspicious.'

'Ugh! Classic DARVO. What a douche.' Susie looks a little confused, so I explain, 'Deny the wrongdoing, Attack the victim, Reverse Victim and Offender so that he seems like he's the one who's being wronged. It's a move often used by sociopaths and abusers.'

'Oh, I know what DARVO is, Saffy, I am literally on Instagram all the time. I was wondering about "douche".'

'It's . . .' I sigh. 'Never mind.'

'Anyway, Finlay's not a sociopath.'

'How do you know?'

'I think I could tell a sociopath if I met one.'

Oh Susie, you sweet summer child.

'Anyway,' I say. 'We'll go shopping tomorrow. And I'll book us in for facials. The best revenge is looking good, and posting selfies online. You'll glow, and Finlay will eat his heart out.'

I think, with relish, about how much I would enjoy watching Finlay literally eating his heart, and drink my tea.

* * *

Later, after I've made my sister eat some vegetables and we've polished off another bottle of wine, I tuck Susan up in her bed with a pint of water and two milk thistle capsules on her bedside table, and sit beside her until she falls asleep. She looks younger when she's sleeping, like the little girl I used to tuck in and read to every night, story after story. She used to love anything to do with princesses or elephants.

I sit there for a while, listening to her breathing, being glad she's alive.

In the living room, I tidy the mess she's made: throw away the rest of the junk food, straighten the sofa cushions, clear up the piles of used tissues. Her phone is on the coffee table. I unlock it (she's used her birthday for her lock code, like nearly everyone else out there) and scroll through her messages, both sent and received. At least Finlay the Tosspot has had the good sense not to respond to the four drunken, pleading messages my little sister has sent to him in the past twelve hours.

I delete her messages; with any luck once she's sobered up she'll have forgotten she wrote them. Then I block Finlay and delete his details from her contacts. She doesn't need any more temptation.

Then I make myself a cup of hot water and fresh lemon (because no matter what my sweet Susie-san believes, my complexion doesn't take care of itself) and while my sister sleeps, I consider my options.

Naturally, I want to kill him. Nobody – and I mean nobody – gets away with hurting my little sister. I know where he lives; I was there last month for a macrobiotic, organic, high-protein dinner party. He has a loft in Shoreditch. The walls are thick Victorian brick, and all the windows are double-glazed, and Finlay's even had the place fitted with extra soundproofing because he plays the saxophone. If I were a petty person, the saxophone-playing and the macrobiotic dinner party alone would be enough to sign his death sentence.

The CCTV camera over the entrance has exposed wiring which would be child's play to cut, and the flat below his is owned by a Chinese businessman who very rarely makes an appearance. And his kitchen is full of lovely, lovely sharp Misono knives.

I close my eyes and indulge in a pleasurable vision of Finlay Smythe duct-taped down on his Danish blond-wood dining table, his smug mouth stuffed with one of his athletic socks, while I test exactly how sharp those Misonos are. I'd been thinking of getting some for my own kitchen anyway, so there would be some useful consumer information to be gained.

But it's a pleasant fantasy, and that's all. This would be a bad way to kill Finlay. It would be messy and obvious and anyone looking for someone with a motive would think first of my little sister.

More importantly, if Finlay were murdered, Susie would be really upset. She's still half in love with him, jerk that he is. If he died, he'd become a saint in her eyes despite whoever Ulyana is. She'd make up this whole fantasy in her head that this other woman was only a fling, and he would have come to his senses and reunited with Susie, prostrating himself with love for her, begging her to take him back, probably brandishing an engagement ring. If only he hadn't been senselessly and tragically murdered before he could do so.

My sister is big on happy endings, despite all the readily available evidence to the contrary.

So as much as I'd love to kill him for breaking Susie's heart, I can't even think about doing it until she's over him.

Plus, and this is a big plus: I've got my own little project going on right now. I'm building the perfect love story for Jonathan Desrosiers and me. I can't afford the distraction of murdering random scumbags. I've promised myself that I'll put my hobby on hold until I've got my man. It's time to make love, not corpses.

But who's to say? Maybe in a year or two, once Susie's found someone better, once Jon and I are blissfully coupled up, I could arrange a little accident for Finlay Smythe. A failure of the brakes on his SLX while he's driving too fast on those twisty Welsh roads, on the way to his latest race. A gas leak in his soundproofed loft. *Clostridium botulinum* bacteria in his miso soup. Yes ... that would be good.

I put down Susie's phone, do a final sweep of the living area for any stray tissues, turn off the lights, and do one more quick check to make sure she's safely sleeping. Then I get myself ready for bed in her guest room, where she keeps a spare toothbrush for me in the en suite and a pair of pyjamas in the wardrobe. I like to get an early night when I can. I set the alarm for six thirty, so I can be up in time to make her breakfast. Before I drift off to sleep, I indulge in another little fantasy of Ulyana-whoever-she-is opening the door of Finlay's bathroom to find him collapsed on the tiles, trousers around his ankles, shit stains on the floor, lips blue from respiratory failure.

I can bide my time. I'm quite good at that.

15

THE ADDRESS THAT SAFFY TEXTED him was a mews house in Kensington, set on a cobbled street of white-painted brick houses, blooming flower boxes, climbing wisteria, and perfectly trimmed topiary trees in pots. The whole street smelled of jasmine and artisan coffee. As Jon and Girl turned into the mews, actual classical piano music drifted from an open window of one of the houses. Jon glanced down at his mud-spattered anorak and boots, the dog of frankly dubious parentage, and thought his odds of being arrested were pretty good.

Saffy's house was the last one on the cul-de-sac on the right. It had a saffron-yellow door flanked by potted palm trees, a matching yellow garage door, and a little balcony dripping with geraniums. It looked like a house inhabited by the beautiful, perky heroine of the type of romantic comedy films that Amy used to watch. Maybe Saffy *was* one of those heroines. He hadn't been wrong about her being rich, anyway – this *bijou* little property must have cost millions of pounds.

He unlocked the door. Girl hesitated on the threshold, whining softly. 'It's OK,' he told her, picking her up. 'I feel exactly the same way.'

It opened directly to the living room, which was all gleaming parquet floors and white upholstered furniture, silver candlesticks and pristine magazines on the glass-topped coffee table. One wall was entirely taken up by a vibrant abstract painting in blues and greens, resembling light on a lily-strewn pond. Jon took off his shoes. 'Try not to shed any hair,' he told Girl.

A minimalist wooden staircase led to a large master en suite bedroom, which looked as if it was twice as wide as the living room downstairs, presumably because of the garage below. It was clearly Saffy's own room – it even smelled faintly of her shampoo – so he went back downstairs to find the guest bedroom, where he dropped his rucksack.

The kitchen was in the back of the house: sleek and modern, spotless white surfaces and white marble countertops. The back wall consisted of glass doors looking out over the double-width courtyard garden, populated with tasteful wrought-iron furniture. There were actual lemon trees in pots. Jon poured himself a glass of water, sat at the kitchen island on a stool that probably cost half the advance of one of his books, and googled Saffy Huntley-Oliver.

She was an heiress – a triple heiress to the Huntley family, from her mother, and the Oliver family, from her father, and the Lyon family, from her stepfather. There were a good number of photographs of her at parties, sometimes on the arm of a handsome man. A different one each time, he noticed. She'd had a brief career as a model in her early twenties, when she'd been a muse to the late fashion designer Carlos Badanucci. He found photos of her in plastic evening gowns and odd hats. Now she was on the board of several charities.

It was a whole other world – not just from his damp cottage in the Highlands, but from his middle-class former life in Shepherd's Bush, or growing up in Putney as the son of a Met detective. These photos, this mews house, all of them naturally tasteful and perfect: it would be easy to imagine that Saffy Huntley-Oliver never had a single problem in her life. Except boredom. Was that the real reason she'd insisted that he stay here?

Stop it. He had enough to think about without wondering about the motivations of a woman he'd barely met. Sometimes the simplest explanation was the best; and besides, he didn't always need to assume the worst of everybody. Saffy took on charity cases: that was why she let him stay here.

Jon sighed. He took his phone out of his pocket, along with DI Atherton's card.

*　*　*

'What do you call *that*?' Atherton's thick finger pointed at Girl, sitting at Jon's feet.

'I think – though I can't be sure – that it's a little-known creature called a dog.'

Atherton grunted. 'I like dogs. That . . . is an overgrown rat.' He slid into the seat across from Jon's and put his pint on the table. It appeared to be Pepsi.

'You don't want a beer?' Jon said, surprised. 'It's after hours.'

'Not every single cliché about coppers is true, you know.'

'Could have fooled me.'

Atherton took a look around, at the old polished oak and the brass railings, the etched Victorian glass. 'Nice boozer.'

'Yeah. I'm staying around here.'

'It's all right for some.'

Jon sighed. 'Listen. I heard you wanted to talk with me, but if not, I'm perfectly happy to fuck off back to my perfectly happy life.'

'Are you, now? Perfectly happy?'

He closed his eyes. Was it written all over him: his defeat?

'Listen,' Atherton said. 'I'm aware that you didn't have to call me. I appreciate that you did.'

'It's not you. It's the family of that poor man, whoever he is.' Jon's pint was nearly empty. 'You haven't identified the sixth victim yet?'

'No head, no hands. No DNA match on our database.'

'No identifying marks? Tattoos?'

'Nada. White male, about thirty-five years of age. In good shape. Dark hair on his head, if what's on his body is anything to go by.'

'Why didn't Cyril keep his head with the other ones?'

Atherton shrugged. 'Guy's a psycho, mate.'

'And why did he leave it on *my* doorstep? When the other ones were left in abandoned buildings, or on waste ground?'

'Clearly, he was trying to get your attention. Has been for some time, hasn't he? He got in touch with you for the Lianne Murray incident.'

'Yes, but I mean . . . was this a killer thing, inserting himself into investigations? Or was it . . . did it have something to do with . . . me?'

Jon heard his own voice. It sounded pathetic.

And of course it had something to do with him. Wasn't that what Atherton had said, on their first meeting? Hadn't Atherton strongly implied that all of this was Jonathan's fault? It was another of those voices that he heard in his head during sleep-less nights, when the rain was sheeting down, and leaking through the roof, and he was lying on his bed with his eyes open trying hard not to think.

'Might have been,' Atherton said. 'But let me give you some advice. You've got to stop taking these things personally. Guy's a psycho, like I said.'

'That's not what you implied when you interviewed me.'

'Yeah, well, then you were a person of interest.' Atherton took a long pull of his Pepsi, and grimaced. 'Don't get me wrong, I still don't like you. But we need that sixth victim ID'd, and Walker insists that he won't talk to anyone but you.'

'Why?'

'Get ready for this. He admits to the first five murders, and that he kept his victims' heads in his freezer. But he's denying that he killed the sixth victim.'

'What? That's the one that led me to him.'

Atherton nodded grimly. 'He claims that you planted the body yourself, to make him look bad.'

'*What?*'

'I know, right?'

'But . . . you don't think that, do you?'

'I believe that it's highly unlikely that there are two serial killers decapitating young men and leaving their headless, handless bodies in bin bags. No – Cyril Walker killed all six of those lads. He's denying the last one purely to screw us over.'

'What happened to the hands, by the way? They weren't in the freezer.'

'You don't want to know.'

Out of habit, Jon opened his mouth to ask again, but then he realised that, in fact, he *didn't* want to know.

Atherton was looking under the table. 'Seriously, where did you get this creature?'

'She fell down a well. I rescued her.'

'Are you sure you shouldn't have left her there?' But Atherton bent down and scratched Girl behind the ear, and Jon liked him marginally better.

'Why does Cyril want to talk with me, if he thinks I framed him?'

Atherton straightened. 'Good question. I suggest you ask him.'

'In prison?' Jon asked.

'Yes. Talk to him. Listen to him. Butter him up. See if you can get any details about the sixth victim.'

'So basically: ask him where the sixth head is, and if he denies it, try to manipulate it out of him.'

'That would be nice.'

'Does it harm the case against him? If you never find the sixth head, and he keeps on denying he did it?'

'Five counts of murder should be enough to put him away for a while. Six would be better. And it's going to save the taxpayer a lot of money, and the victims' families a lot of grief, if we can get him to plead guilty to all six.'

'Right.'

'I'd expect Walker to be upset with you. You were his friend, you betrayed him, yadda yadda. Animosity can be useful in discovering information, with certain people. He's going to want to prove that he's smarter than you. On the other hand, maybe he'll be glad to see you. Maybe he'll think you're writing a book about him.' Atherton looked at him hard. 'You're not writing a book about him, are you?'

'I'm really not.'

'OK.' Atherton reached into his inner jacket pocket and took out an envelope. 'Here's a visiting order for Monday.'

He took the envelope. 'I'm going to have to find someone to look after the dog. It's all white upholstery, where I'm staying.'

'That is very much your problem.' Atherton stood up, scraping the chair across the floor. 'Right. Keep me updated. I'm getting out of here and going for a real pint.'

'I thought you didn't drink?'

'Wrong,' said Atherton, over his shoulder. 'I don't drink with *you*.'

*   *   *

As soon as the dog and he got back to the mews house, his phone buzzed with a text. He looked at it, expecting more misery from Atherton.

Entirely your fault that I had to give my housekeeper a bottle of M&S gin. Sxx

In spite of himself, he smiled. He bloody hated kisses on texts. Only thing worse was emojis. Still, from what he knew of Saffy, it was typical. He texted back: *I think it was your idea.*

Yeah yeah yeah blame the lady. Misogynist pig. Dinner this weekend, or will it threaten your masculinity? Sxx

His stomach growled, and he realised he'd forgotten to eat since a cheese sandwich before he got on the train. He'd fed Girl, but not himself. And he'd had two pints and before that, nearly half a bottle of whisky.

I'm hungry now, he texted. *Want to go for a very macho burger?*
He was flirting. What the actual hell.

Her reply pinged back immediately: *Busy tonight, soz. Sunday?*
I know just the place.

It's a date, he texted back.

And then he put down his phone and said aloud, 'Shit. What if it *is* a date?'

16

I DON'T KNOW WHAT IT'S LIKE for anyone else, but for me, the third murder was when it stopped being expedience or self-defence, and started being a lifestyle option.

I was twenty, and doing some modelling in New York for Carlos Badanucci's atelier in the summer vacation from university. Fortunately for me, Harold's estate had included a *pied-à-terre* on the Upper West Side which was not so much a *pied-à-terre* as a four-bedroom flat in a luxury block with stunning views over Central Park. I'd thought modelling would be glamorous and fun. That was before I realised how much of it consists of standing around in uncomfortable shoes, getting your body pinched and prodded, and listening to everyone around you constantly bitching about everyone else. Carlos was a sweet old man, and within five minutes of meeting him I knew I would do anything for him, but I was glad I had a comfortable place to crash at the end of the day.

The building was one of those legendary New York institutions where the apartments only came up for sale once in a blue moon. About seventy per cent of them were owned by elderly couples, and the rest were owned by young up-and-comings who gazed around the lobby as if they couldn't quite believe their good luck. It reminded me of *Rosemary's Baby*, though I didn't personally witness any evidence of Satan-worshipping going on.

So it was a matter of huge interest in the building when old Saul Bernstein had a heart attack and the penthouse apartment came up for sale.

Mrs Liebmann, who owned a front ground-floor apartment and took this as God-given permission to spend her days watching everyone who came in and out of the building, waylaid me every morning and evening on my way to and from Carlos's. 'It's been sold,' she informed me as if she were communicating state secrets. 'To a couple, look like they're in their thirties. He's something big in drugs, but not the illegal ones, the big pharma ones.'

I liked Mrs Liebmann. I'd known her since I was a kid. When we were staying in the city I'd sometimes come down to her apartment with Susie for raisin and walnut *rugelach* and tea with lemon. When I'd moved in by myself, she'd given me the same pastries and the same tea, and told me, in an undertone, that she didn't like to speak ill of the dead but she thought my stepfather, Harold Lyon, was one of the sneakiest sons of bitches she'd ever met, and tight besides. 'He never tipped the doorman, not even at New Year,' she said, with her quiet, implacable outrage.

'What do you think of the new penthouse couple?' I asked her now.

'He's sneaky,' she said straight away. 'Sneaky' was her epithet of choice. It applied to child molesters, rapists, politicians, telemarketers, and people who didn't clean up their dogs' mess in the street. 'And a show-off. She's a pretty little thing, though.

She asked me about the best local dry-cleaners, best place to get takeout, hairdressers, if I knew any good cleaners, all that. 'They're from Minnesota,' she added, as if that explained the whole thing.

'Well,' I said, 'you keep an eye on them for us, Mrs Liebmann.'

'Don't you worry, Seraphina. I will.'

The Bretts held a housewarming party soon after they moved in, which pretty much confirmed Mrs Liebmann as an excellent judge of character. No expense was spared on the catering, the champagne, the flowers or Chad and Amanda Brett's clothing. Amanda was tiny and cute, snub-nosed and freckled, and she clearly hadn't taken Mrs Liebmann's advice about hairdressers because she didn't have a blue-rinsed perm. Chad was a show-off with a penchant for looking down cleavage and talking about his smart investments in pharmaceuticals.

'Sneaky,' muttered Mrs Liebmann to me, passing a plateful of tuna carpaccio and caviar.

So I was intrigued to see him slipping off, in between bragging sessions, and leaving the apartment. I put down my flute of Bollinger and followed behind.

He went through the fire exit that led to the stairs to the roof. I waited a few minutes and then went up too, taking out the pack of cigarettes I always kept in my handbag for emergencies. All the most indiscreet conversations take place in smoking areas, among the brotherhood of the nicotine.

As I expected, he was standing near the low wall by the edge, where there was the best view over the park, hunched over something he was holding in his hand. When he heard my deliberately loud footsteps behind him, he swivelled his head, wiped his nose quickly, and smiled his big toothy whitened smile. Some host he was: he had crept off to do his coke in secret so he wouldn't have to share.

I held up the cigarettes. 'I didn't like to practise my bad habit on your balcony,' I said.

'We're birds of a feather,' said Chad, taking out his own pack of Marlboros. 'Mandy hates it when I smoke.'

'Got a light?'

He lit my cigarette (sneaky glimpse at cleavage) and we stood together, looking out over the park, smoking. He talked. In the time it took to smoke a cigarette, he asked me exactly zero questions about myself, and allowed me to get no words in edgewise about anything.

'Well,' I said, twisting the butt of my cigarette out under my shoe, 'guess it's back to the party.'

'I'll be down in a minute,' he said, shifting from foot to foot, eager to take some more cocaine without having to share it. I thought about calling him on it, but decided it might be more useful if he thought I didn't know his secret.

From that day, I made semi-regular trips up to the roof, and often ended up joining him for a cigarette. I wasn't quite sure why I was doing it; unlike most of the models I worked with, I wasn't mad keen on smoking, and his company certainly wasn't a pleasure (though he thought it was). But Mrs Liebmann thought he was sneaky. Maybe he was sneaky about something other than class A drugs: something worth knowing.

I didn't see Mandy very much. Occasionally I glimpsed her on her way in or out, toting a rolled-up yoga mat or shopping bags. She wore sunglasses, those big Jackie O ones that covered most of her tiny face. During the hottest New York June on record, she wore long-sleeved shirts.

I mentioned it to Mrs Liebmann. 'She had a limp last weekend,' she said, over *rugelach*. 'I don't like it. But what are you going to do? She won't talk to me, always says she's in a hurry. I can't call the cops unless I know. If Mr Liebmann were alive, he'd talk to that husband of hers. But a woman, he'll just laugh in my face.'

'I'll try to talk to her,' I promised.

I told Carlos I had the flu, put on my running clothes, and lingered across the street in the park until I spotted Mandy Brett coming out of our building with her arms full of dry cleaning. Long sleeves, long trousers, Jackie O sunglasses, and a scarf around her neck. It was a simple matter of crossing the street a block ahead of her, popping in my ear buds, and jogging back in time to collide with her full tilt, knocking her cleaning from her arms and her sunglasses from her face.

'Oh my God! I'm so sorry!' I exclaimed, reaching for her glasses and taking a good look at the bruise around her eye. It was purple and swollen, recent. Give it a few days and it would mature into a very impressive shiner.

She snatched the glasses from my hand and instantly bent to pick up her cleaning.

'Are you all right?' I asked.

'I'm fine.'

'I'm really sorry, I didn't see you. I shouldn't be allowed to jog on the sidewalks, to be honest.' I picked up a suit, which had fallen off a hanger. 'Right, well, I will pay for this cleaning. And I'm buying you a coffee to apologise for scaring the shit out of you.'

'There's no need, I'm OK.'

'I insist. And a pastry; you need the sugar to get over the shock of being knocked over.' I kept a tight hold on Chad's suit in case I needed a bargaining chip.

When she realised I wasn't going to release the suit, she reluctantly agreed to accompany me to the Italian deli down the street. I kept up a stream of friendly chatter and inconsequential questions until we were at a quiet table in the corner and both well supplied with cappuccinos and cannoli, and then I asked her point blank: 'What happened to your eye, Mandy?'

'Oh.' She still had her sunglasses on, inside. 'I . . . ran into a door. I'm still not used to the apartment, I guess. The doors open the other way from our house in St Paul.'

'I don't believe you,' I told her. And before she could react to my blunt comment, I reached over and pushed up one of her sleeves. Sure enough: bruises all around her wrist. 'Where did these come from?'

'Oh it's . . . it's . . . I shut it in a taxi door.'

'Do taxi doors open differently here than in St Paul, too?'

'No, I'm just, I'm just so clumsy. A total klutz, that's me.'

I lowered my voice. 'This doesn't have to keep happening. You could walk away.'

Her eyes were invisible behind the sunglasses, but she bowed her head.

'I don't want to talk about it.'

I'd expected her to get angry and defensive. I'd been ready for that. Not this resigned submission. It must be worse than I'd thought.

'There are people who can help you,' I told her. 'You're not on your own.'

'No,' she said. 'I am on my own. And it's not any of your business anyway. You don't know me.'

'I don't,' I said. 'But I've met plenty of people like him.'

'Please,' she said. 'I'd just like to be left alone.'

She stood and gathered up her dry cleaning.

'Why do you stay?' I asked her. 'Do you love him?'

'Yes,' she said. 'Yes, I love him.'

She left then, and I sat there thinking that of all the crimes Chad Brett had committed or would commit, that was the worst: he had made his wife love him.

* * *

The solution was so obvious that I hardly even had to think about it. Next time up on the roof, drop my lighter, pretend to be picking it up, instead give him a push to his midsection that sent him toppling over the wall and tumbling past his own penthouse window and nine further storeys down. Chad Brett: wife beater, coke snorter, and pavement pizza.

It was ruled accident rather than suicide; there was a small article in the *Post* that mentioned the cocaine that had been found in his system. Because of the drugs and his culpability in his own death, Mandy didn't receive an insurance pay-off, but the money he left behind was substantial anyway. She went back to St Paul. I learned all this from Mrs Liebmann; Mandy never spoke to me again, after that one time in the cafe. In my opinion, the world was a better place without Chad.

I never knew whether she stopped loving him or not.

17

THE QUEEN'S HEAD WAS A large, busy pub on the canal. There was a big dog bowl of water outside the front door, and several dogs lying underneath tables. Girl wagged her tail at a pair of French bulldogs sitting near the entrance, but stuck close to Jonathan's legs. He scanned the customers and didn't see Saffy, so he bought himself a beer at the bar and chose a table by an unlit fireplace, sitting with his back to the wall. He wondered if she'd prefer to sit outside, since it was a warm evening. He wondered if he should buy Saffy a drink, maybe a bottle of wine for the two of them to share. That's what you should do on a date, shouldn't you?

Was this really a date?

If it wasn't a date, what was it? Was she just taking pity on a lonely man? Was she the sort of person who invited random strangers to dinner? That seemed more likely: from what he'd seen of her, she was compulsively outgoing. Confident, in a way that had obviously been bred into her. But she'd made an effort to mention that she was single, when they met again on the train . . .

She arrived in a rush of blonde hair and perfume. 'Hello, am I late or are you early?'

'I'm early.' He stood and she kissed the air on either side of his face. Her cheek rested against his for a brief moment and he was able to smell her hair as well as her perfume.

Then she was talking again. 'I hope this place is OK, I know it's a bit out of the way, but I wanted to make sure you could bring Girl, I hated to think of her sitting alone. Where is she, anyway? Oh, there she is, she's so quiet and good – hello, Girl!'

She stooped and held out her hand but Girl skittered back under the table.

'She's finding London all a bit overwhelming,' said Jonathan. 'To be honest, so am I.'

'On the upside, there are no wells for her to fall into. You're on the beer? Do you mind if I have wine instead?'

'I'll get a bottle and switch over.' He attached Girl's lead to the table leg and went to the bar. Between ordering and receiving a bottle of Sauvignon in an ice bucket, he glanced over to their table. Saffy was sitting back in her chair, scrolling through her phone. Her hair was a bright golden fall and her lips were coral red; her body made a graceful long curve in her chair. Her dress was sleeveless and short, her arms and legs sun-kissed. She wore sunglasses pushed back on her head, and high-heeled gold sandals on her slender feet; her makeup and jewellery were understated but classic. She was the most well-groomed person he had ever seen in real life. Perfect. Like something out of one of those glossy magazines that he never read.

She was way, way out of his league.

'What the hell am I doing?' he muttered.

He looked away from her and picked up a menu instead. Everything was free-range and hand-reared and each dish had a paragraph underneath it explaining every single ingredient.

And the prices started at about what he'd been spending on a week's shop up in Scotland. Quite a difference from his diet lately of cheese sandwiches and Fray Bentos pies.

Once, he'd felt right at home in London. He'd felt like he belonged. Like he was making a difference.

He shouldn't be here.

The barmaid slid over the ice bucket and two glasses, and Jonathan had to take a deep breath before he carried them over to the table. Saffy looked up with a bright smile. 'If I say I'm gasping for a glass of that, you won't think I'm an alcoholic, will you?'

'Tough day?' He tried to sound like a normal bloke, in a normal pub, meeting a normal girl for a normal date. He had no idea if he was doing it right. He had no idea if he *wanted* to do it right.

'I've been building Susie's morale about her ex all weekend.' She plucked the wine bottle from the bucket and poured two large glasses. 'Cheers.'

He touched glasses with her. 'Cheers. How have you been building morale?'

'I plan to kill the toerag as soon as humanly possible.'

'Understandable.'

'So, how was your day?'

He shrugged. 'I've been walking Girl.' It was the only thing he could do to keep his mind off his meeting with Cyril tomorrow.

'Sounds lovely,' she said, before taking a deep sip of wine. 'Ah, I've been waiting for this.'

Small talk. What did people talk about in the pub, anyway? The weather? Sport? He turned his glass in his hand and asked, 'So what do you do?'

'Didn't you google me?'

'Well, I did. But I thought I'd be polite.'

'What did Google say that I do?'

'It said that you used to be a supermodel, and now you're on the board of several charities.'

'"Supermodel" is a serious exaggeration. I did a tiny bit of couture. It's embarrassing to talk about, really.'

'Then tell me about your charities.'

She cringed. 'Can we not? It makes me sound so much like one of those privileged holier-than-thou do-gooders. Which is what I am, I suppose, but it's so boring. It's not a real job.'

'Well, it sounds as if you're doing a lot of good,' he said, surprised at his own diplomacy.

'How about you? You said you were retired. Retired from what?'

'I was a journalist.'

'Oh, that's interesting. What kind of journalism? Heavy depressing news stuff or frothy celeb stuff?'

'I don't really like to talk about it.'

'Ah. OK. So we both can't talk about our jobs. What can we talk about?'

'The weather?'

She shook her head. 'Not the weather, or sport, or politics. So boring.' She sipped her wine, contemplatively.

'What does that leave us to talk about?'

'Films? Music? Books?'

'I haven't seen a film in three years, I only really ever listen to Bob Dylan's *Highway 61 Revisited* and the most recent novel I've read is *Moby Dick*.'

'*Moby Dick* is good,' she said. 'Can't say I remember much of it, though. Really? No films in three years?'

'Before I retired, I was a bit of a workaholic.'

'And since then?'

'I had no way of seeing them. The closest cinema is an hour-and-a-half's drive away from my cottage, and I didn't have a TV or internet. Even the phone reception was iffy. I'm not much of a one for fiction anyway.'

'I hate Bob Dylan,' Saffy said. 'I know he's a genius and all that, but he sounds like a whining old guy sitting on a front porch somewhere. Never understood the appeal.'

'What music do you like?'

'I'm afraid to say that my favourite music is 1940s torch songs.'

'Hmm. Not my thing.'

'Yes, I thought you'd say that.'

'Clearly we're meant to be sitting here in silence drinking and staring at each other,' said Jonathan. Under the table, Girl gave a little sniffle.

Saffy snapped her fingers. 'I know. We'll each ask the first question that pops into our minds, and we answer as quickly as we can. Don't even think about it. I'll go first. What did you think about me when I turned up wanting your help to save a dog?'

'I thought you were wet.'

'That's all?'

'I thought you were annoying.'

'Wet and annoying. Well, that's a good first impression, I suppose.'

'You were so terrified, I thought that you were going to tell me that a child was down that mine shaft.'

Her smile melted. 'Gosh. Really? That's pretty dark.'

'I've got a very dark imagination.'

'You must have a lot of nightmares.'

'That's where the whisky comes in handy.'

He drank his wine, and topped up their glasses. He wondered if they were going to end up drunk again, like they had on the train.

'I suppose it does.' She leaned forward on the table. 'OK, now you ask me a question.'

He wasn't nearly drunk enough for this. But he asked it anyway: 'What is this we're doing? Is this just dinner?'

'We haven't ordered any dinner yet, last I checked.'

'I mean, is it a friendly thing, or is it a date?'

Saffy smiled. 'Well. I think that's a question that needs us both to agree on the answer to make it valid.'

'But from your point of view.'

'From my point of view ... it's a date.'

'But why?' he asked.

'You know. Dating. You spend time with someone to get to know them better. You're familiar with the concept, even though you've been in a shack in the Highlands without a television or internet?'

'I mean – why with me?'

'Because,' she said, still leaning forward, close enough to him so that he could smell her perfume, 'you are the most interesting and attractive man I've met in a very, very long time.'

His throat closed up with something like fear. Jonathan stood up abruptly, and bent to unfasten Girl from the table.

'I'm sorry,' he said. 'But I can't do this.'

He picked up the dog and hurried through the pub to the exit.

It had tipped over from dusk to evening while he'd been in the pub, and the cooling air had made a low mist rise off the canal. He walked rapidly along the towpath, not paying attention to where he was going, just wanting to get out of there.

What on earth was he doing? Why was he fleeing from a perfectly pleasant girl and a decent bottle of wine? His heart was pounding in his ears and he felt as if he couldn't catch his breath, but he walked faster and faster. He thought he might be sick.

Don't have a panic attack, he told himself. *Don't do it.*

He'd had a few panic attacks since Cyril. Since Amy left him. In the cottage. Once, miles from home, driving on an abandoned road. He couldn't tell what triggered them, but when they happened, his body decided it was in danger and it needed to shut down into a maelstrom of fear. Tell him he was dying. Tell him he meant nothing. Heart skipping, breath stopping, limbs shivering, covered in a clammy sweat.

'No,' he gasped out loud, and held Girl closer to his chest. Kept walking. *Think of something else.*

Water condensed in his curly hair, making it heavy and wet against his face and neck. He saw a blur of shadow, smelled grass, and turned into a park. He thought about rain flowing down a window. Silver runnels down glass, drops joining other drops, merging into streams. Dripping onto the ground, soaking deep, deep down, into hidden rivers. That invisible flowing water, cold and numb and black.

And on the back of that: *I'm OK now. I can breathe.*

Girl licked his face. He stopped and put her down onto the grass, and she squatted to pee.

In the mist, someone gripped his shoulder. Jonathan started violently and whipped around, tangling Girl's lead around his legs.

It was Saffy.

'I didn't hear you coming up behind me,' he gasped. Heart hammering again, but he wasn't choking. 'You can do that in heels?'

'I wanted to make sure you were OK,' she said.

'Yeah. Yeah, I'm fine.'

'Only I'm not used to men jumping up and running as far away from me as fast as they can when I say they're attractive. Usually that happens much, much later into a relationship.'

Jonathan laughed weakly, because some response seemed to be expected. She pointed to a bench, just visible in the gloom. 'OK if we sit for a few minutes, or do you really want to be alone?'

Even he knew that he'd already been rude enough, running out on her. He nodded and they sat down side by side.

'You don't have to tell me,' she said. 'I'm a stranger. It's fine. But I was being sincere about why I wanted to see you. In case you thought I was playing some sort of game. I wasn't.'

'OK. I wasn't either. I just . . . can't. I can't date. I was never any good at it anyway, but I can't. Not now.'

'You mean, "It's not you, it's me"?'

'Yes. Well, I mean, it is you. Even if I could date, you're not the sort of person I should be dating. You're beautiful, you're rich, you seem well adjusted, you have social skills.'

'Don't assume too much about me,' she said. 'This whole

148

beautiful rich charming girl act might be to cover up a secret life of crime.'

'Like Bruce Wayne and Batman?'

'Well, technically he was a hero rather than a villain, and also a man, but yes, that's the gist.'

He laughed. It felt better.

'Anyway, you just said it wasn't me that was the problem,' said Saffy, 'and I'm just conceited enough to believe you. So what is the problem?'

'I'm not a good person to date. I'm moody and depressed.'

'You think I haven't noticed that yet? Give me some credit. What's the real reason?'

Jonathan sighed. 'I can't stop thinking about my wife,' he said. 'My ex-wife.'

'Ah.' Saffy was quiet for a moment. 'That's sort of insulting, you know.'

'I'm sorry. It's not intentional. You're amazing – totally out of my league.'

'I'm not going to be fake modest and pretend that's not the truth. Also, I've been very nice to you.'

'You have. It's not you, it's—'

'You already said that.'

'I've just never been very good at relationships.'

'What are you thinking about her?'

'Everything,' said Jonathan truthfully.

'About what went wrong?'

'I know what went wrong. I went wrong. I'm thinking about everything else. Why we were together, what we were like together, what she's doing now, how she is, whether she's found someone else.'

'You don't talk to her?'

'We both thought that was best.' *She thought it was best.*

'Can't you find out how she is by asking one of your friends?'

'She got the friends when we split up. They were all hers to begin with, anyway.'

Saffy was quiet again. Then she stood up.

'Well,' she said. 'If you want to know how she is, why don't we go find out?'

'Pardon?'

'Where does she live?'

'Shepherd's Bush. She got the house.'

'So you know the address. Come on.'

She held out her hand for his. A bit dazed, he stood and took it. Her fingers were cool.

'Do you mean we should go to our – to her house? I don't think she wants to see me.'

'She doesn't need to see you. We can go to her house, stand outside. I'll knock on the door if you want, and you can hide down the street and just look.'

He hesitated. 'Isn't that stalking?'

'Technically yes, but who am I to judge?' She squeezed his hand. 'Come on. You said you can't stop thinking about her, wondering how she is. If you find out, you'll know. Then you can move on. It makes good therapeutic sense. What's her name?'

'Amy.' It hurt to say it, the kind of hurt you got when you kept on poking a sore spot with your finger to see if it was still sore and because it also felt good.

'Let's go find Amy,' said Saffy.

* * *

They got a cab to Shepherd's Bush. Girl sat on Jonathan's side of the cab, panting. He told the driver the address, his old address, thinking how it was funny how it felt so normal and yet strange in his mouth. They didn't say anything on the way. Jonathan looked out of the window, watching the lights and buildings as they morphed from any old buildings to buildings he knew, familiar shops, the Tube station, the charity bookshop where Amy sometimes picked up a couple of paperbacks for a fiver, the cafe where she liked to go before yoga class, the off-licence.

The house was the same as it had used to be: a narrow three-storey brick terrace that the previous owners had painted dark red. The kitchen was in the basement, living and dining room on the ground floor, bedrooms on the first floor, and Jonathan had converted the attic into a recording studio. The main difference was on the front step, where Cyril had left the bin bag. There were new pots of geraniums there.

The curtains on the bay window on the ground floor were also different: they were yellow, instead of navy. They weren't drawn, and the lights were on; from where they stood across the street, he could see right into the lounge.

They'd argued about this. Amy liked to have the curtains open all the time, even at night; she liked the outside to be part of the inside. She said it made the rooms feel bigger and airier. Jonathan liked them closed as soon as darkness fell.

'But people can see in,' he'd protest. 'They can see us. They can see you.'

'If I'm doing something private, I'll draw them,' she'd say. 'Otherwise, why would I care about someone seeing me sitting and watching TV, or cooking dinner?'

And he'd tried to explain to her, how the outside was full of people who were sick. How the darkness hid people who didn't just watch but waited. How everything he'd learned had taught him that people who lived their lives in full view, people who believed in innocence, only made themselves targets.

'I'm not going to let a few people who may or may not be out there change the way I want to live,' she'd responded. And she left the curtains open, except when Jonathan came in and closed them. Shut off her airiness and her light.

Now, Jonathan was the person watching and waiting outside. He looked with hunger through the bay window: saw how she had the same sofa, but different cushions, green instead of blue. The same big round mirror over the fireplace where she would recheck her makeup before she went out for the day; the same one where they'd watched themselves making love on the sofa, some evenings when the curtains had been closed.

No one was in the room. There was a vase of roses on the wooden coffee table. Amy loved flowers. Had she bought these herself, or had someone bought them for her?

'When was the last time you were here?' Saffy asked him quietly. He'd nearly forgotten she was also here.

'Over three months ago.' Irresistibly, he was drawn across the road, not to Amy's house, but Bridie's next door. Bridie was the only neighbour that Jon knew. Amy knew all the neighbours, popped round for cups of coffee, made extra spaghetti sauce for the elderly gentleman down the road who couldn't see very well to cook. Jon rarely exchanged anything but a nod with the people who lived around him. His mind was always in other places. Darker places.

But Bridie had a low brick wall in front of their house which he could lean on and look down into the basement level of Amy's house next door, where the kitchen was.

He'd put up blinds in the kitchen, but they'd been removed. He could see straight through the window. Amy was there.

She was making a pot of tea. Same bright red Le Creuset teapot. Her back was to the window as she reached into the cupboard and took out two teabags (PG Tips, the same) and dropped them into the pot.

Her hair was still in that new short style. Her clothes were new. Her actions, her stance, her shoulders and her back and the side of her face, viewed through the window, from out here in the darkness where she couldn't see him – they were all the same. It was Amy. He would have recognised her anywhere, even if everything about her appearance had changed.

She poured boiling water from the kettle, gave the pot a stir. She took a yellow mug from the mug tree. Without glancing up at the window she picked up the pot in one hand, and the milk and mug with her other, and left the kitchen.

In his mind, he saw her walking up the steps. Past the framed photographs of her family that she'd hung in the stairwell. He could hear the sound her feet made on the stairs. He could smell her, her scent of shampoo and washing powder, see the way she nudged open the living room door with her foot. She appeared in the lounge and as she set the teapot and mug on the coffee table next to the vase of roses, he saw her face.

For a vivid, hot/cold moment, she looked directly at him. His breath stopped and a thousand words rushed to his lips. What would she say at the sight of him? Would there be a flash of recognition, an echo of the smile she used to give him, only to be replaced with dismay?

Then she turned towards the television on the wall, picked up the remote, and he exhaled. She hadn't seen him.

'Is this your first time stalking someone?' Saffy asked. 'I ask only for information. Because you're truly terrible at it, and if you've done this before, I'm surprised you're not in prison.'

Jonathan shook his head, as if coming out of a trance. 'Let's cross the street.'

There was a tree on the corner, with a bit of scrubby browned grass where the neighbourhood dogs did their business. He had always given it a wide berth. Now he appreciated it for the excuse it gave him to stand there with Girl, and the vantage point it offered of Amy's window. Amy had settled onto the sofa with her tea and was watching television.

'*Love Island*,' said Saffy. 'Not to criticise your ex, but did she always have such awful taste in television?'

'I don't know,' said Jonathan. 'I never watched it with her. I was always working.'

'Ah.'

For a while, neither one of them said anything. When someone passed by, they both pretended to be interested in the dog, who at least had a lot to sniff at. Inside, Amy watched TV and drank her tea.

'Does this answer your questions?' Saffy asked, eventually.

'I'd like to stay for a little longer,' he said. 'You can go if you want.'

'I'm just popping off. I'll be back in a minute.'

Amy scratched her cheek. Her new haircut suited her; it accentuated her eyes and cheekbones. He felt as if he'd been away from her for half a lifetime and for no time at all.

In another reality, he would have been able to forget about his job at the end of the day. He would have shut his laptop and sat beside her. Poured himself a cup of tea from her pot, put his feet up on the table, leaned back with his shoulder against hers. Asked her about her day. Watched mindless television and lived in the moment, the two of them, being normal.

How far had he been from that reality? Could he have chosen it at any time? It felt like a choice, now ... but then again, now he was standing outside his soon-to-be ex-wife's house, spying on her in a manner that any sane person would consider grounds for a restraining order.

'Here.' Saffy was back. She handed him a paper-wrapped package, warm and smelling of vinegar. 'I was hungry. We can sit over there.'

She pointed to the low wall of a house for sale, currently empty, a few metres away. They walked there together and sat down. She'd got them both chips. If she'd asked him, he'd have said he didn't have an appetite, but as soon as he opened the paper and breathed in the steam, his stomach growled.

'This isn't much of a date,' he said, glancing at her. 'Sorry.'

She popped a chip into her mouth, unconcerned, as if she often ate takeaway while helping to stalk someone. 'Other people's relationships have always been a bit of a mystery to me.'

'My own relationships are a mystery to me.'

'Why did you fall in love with her?'

He toyed with a chip. 'She was better than me. She was happy.'

'Did she make you happy?'

'She made me the most happy I've ever been. For a while, anyway. I don't know if that's what most people would call "happy". If there's an objective standard of happiness that you can reach.'

'Some people say that happiness is the absence of misery. I don't quite believe that, myself. I think there's more to it than that.'

'I'm not sure what it is,' said Jonathan. 'But she had it. I borrowed some of it from her. Until … I took it all away.'

'Is that why you split up?' Saffy dropped a chip for Girl, who ignored it.

'We split up because I was too wrapped up in my work, and I never really paid attention to her. But really it was because I stopped her from being happy, and I had for a very long time.' He looked at Amy. *Love Island* had apparently finished and she was watching something else, something involving people singing. 'I keep on thinking that maybe if I hadn't been so preoccupied by my work, if I'd spent more time with her, then we'd still be together. But maybe we wouldn't. Maybe we just weren't cut out to be with each other. Maybe if I'd spent more time with her, I'd have made her unhappy anyway.' He glanced at Saffy. 'I have no idea why I'm telling you this.'

'Because I'm a good listener, and also I bought you chips.'

He nodded. 'That must be it.'

They sat on the wall and ate their chips. Girl ate the ones that Jonathan dropped. Amy finished her tea and changed channels to the ten o'clock news. She had her phone in her hand and appeared to be messaging someone. Was this a normal thing for her to do while she watched the news? He didn't know.

'Well,' said Saffy, standing up and stretching, 'I think that's

156

me done for the night. I'm going to find a cab. You?'

'I think I might sit here for a little while longer. I know it's weird, but ... I just want to make sure that she's OK.'

'Change location,' she advised him. 'Otherwise you'll look suspicious.'

He nodded. She took his empty chip wrapper and crumpled it up with her own.

'You know,' she said, 'I still think what I thought about you the first time we met. You're one of the good guys. You might not feel like it, but you are. It's just ... You really need to get over your ex before we go on another date.'

She kissed him swiftly on the cheek and then left him, tossing their chip papers in the bin near the tree.

Jonathan moved over to lean on an ancient white van parked a little way down the road. He pretended to be talking on his phone whenever anyone walked past, so he didn't pay much attention to the man walking on the other side of the road until he turned into Amy's gate and went up to the front door and rang the bell.

Jonathan paused. He stooped and pretended to be tying his shoe. The outdoor light came on, so Jon could see the man. He was in his thirties and had close-cropped black hair. He wore a suit but no tie and his shoes were new. Jonathan couldn't quite tell if he were handsome or not, but he looked fit.

Amy answered the door and Jonathan straightened, more interested in seeing her face than concerned about the possibility of being spotted.

She smiled. Her big, unfettered smile, full of warmth and happiness. The smile that he thought he had erased from her face.

They spoke a few words to each other, though Jonathan couldn't make out what they were. Then she opened the door wider and the man went in. Jonathan did his charade with his phone as he watched them walk into the living room. As he watched the woman he had loved wrap her arms around this stranger's neck, and this stranger put his hands on her waist. As they kissed each other as if they'd been waiting for far too long.

Jonathan's hand tightened on his phone hard enough to turn his knuckles white.

Amy broke away from the man. She went to the window and Jonathan saw her face: the pink on her cheeks, her lingering smile. She looked directly at him, where he stood, phone unheeded in his hand, staring up at her window.

There was no sign of recognition. She pulled the curtains shut.

18

I KNOW THERE'S SOMETHING WRONG AS soon as I put my key in Susie's lock. There's something about the quality of silence on the other side of the door. Or maybe it's a smell: the scent of wheatgrass smoothies emanating from gym-honed pores. I hesitate, gritting my teeth, before I open the door and step inside her flat.

I take it in at a glance. Before I went out, I tidied and cleaned the living room and kitchen but of course it's now a tip again. This is completely typical for Susie and not cause for concern in itself. My sister is basically a human tornado when it comes to mess. But along with the discarded feminine clothing and magazines and wrappers and mugs and cosmetics and socks and post, there is an empty bottle of red wine on the coffee table and two glasses with dregs in the bottom. If I had any hopes that maybe Susie just wanted to use two glasses for the lolz, they are squashed by Susie herself. She's reclining on the sofa in her favourite pink tracksuit, scrolling on her phone, and when she looks up, the expression on her face is pure I've-just-had-sex-with-my-dickwad-boyfriend-but-I'm-pretending-I-haven't.

'Oh,' she says with elaborate innocence. 'You're home. It's early. Didn't the date go well?'

'It was a washout,' I say, hanging up my handbag on the minimalist Scandi hook by the door, which I installed the last time I was here. 'He's still hung up on his ex. Speaking of which—'

'Finlay explained that,' Susie says quickly. 'It was all about some reunion thing for his school. She's organising it and she needed his input.'

'Didn't Finlay go to Eton?'

'His other school, obvs. So what's the deal with the guy you had a date with? Is he soft in the head? There's no way that his ex is as beautiful and smart as you are.'

'You're trying to butter me up and change the subject,' I say, sitting on the arm of the sofa. 'But in fact you are right. His ex is a basic brunette and she dresses like a Head Girl.'

'You saw her?'

'I spent half the evening staring at her.' I sigh. 'It started out well, and then he flipped out.'

'Men suck,' says Susie, and presses 'like' on something on her phone. 'You going to block him?'

I've been wondering this myself, for the entire cab ride home. 'I don't know. He's got a lot of potential, is the thing. If he can get over his basic ex. And also, I've put in so much effort already.'

'Cut your losses.' Susie points at me with a pink-nailed finger. 'That's what you'd say to me. No scumbag dude is worth it.'

'Speaking of scumbag dudes . . .'

I don't get to finish the sentence because at that moment the scumbag dude in question walks in from Susie's room. He's bare-chested and barefoot (which brings up the disturbing fact that his man-sandals are probably festering somewhere in this very room), his hair is wet, and he's drying it with a towel. Unlike Susie, he's not attempting to hide the goofy post-coital expression on his face.

'Oh, hi Saff,' he says. 'I thought you were out on a hot date?'

'Clearly not,' I say.

'Damn. I'm sorry it didn't work out.' He drops the towel on the floor and reaches for something on a side table. With dawning horror I realise it is *my hairbrush*, the one I lent to Susie this morning when she couldn't find hers in the maelstrom of her bathroom. Finlay begins to pull it through his long, wet, man-bun hair.

I watch his every move. I'm not often speechless, but even I can't deal with this level of insolence. I glance at Susie, who's too busy ogling her shagbuddy's tanned and chiselled abs to protest at his unauthorised use of my personal property.

I'm about six inches away from a glass table lamp. I could tip it over right now, smash it on the floor, and shove one of the shards in Finlay's eye, using the pain and blindness to incapacitate him while I get the electrical flex around his throat and strangle the life out of him. Or, I could beat him to death with the wine bottle and then shove my hairbrush down his lying throat. It's my favourite hairbrush, so that would be a shame, but it's not as if I'm ever going to use it again now.

My hatred is burning so hot right now that even the usually more-than-oblivious Finlay Smythe notices that something is up. He finishes brushing his hair and drops *my property* onto a pouffe. Even from here, I can see long strands of his tech-bro, faux-surfer, bleached blondness caught in the bristles.

'Anyway, babe,' he says to Susie. 'Gotta go. Call me.'

I watch, stony-faced and flame-eyed, as this human imper-sonation of a kidney stone finds his shirt behind the sofa, pulls it on, and then unearths his festering man-sandals from beneath the coffee table. He kisses Susie on the mouth and leaves.

Silence fills the room – nay, the entire city block.

Oh my God, I wish I'd killed him.

Susie puts her phone down. 'Chill out, Saffy. It was just a booty call. I was lonely and I wanted sex. We're not back together.'

'Was the sex good?' I ask. Every word a slow drip of poison.

'So good,' she says, leaning back, starry-eyed. 'You can forgive so much when a guy fucks like that.'

I wish I hadn't asked.

'Anyway,' Susie says. 'You just spent the evening with a guy who's not over his ex. So you have exactly nothing to accuse me of.'

'Oh, you're right. Please excuse me. I'm so sorry that I'm worried about your emotional wellbeing and your right not to get screwed over by immature cheating wastrels who have more hair than sense. Of course it's all fine, you can have sex with anyone you want to! I hope that you offered him my toothbrush to use while you were at it.'

Susie rolls her eyes.

'Oh that's mature,' I say.

'Look at you, accusing me of being immature when you treat me like a child. This is my house, Saffy. I can have sex with whoever I want in it. Like a grown woman.'

'A grown woman should have more sense than to let some piece of dick treat her like a disposable sex doll.'

'Sex dolls don't have multiple orgasms.' She bounces up off the sofa. 'You're not my mother or my boss, Saffy. You're my sister, and you're a guest here, and that's aside from the fact that you only ever get involved with men who aren't emotionally available, and tonight was no exception at all. Just because you had a lousy night doesn't mean you can spoil mine, so please keep your opinions to yourself.'

She goes to her messy room and slams the door, and I pick up my defiled hairbrush and hurl it as hard as I can at the wall. It fails to create a massive crater-like dent and instead pings lightly off the plaster and falls to the carpet with a muffled thud.

My phone buzzes in my handbag. I shouldn't check it – you've heard of drunk texting, but that is nowhere near as bad an idea as homicidal impulses texting – but I stomp over and grab it anyway. There's a message from Jon.

'Fucker,' I say, though I don't mean it. Because just seeing his name on my screen makes me go all gooey inside in a weird way I haven't felt before, and I remember what it felt like to kiss his cheek and smell vinegar from his chips, and feel his soft hair brushing the side of my face.

I know, I know, I know. Feminism will never make any strides against the patriarchy until women can stop fancying the pants off of men who don't treat them right. But reader: I open his message.

You're right, it says. *I need to get over Amy. I'm going to try to start making some better choices. Thank you for tonight. You were great, and you keep on being kind to me, and I don't deserve it. I'm sorry.*

I melt a little. Me, the stone-cold killer of men. *It's OK*, I type, even though it really isn't. Because years have taught me that this is what straight men like. They like chilled-out, breezy women who are endlessly fun and forgiving. They like women who don't have feelings other than adventurous sexual ones.

And then I think: hold on. Why am I assuming that Jonathan Desrosiers is exactly like Finlay Smythe? I like Jon. I should give him the benefit of the doubt. There have to be some men who deserve to live, after all.

I erase what I've typed and instead I text: *I was hoping for a better evening, if I'm honest.*

I'm sorry, he replies right away. *It was entirely my fault.*

And when was the last time a man told me he was sorry, unless I was about to stab him in the neck?

How are you going to make it up to me? I text.

It can't be tomorrow. I'm busy. But another time soon?

I settle into the armchair in the messy room, looking forward to a little light flirtation. *What are you doing tomorrow?* I text. *Is it anything fun?*

Well, he replies. *That depends on whether you think it's fun to go to prison.*

19

H E WAS IN THE CHROME and marble guest bathroom, shaving, when the doorbell went and Girl ran to the door, barking. She had a strange bark, half a squeak, as if she really wanted to sound threatening but couldn't quite bring herself to mean it. Wiping the lather off his face, Jon went to the door. Since he'd found a body on his doorstep, he always looked out through the peephole, if there was one, before he answered the door.

It was a blonde woman in a mint-green tracksuit, her hair up in a messy bun. He opened the door and she grinned at him. She had a young, sunny, pretty face.

'Hi,' she said. 'You must be Jon. I'm Susie. That's quite a scar on your shoulder.'

'I got stabbed,' he said, taken aback. 'Are you—'

'I'm Saffy's sister. And I'm pissed off with her but she said you needed someone to look after your doggy while you went to prison to visit a friend, and I love doggies, so I said I'd do it. Also I wanted to see what you looked like. And tell you that if you break her heart, I will fucking kill you with my bare hands.'

'Um ... OK.'

Girl nosed past his legs, her tail wagging frantically. Susie squealed and stooped down. 'Oh my God, you are adorable, aren't you? Aren't you? You're like a corgi gone wrong, you look like you've been in a tumble dryer, you're the most beautiful thing!' She fussed Girl and Girl squirmed with delight.

'She likes you.'

'Oh, we're going to be best friends, aren't we, sweetheart?' Girl licked Susie's face and she giggled. When she stood up, her sweatsuit was covered with dog hair. 'I heard you rescued her from a well.'

Jon looked down at Girl, who was grinning with her tongue lolling out. 'We did, and she can be a little shy sometimes, but not with you.'

'Saffy must like you, because she is super precious about her furniture.' Susie came past him into the house, dumping her large and expensive-looking handbag on the floor. 'God! I am so annoyed with her. Anyway, who are you visiting in prison? Do you know a lot of people in prison? Are you going to put on a shirt first?'

Despite the clothes, it was easy to tell that this was Saffy's younger sister. They had the same eyes, the same perfect skin, the same easy entitlement and outspokenness, a similar trans-Atlantic accent. Susie was shorter and she had a dimple in her cheek when she smiled, and also long pink nails and aggressively groomed eyebrows.

'I'm visiting someone I used to know,' said Jon, 'and I do know a few people in prison but it's not because I personally have been sent to prison, and yes, I plan on putting on a shirt.'

'OK,' said Susie. 'Well, I'm going to call for a Deliveroo, do you think Girl likes noodles? Do you like noodles, Girl? Do you like sushi? Do you like being called Girl? Because you look more like a Doris to me, can I call you Doris, cutie-pie?' She kept up a running monologue to the dog as she walked into the kitchen, Girl following her close behind. Jon shrugged and went to put on a shirt.

* * *

The long wait to see Cyril was both boring and anxious, routine and horrific. His hands were sweating and he felt a little sick to his stomach. Jon had visited prisoners before, and spoken to murderers before, but he'd never spoken to one who had actually tried to kill him, or whose victims he had found. Or who had sat on Jon's own sofa. Up until the moment that he'd discovered the heads in Cyril's freezer, he'd thought Cyril was quite a nice bloke. Cyril had even apologised before he stabbed him. Now that he was in jail for his crimes, the mask would be off, and Jon would be able to see the monster that had been lurking underneath the whole time.

Which was why he was quite surprised that when he walked into the visiting room and scanned the waiting people, Cyril, who was already sitting at a table, grinned and waved at him.

'Jonathan!' he enthused. 'Good to see you, mate! How are you doing? Are you all healed up from the last time I saw you?'

'Um. Yeah, I'm much better, thanks.'

'I didn't want to have to hurt you, you'd always been a good friend to me, but you found my little secret, so . . .' Cyril shrugged.

Cyril's hair was carefully styled. His fingernails were bitten down, but clean. Because he was on remand, he wore his own clothes: jeans and a zip-up sweatshirt with a niche logo. The only way he looked different from before was that his skin was a little paler, without the suntan from his jogging habit.

He didn't look like a monster. He didn't look like a guy who would kill six people and try to kill another with a kitchen knife. He just looked like Cyril. Which was eerie, but also good, in a way, because it made it easier to treat him as a friend. And Jon would need to do that, if he wanted to get information out of him about the sixth victim.

'How's Amy?' Cyril asked.

'She's fine.' But as he said it, he remembered that Cyril knew where Amy lived. He knew what she looked like. He wondered if Cyril had any friends outside who would do him a favour. He kept his voice light and joking, though. 'I don't think you're going to be invited to her next cocktail party, to be fair.'

'Don't worry, Jonathan. Hurting women isn't my thing. Men who hurt women are the lowest of the low.'

'Whereas those men in your freezer . . . ? They deserved it?'

'No. All they wanted was a square meal and a good night's sleep. They didn't deserve to die. That was all down to me, mate. I wanted them too much.' Cyril shrugged again, and a shiver ran down Jon's spine. He was so casual. So matter-of-fact. 'I'm just selfish, I guess.'

Jon glanced at the nearby guard, who was putting on an air of ignoring them while watching them constantly. He lowered his voice.

'Do you mind telling me, why did you keep their heads? Was it so they couldn't be identified?'

'Yeah, partly. Also, I liked knowing they were around. I was pretty lonely after the divorce, and . . . I liked the company.'

'You knew all their names?' Jon asked.

'Their first names, yeah. Or nicknames. But listen, speaking of names, I have a bone to pick with you, Jonathan.'

A bone to pick. Now that was some terrible word choice. 'What's that?'

Cyril leaned forward. 'They're calling me "The Bin Bag Killer". It's all over the press and the news. And the internet's going crazy over it. Sometimes it's "BBK", which is a little better, it's got echoes of BTK, but still. Everyone's focused on the bin bags. Like that's the most interesting part.'

'I think that's because you cut up your victims and put them in bin bags.'

'Sure, but that was expedience, OK? That was practical. You live in a little terraced house in the middle of London that's overlooked by all the neighbours, you drive a van but it's full of tools, you don't have easy access to a river or a field, you have to get rid of a bloody great man-sized body somehow, don't you? You know what I mean, Jonno. You talk about this stuff all the time on your podcast. I wasn't even into the murder that much, you know? It was all about the company for me, and the power. I had to kill them to do what I wanted with them. I didn't *enjoy* that part when they died. And disposing of the body is just a pain in the arse.'

He had tortured each of his victims for days, and now he was talking about their bodies as if they were a minor inconvenience. Like a flat tyre on his van.

'Also,' Cyril added, '"Bin Bag Killer" is an insult to the men I killed. Like I was out there killing bin bags, instead of human beings. I didn't think of them as garbage; they meant something to me. I mean, come on. Think of the victims!'

'I have been,' said Jon.

'Right? Give them some proper bloody respect. Also, the answer to what I should be called is *right there*. It's literally how you found me. These journalists are proper shit.' Cyril lowered his voice. 'This is one of the reasons I wanted to talk with you, actually.'

'What's that?' Jon leaned forward as well. Was this when Cyril told him the name of Number Six?

'I've got two favours to ask of you, and the first one is this. When you write about me, Jonathan, and when you do your podcast, don't call me anything to do with bin bags.'

'I don't think I'm going to write about you, Cyril. It's all a bit close to home.'

Cyril waved his hand. 'Oh, you will, mate. It's too good a story to turn down. Also, I'll do whatever interviews you want. As long as you call me by my proper serial killer name.'

'What's that?'

'The Axe Murderer. It's obvious, right?' He mimed putting on body spray.

'You didn't use an axe, though.'

'Everyone likes a pun.'

Jon glanced at the clock in the corner. Cyril hadn't given him a name yet, or even mentioned the sixth victim. He was going to have to ask outright, and for that he needed Cyril on side.

'OK,' he said. 'Axe Murderer it is.'

'Thanks, mate.' Cyril sat back in his chair. 'Tell me something. Were you scared when I found you in my kitchen?'

'You were proper fucking terrifying,' said Jon. 'I'm not going to lie.'

'You should have seen your face!' Cyril burst into laughter. 'You looked like you'd shat yourself. Did you?'

'No, but it was a close thing. Listen, Cyril. Speaking of the victims, I need to ask you something.'

'Right. I know what you want to talk about. The guy you found. And that's just what I want to talk about, too.'

'Who was it, Cyril? What was his name?'

Cyril shook his head. 'I don't know.'

'You said that you knew all of your victims' names. You said you cared about them.'

'He wasn't my victim.'

'C'mon, man. This is me you're talking to. You don't have to deny it. If you go to prison for five murders or six, it's going to be the same. Let the family bury their dead. Let them bury a whole body. It's the least you can do.'

'I didn't kill him. I'm being straight with you. Those five guys you found, I'm not denying it. I killed them. But that last one, I had nothing to do with. I would never leave a body on your doorstep anyway. I like you. And I like your wife! That would be a crappy thing to do. Let alone spraying the bag with Axe, which would just be stupid. I'm many things, Jonathan, but I'm not crappy or stupid.'

He decided to push a little. 'The police think you did it because you wanted me to find you. It was a cry for help.'

'Bullshit! I was having fun! I didn't want to be found.'

'Some would say that you did, which was why you got in touch with me in the first place. About Lianne's killer.'

'I did that, because I hate to see the wrong man being fitted up for a crime he didn't do. My brother, remember? And now the same thing's happened to me.' He pointed at Jon. 'I don't hold it against you that you caught me. It's a risk I was always willing to take. But I did not kill that last man. Someone is

171

fitting me up. For a while, I thought it was you.'

He faked surprise. 'Me? You thought I killed someone and put his remains on my own doorstep?'

'I thought you were looking for attention for your podcast. But then I realised you don't need an extra body to get attention. All you needed to do was find me. And you're not a killer. You haven't got the heart for it, and besides, I think you're genuinely one of the good guys.'

'Then who do you think did it?'

'I don't know, mate. That's why I wanted to talk with you. I don't trust the police, but I've always trusted you, right from the first time I heard your voice. That's why I'm asking you a favour, and I think you'll do it for me.'

'Time's up,' said the bored-looking guard, appearing behind Cyril's shoulder.

'What's the favour?' Jon asked.

'Come on, time,' said the guard. Cyril stood up.

'I want you to find out who killed that last guy,' he said. 'For his family's sake, but also for me. Do it for me. As a friend.'

'Let's go,' said the guard. Cyril turned to leave. Jon watched him go. Before he left the room, Cyril turned and shouted over his shoulder.

'By the way, no hard feelings about stabbing you, mate!'

20

I'M IDLY HATE-FLICKING THROUGH THE Instagram feed of an actor who's been accused of sexually harassing and gaslighting multiple women (you know who he is) when Susie's doorbell rings, and then instantly rings again. And again.

When I answer it, it's Finlay. He's wearing two pairs of mirrored sunglasses: one on his face, and one on the top of his head.

'What do you want?' I ask him, being somewhat less than my usual effortlessly charming self.

'Hey Saff, I'm looking for Suze?' He steps forward, as if to go past me into the flat, but I don't budge.

'She's not here.'

'Ah, OK, where is she?'

I shrug. Finlay folds his toned arms.

'Yeah, so I feel like you and I got off to a bad start?' he says with that fake-Aussie upward inflection that probably makes all the girls think he's *sensitive* and *respectful*. 'But I like really care about your sister.'

'You've got a strange way of showing it?' I say, copying his tone.

'Look, I explained all of that to her, yeah? Things are fine now. Also, she's a grown woman?'

'She's my little sister, and I know her better than anyone else. Even you, though I'm sure you find that difficult to believe.'

'Hey, hey, listen, I just want to talk with her?'

'Then wait for her to call you, instead of turning up at her house and getting all up in her personal space.'

'That's something coming from you. I thought you had your own house?'

'I'm staying with her because she needs me right now. Because someone hurt her very badly.' I make to shut the door, but he puts his foot in it. He's wearing sandals, and I could break a few toes if I wanted to. Which I do want to. And then, maybe his neck. But instead I sigh, and say, 'Finlay, if you don't take your foot away, I will scream really loud and you're going to have to explain to all the neighbours why you are intimidating a woman who is on her own.'

'Are you really pulling the "poor little weak woman" card?' he asks. 'You're the least helpless creature I've ever seen.' But he takes his foot away. 'Does your sister know that you are a complete and total psycho?'

'Just remember,' I say. 'You might be Susie's hunk of the moment, and believe me, there have been many of them, but I am her sister. I'm her only family, and have been for as long as she can remember. I have picked her up from more heartbreaks than you've had hot dinners, and I'll be picking her up long, long after she has forgotten your name. She and I share the same blood, and we always will. If you try to compete with me, you will never win.'

Then I shut the door in his infinitely killable face.

* * *

I can hear Girl barking inside my house, and to my surprise, before I can turn my key in the lock, Jon opens the door. 'Hey,' he says.

He doesn't look as pleased to see me as you'd expect, given that I'm gorgeous, charming, intelligent and rich, and also letting him stay in my house for free, so I say, maybe a little testily, 'I'm so sorry, am I interrupting something?'

'No! Not at all. Of course not. I'm sorry, it's been a weird day.' He steps aside, and I come in. The dog, who was barking so enthusiastically before, is now nowhere to be seen.

'I really didn't mean to interrupt,' I say. 'I didn't know if you were back yet. I was mostly looking for my sister.'

'She left about ten minutes ago. This guy on a scooter came and picked her up.'

Ugh. 'White guy with long hair, wearing two pairs of sunglasses?'

'That's the one. Is he the bad boyfriend?'

'And he's winning.' I must look as downhearted as I feel, because Jon says, 'Hey, come and sit down. Would you like some of your own coffee? Or some of your own wine?'

'Both,' I say, and we go into the kitchen. The island is strewn with wrappers from all of Susie's favourite takeout places.

'Sorry.' Jon starts picking up the mess.

'Oh, don't worry, I'm used to it. My sister leaves chaos behind her everywhere she goes.' I wave my hand in dismissal, but Jon continues tidying up and wiping down the smeared surfaces. I can't help noticing that he does a pretty good job. It's not to the removing-every-trace-of-blood-and-DNA level, but for a man, it's not bad. Then he puts a pod into the coffee machine and soon the beautiful aroma fills the air. I take a deep breath to calm down.

'This is new,' says Jon.

'What?'

'I thought you were always on top of the situation. Even when the idiot guy you're out for dinner with makes you stalk his ex-wife.' He puts the espresso in front of me and adds another pod for himself.

'It's my sister,' I tell him. 'Why does she always end up with such losers?'

'There are a lot of bad men around.'

'You've got that right.' I drink the coffee in two scalding gulps and hold out the cup. 'Hit me again.'

He gives me the cup he's just made for himself. 'Want to talk about it?'

Normally, the answer to this is *Hell no*. Normally, I am an island unto myself. I treasure my private thoughts and actions. Sometimes this is for obvious reasons, because 'prison jumpsuit' is not my best look, but also, it's been ingrained in me since birth. Feelings make you vulnerable. They're things for other people to exploit and manipulate. Look at how my stepfather manipulated my mother, and my sister, and me, to satisfy his own desires. It's easier and safer never to share your feelings, or at least only to share the slimmest part of them, just enough to prove that you're human.

But I think about how Jon rescued that dog without even thinking about himself. He's not a manipulator, even if I am.

'I've basically been Susie's mum ever since she was very little,' I tell him. 'Our dad died before she was born, and then our mother died when she was four, and then our stepfather – who was a total douchebag, by the way – died when she was six.'

'I'm so sorry. That's a lot of loss to suffer very young.'

'Thank you. Anyway, as a result, I've always looked after Susie. She's the only person I've got. And when she makes bad choices, it feels like I have to save her.'

'But that's not working?'

'No, because she thinks that she's grown up and she can make her own decisions. But you've met Susie. She's a princess. She has no idea of how the world works.'

'And that's because ...'

'I've spent my whole life protecting her. So it's basically my fault. I know. But how can I stop? It kills me to see her heart broken.'

'When someone breaks up with you,' says Jon, 'someone else will always say, "Well, if you've got a broken heart, at least it proves that you've got a heart to be broken." People said it to me when Amy left. All that silver-lining bullshit. All that better-to-have-loved-and-lost bullshit. None of it's true. It's fucking terrible. It rips out your guts and steals everything you love from the world.'

I nod. But I can't say I truly understand. Have I ever had my heart broken? Certainly not by a man. I have never let one get close enough to my real self, not unless I was strangling him at the time. I guess the closest I've come is my mother dying, and Susie being angry with me. Those are both fucking terrible.

'But you know ...' he continues, 'if you're lucky, you live through it. A wise person would say maybe you just have to let Susie make bad decisions.'

My eyes are burning and my throat is tight. I am actually close to tears. Seriously? Am I this good at acting or did Jon just say something that touched me?

'That guy does look like a loser though,' he adds, making a face, and that makes me laugh. I wipe my eyes.

'How'd you get so wise all of a sudden?' I ask. 'You weren't talking about heartbreak like this the other night.'

'Ah.' He pulls up a stool and sits across from me with his new coffee. 'Well, I've had a couple of things happen that added a little perspective. One of them is that I spent today talking to a guy who's killed at least five people because he says that he cared about them so much he didn't want them to leave. That sort of changes your opinion about letting people go, you know?'

Inwardly, I perk up. I didn't think he was going to talk about visiting Cyril Walker, and I'm intensely curious. Trade secrets, and all that. I would've loved to be a fly on the prison wall.

But of course I pretend to be surprised and shocked. 'You went to prison to visit a serial killer? You didn't tell me that. You said you were visiting an old friend.'

'My old friend happens to be a serial killer.'

'Wow. Just ... wow.'

'I didn't know when I became friends with him, obviously.'

'Of course not!' I wrinkle my nose in a way that I know makes me look appealing. 'But ... you told me that you were coming down to London to help someone out. Was it him?'

'No, it was ...' He sighs. 'It's a long story.'

'Well, I have literally nothing else to do today, since my sister's not speaking with me.'

I see him weighing the pros and cons of telling me the truth about himself. Then he seems to make a decision. He downs his coffee, and then he proceeds to tell me about his career, and how he caught Cyril Walker, while I pretend to be surprised.

I think he's really starting to trust me. Isn't that adorable?

21

H E STARTED WITH HIS DAD, though he didn't do his usual spiel about his father being a great detective, and it being passed down through the blood to him. He didn't have any books to sell or a podcast to promote, so he could tell the truth, or at least some parts of the truth. His father might have been a good policeman, but he was a shitty father, drinking from the minute he got off work until he passed out on the sofa almost every night, except for the nights when he was beating up on Jon's mum.

He didn't say any more about his mum.

'Anyway, I was never good enough for him,' he told Saffy, who was perched delicately on one of her own kitchen stools, drinking her third cup of coffee with no noticeable side effects. 'He thought I read too much. He wasn't happy about my doing English A-levels, and when I wanted to go to university, I think I chose journalism just to spite him. He hated the press. Said they were vultures.' Just like Atherton had said. Atherton was like his dad, in a lot of ways. 'Anyway, I did my degree, wrote for a local paper, then freelance for the *Guardian* and *The Times*, though I never got made a full-time member of staff; and then I don't know if you remember when Gabbie Mordant was kidnapped? A little girl, taken from her house in the middle of the night in Twickenham?'

Saffy shook her head. 'I can't say that I really follow the news.' She picked up her phone, tapped something in, and wrinkled her nose in that cute way she had. 'Oh no, that's grim.'

He filled her in on the details. No one knew who did it. The house was locked, not even a window disturbed. The father was suspected, then cleared. A male cousin – the same. And the days were ticking down, every minute less likely that Gabbie would be found alive, and there was no sign of the six-year-old and no suspect in sight. There was something about Gabbie's face that haunted Jon, that made him need to know. He was newly married to Amy, and he'd started spending weekends and evenings poring over all of the coverage, digging into everything he could find about Gabbie's family, about the neighbours, about the school.

'I started a blog with everything I found,' he said. 'That was the thing in those days: blogs. It was a big news item, so my blog was easy to find. And people started writing to me, sending me theories and tips. I passed any bona fide information on to the Met, of course – one of my dad's friends still worked there. And one of the theories, something that I'd written about, turned out to be true. It was a painter who'd worked in the house before the family even moved in. He had a key – he had keys to lots of places – and he'd bided his time. The girl's body was found in Kent. And I was commissioned to write a book about it. And then I started a podcast. And then I wrote some more books. And that's that, I've been profiting off murders for ten years now.' A wry look. 'Do you still think I'm a good guy?'

'That's like saying the police profit off of crime,' Saffy said. 'You didn't cause the murders. You investigated them. You solved them.' She leans forward. 'Was your dad proud of you?'

'My dad was dead by then.' As with his mother, he didn't go into it. 'Anyway, I've got out of the true crime game. Which is why I didn't talk about it when we met. And why I didn't tell you my full name, even though you told me yours. It's been all over the newspapers in the last few months.'

'Like I said, I can't say I follow the news. What are you going to do instead of the true crime game?'

'I don't know.'

She seemed to be thinking about this. 'So ... you met the serial killer who you visited yesterday, when you were doing your podcast.'

'Yes, but I didn't know he was a serial killer at the time. That's ... a whole other story.' He looked at his coffee cup. 'Do you want to go to the pub and get something stronger? It's dog-friendly in there.'

'I can do better than the pub.' She got up, pressed a seemingly random spot on a kitchen cabinet that he hadn't been able to open, and the door slid to the side to reveal a wine refrigerator. 'Hmm,' she said, taking out two bottles and looking between them. 'God, this is a real dilemma. Are you about to tell me a Sancerre story, or is it more of a Pouilly-Fuissé story?'

Jon watched her in something like amazement. How had he started the day in prison and ended up here, in the kitchen of someone whose biggest dilemmas of the day were her sister's shitty boyfriend and which type of expensive wine to day-drink?

'I think it's more of a Chianti-and-fava-bean-type story,' he said.

'Right. Give me a minute.' She turned back to the wine fridge and in a moment emerged with another bottle. 'I don't have a Chianti but I do have an Amarone. OK with you?'

She'd taken his comment so seriously that he wasn't sure if she'd ever seen *Silence of the Lambs*. To be fair, she seemed more like a romcom person than a horror person.

'Amarone sounds great,' he said. As if he knew the difference. It was red.

'OK, so who did you visit yesterday?' She put the bottle on the island and opened another cupboard for glasses.

'His name's Cyril Walker.'

'That sounds familiar for some reason. Cyril with a C?' She abandoned the glasses and picked up her phone again. After a moment, she said, '*Oh.*'

'Yup.'

'Holy shit, you got stabbed?'

'Uh-huh. It's fine though,' he added hurriedly.

'Oh my God, you found all those *bodies*?' She turned to him with a shocked expression. 'On your doorstep? Like, the doorstep that you and I sat across from eating chips?'

'Only one body on my doorstep. The rest in Cyril's freezer.'

'Oh my God, that's so dark. Ugh. It puts me right off fish fingers, like forever.' She shuddered. 'I had no idea that you'd been through all of that. It's horrible. I'm so sorry. But you know, even more amazing that after you were literally stabbed, you didn't even hesitate to help a strange woman and a dog.'

'Oh. Well.' He waved his hand, and instinctively looked down for Girl. She wasn't at his feet as she usually was. Probably napping off the effects of Susie's shared takeaway.

184

'So this morning you went to see the Bin Bag Killer.' Saffy put two glasses on the island and opened another drawer for an opener.

'He doesn't want to be called that. He wants to be called the Axe Murderer.'

Saffy, her back turned to him as she rummaged in a drawer, made a strange sound.

'Are you OK?' he asked.

'Oh, yes, I just couldn't find the corkscrew. Here it is.' She used the little knife to cut open the foil on the bottle. 'Are all serial killers so sensitive about what they're called?'

'Not all. But lots of them are. They tend to be narcissists, and narcissists like to get full credit for their work.'

'Well, I can understand that part. I'm a narcissist, but it's only because I'm brilliant and beautiful, and I want everyone to know it.' She winked at him and seriously, this was by far the best he'd felt all day. And he hadn't even had a sip of expensive wine yet.

Then his phone rang, and once again, it all went to hell.

22

AMONG MY MULTITUDE OF OTHER talents, I'm pretty good at reading upside down, even when I'm opening a wine bottle. Which is why when Jonathan's phone rings, I know it's the police – someone called DI Atherton – even before I see his expression transform from relaxed to tense and pained.

'Sorry,' he says. 'I've got to take this.'

He picks up his phone and walks rapidly out of the kitchen. I wait until I hear the guest bedroom door close, and then I put the wine down, slip off my shoes, and silently creep after him to listen to his side of the conversation.

Through the door, he sounds testy. 'No, I got nothing. He's still denying it. He's more concerned about his press.'

A pause.

'Well, he did say he was sorry for stabbing me. I got that, at least.'

He's quiet for quite a long time, and then: '*What?*'

It's a shout, loud enough for me to recoil in surprise. I blink, and then lay my ear to the closed door again.

'You couldn't have told me that before I spent the day in prison, at your request? How did you ... well, that's ... um ...

Seriously? Today? I've already ... OK. OK, whatever. I'll be there in half an hour.'

I hotfoot it silently back to the kitchen, slip on my shoes, and I'm pouring wine into a second glass by the time that Jonathan reappears. He's flushed and looks angry.

'Uh-oh,' I say. 'Do you need this?' I push a glass towards him.

'I'd better not,' he says. 'Sorry. I need to go out.'

'Why?'

'That was the detective in charge of Cyril's case. He says they identified the sixth victim – the one that I found on my doorstep – and they want to talk to me about it.'

Ooh, the plot deepens. 'Who is it?'

'They didn't say. Sorry about this.' He gestures to the wine. 'We'll have to resume our conversation another time. Actually ... if you're not busy, would you mind staying here with Girl while I'm out?'

'No way,' I say.

'Absolutely, that's fine. You've done so many favours for me already, and you've got a life. I'll just—'

'What I mean is, there's no way I'm letting you go to the police station to find out who you found dead on your doorstep, on your own. What if, God forbid, it's someone you know? You should have someone with you.'

'Oh. Thank you, but that's not necessary. I'm used to being on my own, and also I don't want Girl to mess up your flat.'

'You have clearly never tried to talk a Huntley-Oliver out of something when our minds are made up,' I say. 'Believe me, it's a hopeless cause. I'm driving you to Scotland Yard, and Girl can come with us. If you don't want me to come inside, she and I will sit in the car and wait. No arguing. Find Girl, and let's go.'

I watch as he struggles with this. He clearly doesn't want me to come, but also he does. Poor man, he's so lonely. He hasn't had anyone to confide in for ages. It makes my heart ache, really it does.

'OK, thanks,' he says at last, and goes off whistling for Girl. Unfortunately he takes his phone with him in his pocket, so I don't have any time to snoop about how much contact he's had with the police lately. Just out of interest. You know.

He reappears with Girl on a lead. She very deliberately doesn't look in my direction, but she happily goes along with him out of my side door into my garage. Jon pauses a moment when he sees my understated Mercedes sedan: black and sleek, almost too big for the mews house garage.

'I expected to see another sports car, or a Chelsea tractor,' he says.

'Of course not, darling. This is Kensington.' I wish I had a sports car – it's so much more fun to drive around London in a convertible – but while I'm in the city, I need the boot space of a sedan, at least. It's impossible to move bodies around on public transport with any sort of discretion.

As soon as Jon opens the car door and tries to get Girl to jump in, she baulks. She places her paws four-square on the concrete. Her ears go down and hackles rise, and she growls, low in her throat.

'Maybe she's had a bad experience with a car,' Jon says, and crouches to speak to her softly and encouragingly. This dog is far from stupid. She remembers very well what happened the last time she got in a car of mine.

I go round to the side and spread a travelling rug over the

back seat. (Yes, I have an old-lady travelling rug. I got it from a National Trust shop. They're super handy for impromptu picnics and also wrapping things that you don't want to be seen.) But Girl refuses to get into the back seat at all, so in the end, Jon has to sit in the back seat with her on his lap, and I have to drive them like a chauffeur.

'Sorry,' he says as I pull out onto Exhibition Road. 'I don't know what's wrong with her today. Maybe it's because I left her earlier.'

'It's fine,' I say. 'My ego is healthy enough not to be damaged by a pet.'

'She adored your sister. She was literally eating out of Susie's hand.'

'Ahh, bribery with food. I'm going to have to try that one. So, why do the police need to talk to you, do you think? Are you helping them to solve the case? Is there even a case to solve, if you know who did it?'

'As of this morning, the sixth victim hadn't been identified. I went to talk to Cyril to try to see if he'd tell me who it was. Cyril had to have left the body on my doorstep for a reason.'

'What kind of reason would someone have for leaving you a dead body?'

'Maybe he wanted to be found. Or maybe he just wanted the attention.'

'Like ... a cat leaving a dead mouse on your kitchen floor?'

'He wants me to write about him. Maybe it's some twisted bid for fame. That's what I thought, anyway. But this morning he denied killing the sixth victim at all. Which is implausible, but ... why would he deny it, if he was looking for attention? He actually asked me to try to figure out who did kill that man. None of it makes sense.'

Driving in London is something no sane person would do. The traffic and the stop lights and the lumbering buses and the mad taxi drivers and the angry cyclists and the precarious e-scooters and the unpredictable motorcyclists and the Deliveroo bikers trying to make enough money to live on in a gig economy and the tourists who have no idea which way to look when crossing the street. Every single person on the road hates every other person on the road and has the potential to kill them in an instant. Personally, I love it. Sometimes I go for a drive around rush hour just to witness what the world would be like if more people were like me.

I hum and tap the wheel while I drive, feeling very zen, and in the back seat, Jon murmurs soothing words to his dog. I can tell he's trying to calm himself down, as well as Girl. He must be worried about the identity of this guy, whether he knows him, going through the names of people who he hasn't seen lately. He's probably anxious, thinking that he's somehow responsible for a man's death. He's thinking about the family of the victim and what they'll feel like when they find out, or whether they've found out already and are grieving. I glance in the rear-view mirror and his brow is furrowed and he strokes and soothes a helpless animal. I've spent so much time thinking through the thought processes of bad men, trying to keep one step ahead of them, that it's fascinating and rather lovely to read the thought processes of a good one.

Of course there's no place to park outside Scotland Yard so I drop Jon off outside, telling him I'll drive around or park somewhere and come pick him up when he calls me. Finding a parking spot in London is another one of my favourite competitive games, though, so I find a place within a few minutes. I turn off the engine, and it's just me and the dog in the car.

Jon left a window cracked, but the dog is panting. She's sitting as far away from me as possible, in the corner of the passenger side back seat, and her hackles are raised again. I notice that there's a good deal of wiry white hair on my National Trust blanket.

'I know we got off to a bad start,' I say to the dog. 'But on my side, it wasn't personal at all. Like everyone says, serial killers start out their career by harming animals, but I have never ever enjoyed torturing an innocent creature. I'm a vegetarian. That might be hard for you to believe. Everything I did, I did to get closer to him, not to hurt you. It's not like I chose you specifically because you'd fit in a well.' I consider. 'Well, I sort of did. But I didn't know you then.'

The dog is looking at me side-eyed.

'Yes, and I still don't know you, because you hate me and won't get close to me. But let's face it, you didn't get hurt in that well and you've got a great life now, much better than you did before when I found you in the shelter! So you should be thanking me for that.'

She doesn't move. Somehow, she is still shedding.

'The thing is, he likes you. And you like him. And I like him. More and more every day. He is super adorable, and I think he's even more adorable because he's bonded so quickly with a dog who he didn't want in the first place and who is, if we're being frank, quite funny-looking.'

Narrowed eyes.

'Oh, don't deny it. You're not winning Crufts any time soon.'

A pedestrian slows down, and smiles at Girl through the window.

'OK, whatever, you're cute. So we're going to have to find some sort of truce, somehow. What will it take? Sausages?'

She doesn't answer.

'Chicken? Filet mignon?'

Silence.

'Please don't tell me you're into human flesh. Even I draw the line somewhere.'

I sigh and mentally start compiling my next order from Fortnum's.

*   *   *

We wait for ages, and Girl and I have not got any further into the terms of our truce. I'm considering trying to let her out to have a wee, but I'm afraid she'll take the opportunity to bolt, and that would not make me popular with Jonathan if I lost his dog. So basically I'm praying that she will not relieve herself all over my leather upholstery, when my phone finally rings.

'Hey! How'd it go? How are you doing? What did they say?'

'I'm ready to be picked up,' he says. And then he ends the call.

'Rude,' I say to the disconnected phone, but I still start up the car and drive immediately to the spot where I dropped him off. He's standing there, alone on the pavement, hands shoved into his jacket pockets, head bowed. He doesn't seem to notice when I drive up, until I beep the horn. Then he looks up, comes to the car, and gets into the back seat. Girl immediately climbs onto his lap again, with a whimper.

'What happened?' Someone honks their horn behind me, because I'm holding up traffic. I ignore them. 'Are you OK?'

'I've been told not to leave town,' he says. His voice is detached, as if he can't believe what's going on. 'Apparently I'm now the number-one suspect for the murder of the man I found on my doorstep.'

23

H E COULDN'T BRING HIMSELF TO explain more until they were back in Saffy's house, and halfway down the bottle of red she'd opened before. His mind was too crowded. Despite all of the crimes he'd investigated and written about and talked about, he'd never imagined being an actual suspect in one. He sat in her kitchen, Girl pressed up against his leg, and drank rich red wine without tasting it, until the alcohol shook some words loose. When it did, they were unexpected to him.

'I just kept on seeing Cyril's face,' he said. 'All the time that Atherton was speaking to me, I kept seeing Cyril that first time I met him in person in a pub, before I knew what he was, when he was a witness in Lianne's murder. When I asked him why he'd got in contact with me, and he said, "I can't stand to see an innocent man go to jail."'

Saffy sat across from him. She was uncharacteristically quiet, and her lips were pressed together as she watched him intently.

'Are you scared to have a man who's suspected of murder in your house?' he asked her, and she immediately shook her head.

'No. And also you didn't do it.'

'How are you so sure? You hardly know me.'

'I know you well enough to know that you don't kill people.'

He nodded. 'Thanks.'

'Oh my God, Jon, that's the *bare minimum* of loyalty you want from your friends – for them not to believe it when you're suspected of murder. I like to think I can do better than that.'

'He told me not to leave London. I had to give him your address. But I'll move out and get a hotel.'

'What? Why would you do that?'

'Because who knows how long this will take, and this is your house. I can't stay here indefinitely while you stay with Susie, especially if you're arguing with her.'

'I have to stay with Susie if I'm arguing with her,' Saffy said. 'If only to make sure that she doesn't move that toerag Finlay in with her. Listen, I want you to stay here. We don't know each other very well yet, but I know I can trust you. And I don't trust many people, to be honest. Basically myself, and Susie. So you will be mortally offending me forever if you don't stay at my house for as long as you need to.'

He used to be a man with pride, but that tended to get knocked out of you by news like today's. Also, Saffy's house was wonderful, and it was interesting to see how the one per cent lived. And then there was Saffy herself . . .

'OK. Well, thank you. The next bottle of wine is on me.'

She grimaced.

'All right then. I'll buy you a proper dinner.'

'I choose the restaurant.'

'Deal.'

They smiled at each other, and that was a little miracle.

'I don't understand how I just randomly met you, and suddenly you're my confidante,' Jon said. 'This has never happened to me before.'

'Me neither. It must be kismet.' She poured more wine. 'So if I'm your confidante, please tell me what's going on and why they suspect you, because I'm going literally crazy here from the suspense.'

They'd led him to a formal interview room, first off, which was different from the last time he'd been in Scotland Yard. Jon sat there in the bare room by himself for several minutes, and even though he knew he was being left alone specifically in order to make him nervous, he was still nervous. When DI Atherton entered, his expression, never anything that could be called friendly, was downright stony. Even the grudging cynical humour he'd had the last time they'd met in the pub was gone. He didn't ask how Jon was or about the dog or about his visit to Cyril. He'd sat down across from Jon, his cheap suit straining, and put a closed file on the table. He said, 'We know who the sixth victim is.'

'Yes, that's what you said on the phone. Who is he?'

Atherton didn't answer.

'If you knew who he is, why did you send me to talk with Cyril?'

'We found out this morning. We had a DNA hit.'

'Why did that take so long?'

'Because it wasn't in the UK database. The victim was an Italian national with a prior conviction in the Czech Republic. So we had to go through Interpol. A match that used to take fifteen minutes took six weeks.'

'Brexit, eh?'

Atherton grunted, then said, 'So. Do you want to tell us about him?'

'Me? I have no idea who he is. That's why I went to ask Cyril. Like you told me to.'

Atherton just looked at him.

'What's going on?' Jon said. Nervousness was edging into fear. 'Why am I in an interview room?'

'If you write about this, or talk about this, or even open your mouth so much as a fucking centimetre in public, I will have you in jail for interfering with an investigation.'

'I told you: I'm not writing about this case, or anything. I've had enough murder to last a lifetime.'

Atherton opened the file. Inside was a mugshot of a man in his thirties with a shaved head and an aggressively square jaw covered with black beard stubble.

'Look familiar?' asked Atherton.

'Never seen him. Who is he?'

'Francesco Fanducci.'

Jon shook his head.

'You might have known him as "Big F".'

'I've never met him.'

'Keep looking at the picture for a little while, Jon. Think back.'

'I don't need to. I've never seen his face.'

'You're sure?'

'Yes. What was his connection with Cyril?'

'None, as far as we can tell.'

'When I talked to Cyril this morning, he said again that he didn't kill the man I found. Are you thinking that he might have been telling the truth?'

'Cyril Walker's known victims were all homeless men in their twenties. Four out of five of them – maybe all of them – had worked as rent boys. They were addicts and Walker lured them to his house by promising them drugs – which he gave them, according to the post-mortems. It may be how he kept them under control while they were in his house. All of them had engaged in, or had been forced into engaging in, anal sex within thirty-six hours of their bodies being found.'

'Oh God.'

'Fanducci was not homeless. He owned a nightclub in Peckham. He was thirty-six years old, married with five kids and has a semi in Croydon, where he played cricket for the local team.'

'What you're saying is that he doesn't fit Cyril's victim profile.'

'Aren't you a clever boy. Got it in one.'

'What was his conviction for in the Czech Republic? Drugs?'

'Assault and battery.'

Jon wasn't in the interview room anymore. He was in Cyril's house, in his kitchen, the scent of Axe in the air, the space redolent of so many other lonely places he had read about and looked at online.

'Dennis Nilsen's victims weren't all homeless, or gay,' he said. 'Ockenden was a student. Two of them were children. To a certain extent Nilsen was opportunistic rather than having a definite victim profile. He also said he killed because he was lonely, which is something that Cyril also said to me. Lonely people aren't always picky.'

'Pardon me, I wasn't aware that I was talking with a walking encyclopedia of crime. Should I turn this investigation over to you?'

'No.'

'Because I have a spare detective badge in my office. You might want to put it on.'

'Sorry.'

'Alternatively, you might want to answer my questions for once, instead of asking them.'

Jon took a deep breath of the institutional air. This place wasn't very unlike the prison where he'd been this morning.

'I didn't know Francesco Fanducci,' he said. 'I don't frequent nightclubs. I don't play cricket, and I actively try to avoid Croydon. His face doesn't look familiar to me. If you showed me a photograph of his ankles and feet, I might recognise them, from when I found the body. But no, I don't know him, and I don't know what his connection would have been to Cyril.'

Atherton said nothing, only watched him.

Jon waited as long as he could, and then burst out: 'Was Fanducci sexually assaulted, too?'

Atherton slammed his hand down on the table. 'Enough. Enough. I am not here to answer your questions. It is none of your business, unless you know the answer already. Do you?'

'Unless I know already? What do you mean? Do you think—' Jon's eyes widened. 'Wait. Are you saying that I'm a *suspect*?'

'I'm saying that I'm telling you not to leave town, in case we need you to assist with our enquiries.'

'Do I need to get a lawyer?'

'That's up to you. I'd like to ask you some questions about your whereabouts on the day that Fanducci was last seen alive.'

* * *

Now, Saffy listened to him with wide eyes and her mouth half-open in astonishment. At a time like this, he shouldn't notice that her eyes were so bright blue, or that her teeth were white and that her lips were plump and wine-stained, the texture of soft velvet. Maybe it was the effects of the news he'd just had. Wasn't death supposed to make you want sex? Maybe the same thing was true of being suspected of murder.

He watched as she licked her lips and he shifted in his chair.

'Do you need a solicitor?' she asked. 'I have a really good one. She doesn't do criminal law but she'll be able to recommend someone. Do you want me to call her?'

'No. I mean . . . not yet.'

'You have an alibi, right?'

'Well. The thing is, I don't. Fanducci went missing on the fifteenth, and that's the same weekend Amy was away with her girlfriends for a hen do in Brighton. I spent the whole two days in the house, working. She came home on Sunday night. But I didn't see anyone who could confirm my story.'

'But . . . why would you dump the corpse of a man you killed on your own doorstep?'

He shrugged. 'Murderers sometimes like to insert themselves into their own crime scenes. It's a well-known phenomenon. I'm pretty sure that when Cyril spotted Timothy Bachelor, he was out hunting for his own victim.'

She was looking at him in a strange way.

'What?' he said.

'Did you say that when you visited him this morning, that Cyril asked you to find out who killed the man you found? What's-his-name, Fandango?'

'Fanducci.'

'Right. Him. Number Six. Didn't Cyril ask you to solve it?'

'Yes, but at the time I thought he was playing some game.'

'But you have solved crimes before, right? You caught Cyril, for example. And you said you helped to catch what's-his-face, who kidnapped that girl. And Timothy Bachelor.'

'I just looked at evidence. I didn't really—'

She leaned forward. 'But ... what if you did figure out who killed Number Six? Wouldn't that clear your name, too?'

He blinked at her. Four months ago, he would have been champing at the bit to investigate this crime, and put it on his podcast, and write the book about it. Watch the listener numbers go up and up. Go on another book tour.

'I promised Atherton that I wouldn't say a word about it in public.'

'Which is fine, if we investigate in private.'

'We?'

She spread her hands. 'Are you kidding me? Of *course* I'm going to help you. I read every single Nancy Drew book when I was a little girl. I probably even have a magnifying glass around here somewhere.'

Jon thought about it, furrowing his brow. What were his options, anyway? Sit around and wait for the Met to clear him? Hope that Cyril changed his mind and confessed to the last murder after all? This body had been on his doorstep.

'This wasn't just murder,' he said, slowly. 'This was personal.'

'So you'll look into it?'

'I think ... I think maybe I have to. I think maybe it's what I've had to do all along. Maybe Atherton was right ... maybe this *was* because of my podcast. In which case ... it's my *duty* to find out what happened.'

She was watching him intently, her cheeks flushed. 'Maybe I've got a morbid streak, but for some reason I'm finding you incredibly sexy right now.'

Heat flushed through him and his mouth went dry. Jon swallowed hard, reached for his wine glass and found it empty.

'I'll open another one,' Saffy said. She got up and bent over the wine fridge. She wore white linen trousers that tightened over her backside, and her jumper rode up a bare half an inch to show him a strip of golden skin.

He cleared his throat and looked at the marble countertop.

What was this? He was still heartbroken over Amy. He was a suspect in a murder case. He was homeless, jobless, and responsible for an odd-looking dog. Saffy was so out of his league that she might as well be on another planet.

He could hear her taking out a bottle, and the rustle of her clothes as she opened it. Her remark about finding him sexy hung in the air between them. He could almost taste it, like a terrifyingly expensive wine.

'Amy's seeing someone,' he blurted.

'Oh?' The cork popped. 'How do you know? Are you in touch with her?'

'No. I saw them together, that night when I was sitting outside her house. After you left.'

'Speaking of returning to the scene of the crime,' she said lightly. He was deliberately not watching her so he was startled when she placed her hand on his wrist. Her skin was cool, her fingers slender. She squeezed his wrist and he looked up at her.

'Listen,' she said. 'I can see what's going on.'

'What's going on?' His voice sounded rough to his own ears.

'I flirt with you, and you instantly bring up your ex. You're giving me the message, loud and clear, that you're not ready to get involved with anyone else. I get it. And I'm not into competing with another woman, anyway, so yes, I really do get it.'

That wasn't what he'd meant – not consciously, anyway. He'd said it aloud, almost as if to give himself permission to find another woman attractive. But she was right: it was a subconscious distancing strategy. And the fact that he felt he needed permission showed that he wasn't over Amy yet.

But.

He lifted his hand so that he could clasp hers. Her hand was small and delicate compared to his. He turned her hand over, so he could run his thumb down the centre of her palm. Saffy's skin was ridiculously smooth, incredibly soft. A woman who'd grown up in privilege, a fairy princess. He wondered what it would be like to raise her palm to his face, rub his cheek against her. Kiss the centre of her palm. Take one of her slender fingers into his mouth, and hear the intake of her breath.

'I think you're sexy too,' he heard himself say. 'Very sexy. And very beautiful, and kind, and generous.'

He met her eyes and she was biting her lip. *He* wanted to bite her lip. This was an incredibly bad idea.

'This is an incredibly bad idea,' she whispered in a way that made it sound like an incredibly good idea.

For a long moment, they gazed at each other, the air heavy. Then he let her hand go. Saffy stepped back.

'I'm sorry,' he said. 'I think I've been lonely. And it's not fair to ask you to—'

'No, you're right. It's too fast. It's too soon. I guess I'm frustrated. I haven't had sex for so long I've forgotten who gets tied up.' She laughed, a breathy laugh that sounded fake.

'*Grosse Pointe Blank*,' he said.

'I should have known I couldn't get a serial killer reference past you,' she said. She shook back her hair, and wound it around itself to make a loose knot at the back of her neck, and refilled their wine glasses. Then she took hers and retreated to the other side of the kitchen island, where she'd been sitting before.

'So,' she said. 'Are you going to investigate Number Six?'

'I don't think I have a choice.'

'And are you going to let me help you?' She smiled, that dazzling, charming, winning smile. 'Your own personal Nancy Drew?'

'I don't think I have a choice about that either, do I?'

Saffy squealed and clapped her hands. 'Yes! I've always wanted to catch bad guys!' She held up her wine in a toast, her eyes sparkling. 'Oh, this is going to be so much *fun*.'

24

I'M IN SUCH A GOOD mood that when I get back to my sister's flat, late and more than a little drunk, and find Susie and Finlay the Man-bunned Love Rat sprawled on the sofa both playing *Grand Theft Auto*, I don't even think about reaching for a knife. I simply glide silently and serenely to my boudoir, where I kick off my shoes and land rather less than gracefully on my bed.

I have handled all of this astonishingly well, if I do say so myself. The wine; the intense and sympathetic listening; the sexual tension; the artless suggestion that we should investigate Number Six together; the carefully calculated vulnerability. The *Grosse Pointe Blank* quote.

I think what clinched it was that little moment when our eyes met, and our hands touched, and the air crackled, and yet I stepped back. There is nothing better than self-denial to whet a man's romantic appetite. They say it's a typical women's game to play hard to get, but what I like even better is to play easy to get, but hard to keep.

And the irony is, that it's working on me, too. I have not been this horny in years. Maybe ever. The thing is, that Jon knew I wanted to have sex with him. And I knew he wanted to have sex with me, too. We could have ripped each other's clothes off and gone at it on the kitchen island. But this time it wasn't his ex keeping us apart . . . it was his own honour.

I roll across my bed, pleasurably drowning in unfulfilled lust. God, I want to take that man, and throw him on a bed, and rip off his shirt, and *lick* that knife scar, and then . . . and then . . .

There's a tap on my door. I sit up quickly enough to make myself dizzy, and adjust my clothing. 'What?'

Susie comes in, closing the door behind her and sitting on my bed. 'Oh my God, you're drunk!'

'No I'm not.'

'You never get drunk!'

'I forgot to eat dinner. Or lunch.' I think about it. 'Or breakfast. Hey, do you know what I really want? Doritos. Do you have any?'

My sister stares at me. 'What is wrong with you?'

'Nothing's wrong with me! Everything's great.' I loll back on the bed again, vaguely aware of a goofy grin on my face. 'Did you meet Jonathan? What do you think of him?'

She considers. 'He's hot, I guess. In a geeky way. He could use a wardrobe refresh and a haircut . . . Wait. Did you just spend the evening with him?'

'Maybe.'

'Did you sleep with him?'

I glare at her, offended. 'Do I have the hairstyle of someone who has been having lots of amazing sex?'

'No, but you could have been standing up or something.'

Standing up. Against the kitchen counter. Against the refrigerator. Against the Jeff Koons . . .

'Oh my God!' squeals Susie. 'You are in love!'

'No I am not,' I say from the pillows.

'You so are.'

'I am not. I am in lust.'

'Doritos?'

Susie does have a point.

'I am *badly* in lust,' I concede. 'I want to fuck that man five ways from Sunday.'

'Why aren't you?'

'Because he is hon-our-ab-le.' I string out the word with relish.

I decide not to mention the whole being-suspected-of-murder aspect. Susie wouldn't get it.

She's looking cloudy, however. 'Listen, Saffy,' she says. 'I came in here because I don't want to argue with you anymore.'

Ugh. She is killing my lust buzz with discussion of Finlay.

'It's OK,' I say to her. 'You're a grown-up, and you have to make your own decisions. I can't step in and make them for you. I will support whatever you want to do, and I will be here if things go wrong. In fact, if things go wrong, I will carve a bloody swathe across London.'

'Saffy. Be serious.'

'But if things go right, I will be the world's biggest cheerleader for you.'

She smiles. 'Thank you. I love you.'

'I love you too.' I shove at her leg. 'Now go get me some Doritos. And then leave me alone so I can wallow in sexual frustration in peace.'

25

WHEN HE SLEPT, FINALLY, IT was only to dream about Francesco Fanducci. Jon was on the neatly brick-paved front path of Fanducci's house, which in his dream was a 1930s mock-Tudor semi, draped with Italian flags. The number on the front door was six. When he knocked, the sound of playing children drifted out of the open front window. A woman opened the door. She was in her forties, with curly salt-and-pepper hair. Just like his mother's.

'Hello, Jonny,' she said to him, and though her face was different, her voice sounded like his mother's, too.

'Mrs Fanducci,' Jon said. 'I have something for you.'

He had something in his hand, which he gave to Francesco Fanducci's wife. He only realised what it was after she took it. It was a black plastic bin bag.

He opened his mouth to tell her not to open it, not to look in it, to give it back to him so he could take it away from her. But he couldn't get a single sound out.

Then she opened the bag and pulled out what was inside, by the hair.

'Oh, thank you, Jonny,' she said to Jon in his own mother's voice.

The head she held, blue-skinned and frozen, broken-veined and dead-eyed, crusted at the neck with blood, did not belong to Francesco Fanducci.

It belonged to Jon's father.

* * *

After that, he gave up on sleep. He left Girl snoring at the bottom of his bed and went to the kitchen, where he put the empty wine glasses in the dishwasher, put the empty bottles in the recycling bin, and made himself a cup of tea. Then he sat outside on the patio next to the lemon tree, in the cool clear night. In Scotland he'd be able to see the stars, but here in the centre of London he could only see an orange glow.

The meaning of his dream was clear enough: Francesco Fanducci's death, dismemberment and disposal were somehow personal. He had a connection to this man he'd never met. The police thought it was a deadly connection. Jonathan knew otherwise. But he had to prove it.

And to do that, he had to start close to home.

He turned on the Wi-Fi on his phone and punched in the code that Saffy had given him. He started with his private email. He'd deleted the mail app months ago, so he went to webmail, held his breath, and entered his password.

He had over a hundred unread messages. He didn't look at any of them; he went straight to the search bar and typed in 'Francesco Fanducci'. There were zero exact matches, and equally nothing for 'Francesco' or 'Fanducci'. He tried 'Frank' and came up with a lot of hits, which he scrolled through. None of them seemed related to the case.

The podcast email address was riskier, and also more likely to be relevant, because that was public. There were several thousand unread messages in that inbox, none of which he had any interest in reading, so for this account he did a more detailed search, looking for emails before the date that Francesco had disappeared. He had to scroll through a lot more messages here. None of them jumped out, though he'd have to go through them more carefully at a time when he wasn't blurry from nightmares on top of two and a half bottles of strong wine.

Jon wasn't much of a one for social media, even before his self-imposed exile – that required more sociableness than he could usually tolerate – but the podcast had an Instagram account, where he posted photographs of the people he talked about and any relevant evidence. He reinstalled the app and tried to log on to that now, realised he'd forgotten the password, and had to go through the whole rigmarole of resetting it before he could access it.

The account had nearly half a million followers. For the first time, he wondered, who were all these people? What type of person listened to him talk about death, and was so interested in it that they wanted to look at photographs, too? Were they people whose lives had been touched by murder? Were they curious, horrified, fascinated?

Were some of them killers? How many of them were now dead?

'You're a vulture,' Atherton had told him. He agreed. Five hundred thousand people, all obsessed with death. Their obsession bought his food, paid his rent. It would settle his divorce.

In disgust, he went to his account settings and his finger hovered over the 'Delete my account' option. But this wasn't just a morbid Instagram account anymore. It was evidence.

The police might have already looked at his public profile and the comments on his posts. But they couldn't access his messages – at least not yet. Until they got a subpoena, he had this information all to himself.

He tapped the paper aeroplane icon to access his messages, intending to scroll through to look for Fanducci's name or picture, as he had with his emails. But his thumb froze over the screen when he saw his message requests.

Over and over, all the way down his screen. Dozens of messages. Different accounts, different profile pictures, the same words.

COME BACK OR I WILL KILL YOU.

26

A LOT OF WOMEN CARE ABOUT fashion, but I think I can confidently say that with the possible exception of drag queens, no one spends more time thinking about fashion choices than an efficient female serial killer. Of course I mean things like choosing colours that won't show blood, or a dress cut that won't pop a boob when you're strangling a man from behind, or materials that take well to stain removal and home washing, and always having a pair of flat shoes in your bag in case you have to run from the rozzers; but it's much more than sheer practicalities. For one thing: clothes project an image. They hide the truth and cultivate a different, chosen truth. I'm not just talking about a skirt that conceals the effects of a PMT carb binge – it's something even more serious than bloating. When you have a number of murders under your belt, you have to make sure that the said belt portrays an image of a woman who is both stylish and completely not sociopathic.

(Obviously leopard print is out.)

Despite this, I'll admit that choosing an outfit for tonight took even longer than it usually does. Of course it's second nature for me to wear clothes that are stylish, expensive, classy and of impeccable taste, while screaming definitely-not-a-serial-killer, so I barely have to think about that part. But tonight I also want to look sexy, without looking as if I'm trying too hard. I want Jon's honour to be tempted. But at the same time, we're going to a nightclub and I don't want random strangers to try to feel me up. It's gross, and also I've made that decision not to kill anyone while I'm focusing on my new relationship.

I slept later than I meant to, because of a teensy hangover, so it was already noon when I braved the shopping wilds of Chelsea and Mayfair. I skipped Knightsbridge because I cannot cope with Kardashian-alikes when I've got a headache. I had almost no luck until I rocked up to a never-fail boutique in a hidden corner just west of Bond Street run by this adorable Albanian called Gustav, who dresses Cate Blanchett when she's in town. I brought him a coconut milk flat white with an extra shot, his favourite. 'I need to look like a grown-up Nancy Drew, but hotter,' I told Gustav, and he understood what I meant immediately, even though I'm not sure they had those books in Albania. I walked out with a Helmut Lang ruched-effect faux leather midi skirt (so practical – everything wipes off), and a clingy Stella McCartney cream silk French-cuffed blouse, which is admittedly less practical for bloodstains but otherwise will go with everything, so not only a killer outfit but also a good investment.

Decent underwear, a pair of heeled ankle boots, and a swipe of red lipstick later, and I'm ready for anything.

(I'm joking. It took at least three more hours to get ready. This lady goes nowhere without a blow-dry, a manicure and a wax.)

I'm meeting Jon at the Berkeley for cocktails before we go to the club. I arrive ten minutes late – a calculated move to make him a tiny bit anxious and more glad to see me, but it's a difficult one to make. I'm dying to see him, and also for him to see me.

But when I arrive, he's sitting at a corner table by himself, a beer in front of him, scrolling on his phone, and he doesn't even notice me walking in.

'Hi,' I say when I've reached the table.

He starts and stands up hurriedly, phone in hand. 'Oh, hi,' he says, looking guilty.

I hold up my hand. 'No. You did that wrong. This outfit deserves a proper hello. Shall we start again?'

He nods and puts down his phone. Then he actually sees me.

'Wow,' he says. 'You look ... wow.'

'That's better.' I smile and offer my cheek to be kissed. Then I sit down, order a Manhattan, and assess this man I've got the hots for. He has not spent his day shopping, though he has seemingly made the effort to shave and to iron his shirt. As usual, his hair looks as if he's run his hands through it. White dog hairs cling to the shins of his trousers.

I still have the hots for him. Human sexuality is a mysterious thing.

'What were you looking at on your phone?' I ask him. 'I think that's the first time I've ever seen you on it.'

'Oh, just chasing up a lead,' he says.

'Ooh, a lead? What is it?'

'It didn't pan out.' He turns off his phone and puts it in his pocket.

He's lying. I don't allow my face to change, but inwardly I am adding a red cross to a checklist that up to now has been nearly all green ticks. Has he been in contact with Amy?

'So,' I say. 'What's our strategy tonight? We didn't get any further than deciding to go to Fanducci's nightclub and look around. But I'm assuming you have some sort of plan.'

'Talk to people.'

'That's it? It's a nightclub. Aren't we going to dance?'

'I'm not the dancing type,' he says. 'Anyway, you can learn a lot by talking to people. In general, most of us love to talk about our lives.'

'Unless we're hiding something,' I say, a deliberate jab at his phone behaviour.

'Right. But even then, you can often get a hint just by how they hide it.'

'At the same time, we have actual questions that we want to get answered, right?'

'If we can.'

My drink arrives, and I take a sip. Perfect: sweet and smoky.

'Let's get started,' I say, and I take a Moleskine and pen out of my handbag.

'Um,' says Jon. 'Sometimes it intimidates people when you write down what they say. It's best to keep it casual at first.'

'I'm not totally clueless,' I tell him. 'I'm not going to go around a nightclub with a notebook like some sort of comic-book cub reporter. I just think it's a good idea for us to gather our ideas together before we plunge into the breach. So.' I open the notebook and write three headings in bold black ink.

MOTIVE?
KILLER?
WHY ON JON'S DOORSTEP?

'You've been thinking about this,' says Jon.

'Obviously. So the first thing I was thinking, is drugs. Was his nightclub a front? Was he laundering money?' I write *drugs* and *money* under the first section. 'If that's the reason, the murderer might be someone from a drug or crime syndicate. Why dump the body on your doorstep, though? Have you pissed off any drug or crime syndicates?'

He shrugs. 'Not that I know of, but it's possible. Bachelor had some drug connections, for example. Maybe he's got friends outside of prison. But why would they frame Cyril? The more likely reason is that whoever killed Fanducci was deliberately trying to pass it off as one of the Bin Bag Killer's victims, to deflect attention from them. And they left the body outside my house because they knew I'd make the connection.'

'Had you talked about the Bin Bag Killer on your podcast?'

'Yes, after the fourth body was found. About six weeks before Fanducci disappeared.'

'Sounds plausible.' I write all of this down in the appropriate columns. 'What else?'

'Most murder victims know their killers. It's always worthwhile looking at the family.'

I write *family – wife?* under KILLER and under MOTIV-ATION, I write *jealousy* and *family problems*.

'We always have to consider that Cyril's lying, and he did kill Fanducci after all,' I say. 'It's actually the simplest answer, and it also ticks all the boxes.'

'Except that Cyril really does have a passion about people being punished for crimes they didn't commit. His brother's story checks out: Phil Walker was sent down for a robbery that he was later found not to have done. Cyril has no reason at all to lie.'

'Except to mess with your head, which he has a lot of motivation to do. You busted him.'

'Also,' said Jon thoughtfully, 'Cyril's victims were all sexually assaulted. Atherton was cagey about whether Fanducci was. So I think he wasn't.'

'So maybe Cyril didn't fancy him.'

'It's a big change in motivation, if so.'

'Don't some murderers just randomly kill sometimes? Without the whole motivation and signature thing? It seems like a lot of rigmarole.'

'Not serial killers. The motivation is the whole point. Cyril killed because he wanted love. Killing for another reason, or for no reason, would be pointless to him. He'd probably even think it was morally wrong.'

Oh my God, this man totally understands me. My underwear is *so wet* right now.

'Well, I'm going to write it down anyway,' I say. 'Both Cyril, and random killer. There's a chance that your doorstep was a random place, too.'

'I don't think so,' Jon says. 'I think it was targeted. We only need to know why.'

'Random things do happen,' I tell him. 'For example, once I got into a cab at St Pancras Station, and I saw something shiny between the seat cushions? And when I dug it out, it was the necklace I'd lost on my way to the station five days before! The exact same necklace. Which is totally random, that I got the same cab, and also sort of gross that the seats hadn't been properly cleaned the whole time I was in Paris.'

He nods, though he still doesn't look convinced. I write *Cyril* and *random psycho* in the correct places in my notebook.

'Anyone else?' I ask. 'Is there anyone who's out to get you?'

He frowns, and takes a long sip of his beer. 'Well,' he says, 'I might have some enemies, I don't know. But what are the odds that I'd know more than one actual killer?'

'Unless they're caught, you'd never know.' I survey my list. 'Well, that's something to start with, I guess. Have you found out anything about Fanducci from your research?'

'The police haven't released his name yet, but I know from their questioning that he went missing between 2 and 4 a.m. on the fifteenth. All I could really find out online was the name of the nightclub he owns, and the fact that he used to own another one in Brixton. I found his address, and I believe that his wife used to be a primary school teacher, though I couldn't find any current employment details. Atherton said he had five kids, and a conviction for assault in the Czech Republic. Also, he plays cricket for the local team.'

'Cricket.' I hover my pen over the notebook, deciding whether to put *cricket-based conspiracy* under MOTIVE.

'However, I think we can safely say that he wasn't killed and cut into pieces by a cricket bat.'

'I don't pretend to understand sports.' I write it down anyway, because an Italian playing cricket is weird. Then I close the notebook and snap the elastic shut. 'Well, that gives us a few avenues of enquiry.'

'Also, we need to keep an open mind,' Jon warns.

And I can't help myself. I allow myself a sleepy, sexy smile, and I drawl, over the lip of my Manhattan glass, 'Oh, I have a *very* open mind.'

And in the moment that I say it, I guarantee he's *not* thinking about whatever it was on his phone.

27

FANDUCCI'S CLUB, MAJICKS, WAS LOUD and nearly empty. There were a lot of mirrors and neon signs saying things like DIVA and DANCE LIKE YOU MEAN IT. The music, this time of night, was mellow funk. No one was dancing, though there were a few people drinking at tables and the bar. 'We should talk to the bouncer,' Saffy whispered, taking Jon's arm. 'Bouncers see everything. My sister dated a bouncer once for about five minutes and she learned so much gossip, it was insane.'

Jon nodded. 'Let's get a drink.'

He couldn't remember the last time he'd been in a nightclub – probably not since he'd been a student. But Saffy strode in, instantly at home. He suspected she'd be instantly at home anywhere, even in Peckham. He noticed a table of men watching her and his emotions were strange: a mix of annoyance that other men stared at her, and pride that he was with a woman worth staring at – along with worry that her attractiveness would make them stand out when they were on a fact-finding mission.

It was easier doing this sort of thing on his own.

At the bar, he ordered a beer and she ordered another cocktail. While the bartender filled a shaker with ice, Jon said casually, 'We've never been here before. When does it start getting busy?'

The bartender shrugged. 'We're getting a hen party any minute, mate.' He nodded at a corner of the club festooned with L signs and silver balloons. 'Other than that, we're pretty relaxed on a Thursday.'

'More hectic on a weekend, eh?'

'Not so much these days, mate.' He poured liquor into the shaker with a flourish. 'I'm looking for a job with better tips, to tell you the truth, bruv.'

Jon dropped a £10 note into the tip jar. 'I'm surprised to hear it,' he said. 'I play cricket with Francesco, and he's always talking about what a success this place is.'

'He would, wouldn't he.'

'I haven't seen him in ages, though. You know what's happened? Has he gone on holiday?'

'Can't talk about that, don't know nothing.' He strained Saffy's cocktail into a stemmed glass, slid it over and then poured Jon's beer. 'Anything else?'

At a table, Saffy sipped her drink and winced. 'No wonder he doesn't get any tips.'

'Another motive, though. If the club is failing, there might be money problems.' He looked around the room. There was another bartender, this one female, and a few waitresses gossiping at the end of the bar. The DJ in his booth. The bouncer outside. Slim pickings.

They sipped their drinks and chatted, mostly about the decor, and Saffy told him a long, involved story about one time that a former business associate of her stepfather's had tried to get her to invest in a nightclub in Manhattan that had turned out to be a recruiting ground for an apocalyptic multi-level-marketing cult. The hen party came in, screeching and giggling, and the music cranked up as some of the women hit the floor.

She emptied her drink, grimaced, and stood. 'OK, I'm going to try to buy some drugs.'

He half-stood. 'Are you sure? Do you feel comfortable?'

'Darling, I'm a socialite with a string of City boyfriends. I know how to find cocaine.' She strode off towards the ladies' room, and Jon (and probably every other man in the room) watched her go.

Before he'd met her in the hotel, the evening hadn't started out well. More threats had appeared on his Instagram account, and now that he'd gone through his professional email account in detail, there were threats in there too. Most of them variations on a theme, telling him to start up his podcast again if he didn't want to be hurt. They were all from different, obviously fake accounts. He wasn't frightened, of course – trolls were cowards. And they didn't seem to have his personal information, because all of the threats were on his public accounts. He'd lied about it to Saffy because it seemed ridiculous, though unpleasant. It brought up all kinds of questions about what sort of person his show and books were appealing to, and what kind of behaviour he was encouraging.

But now, almost in spite of himself, Jonathan realised that he was having a good time. Ever since he was a kid, he'd loved solving puzzles. It was the best part of his journalism: not the writing or the presenting or the listener numbers or the TV appearances or the crowds at his book signings, but the hands-on work of gathering information and figuring something out. And tonight he was doing it in the company of a beautiful, clever woman. This was fun. And not long ago, he'd thought all of the good times were over.

A waitress turned up and he ordered another couple of drinks. When he tried to chat with her about the owner, she shook her head. 'I don't know nothing about that,' she said, and left. Saffy returned a few minutes later, also shaking her head.

'That's one theory down,' she said. 'If this place is a front for a drug ring, they're doing a terrible job. You'd be hard-pressed to get a vitamin.'

He stood up and held out his hand. 'Let's dance.'

'Dance? I thought you weren't the dancing type.' But her eyes sparkled, and she took his hand.

'We're in a nightclub, and we want to blend in.'

He led her to the floor. Most of the hen night were on it, now, in glittery dresses and deely bobbers and feather boas. Saffy, in her long skirt and modest blouse which nevertheless clung deliciously to every curve, looked cool and classy, like a Hitchcock heroine. The coloured lights lit up her skin and hair, made her red-painted lips look almost black. He couldn't look away from her.

But when they were in the middle of the frenzy of dancing hens, he realised that the DJ was playing OutKast and he had literally no idea how to dance to it without looking like an utter fool.

Saffy saved the day – again. She stepped close to him and put her hand on his shoulder. In heels, she was as tall as he was. His arm automatically curled around her waist.

'I only slow dance,' she murmured.

He drew her closer, resting their joined hands on his chest. She smiled at him, eyes glittering, and they began to move slowly together, ignoring the blasting music. Ignoring everything. She smelled wonderful – like flowers and spice – and she moved with him seamlessly, light and supple in his arms.

The last time he had danced was at his wedding. And it had been at Amy's insistence. He'd danced with her in front of all their guests, and he'd felt silly, embarrassed, wanting the music to finish. He had known that she loved to dance and that his awkwardness was ruining this moment for her, and that made him feel more awkward. He'd promised himself that he would take lessons, take her out dancing sometime. He never had. Maybe the new man in her life liked to dance. He hoped so.

The music changed and melded from one song to the next, and Saffy leaned a little bit closer, close enough so that her cheek brushed his. Amy had moved on, his marriage was over. He had to get on with his own life, too. And this woman, this beautiful, sexy woman, wanted him. This woman who trusted him, who thought he was worth her time, who enjoyed what he cared about. If he tilted his head, caught her eye, spinning slowly on the dance floor, he could kiss her.

'Jon,' she whispered, and her voice was honey and promise. She could say anything to him right now and he knew he would say yes.

'Mmm?' His heart thumping, his mouth parting to kiss her.

'The bouncer just walked through on his way to the back. I think he's on his break.'

'Oh.'

'Should we go talk to him?'

'Yeah. Yeah, let's go.'

'OK,' she murmured. 'Buy a couple of bottled beers and meet me by the toilets.'

Feeling stunned, he followed her off the dance floor. She disappeared out of sight while he bought the beer and made his way to the loos. She was standing on the other side of them, next to a propped-open fire escape door. When she arrived she opened her tiny handbag and took out a pack of Marlboro Lights.

'I didn't know you smoked,' he said, stupidly.

'I don't, but it's a great excuse to hang around outside with the bouncer who does.' She winked at him and pushed open the door. It led to a little courtyard furnished with a couple of plastic lawn chairs. The bouncer who'd let them into the club stood under a light, smoking.

'Oh thank God, have you got a light?' Saffy said to him, bouncing over to the big man, holding out her Marlboro.

'Punters aren't supposed to be out here,' said the bouncer.

'Ugh, you think I'm going to smoke on the street? I won't tell if you don't.' She gave him a winning smile.

The bouncer shrugged and dug in his pocket for a lighter. As he lit Saffy's cigarette, he glanced at Jon, who smiled a little foolishly and held up one of the beers. 'Are you allowed one of these?'

'Hell no, but I'll have it.' The bouncer took it and he and Jon clinked bottles. 'Thursday is the new Friday, right?'

Saffy inhaled deep. For a woman who didn't smoke, she did a good impression. 'Not here, it isn't,' she said. 'This place is dead. If I were the owner, I'd be looking for a new investment.'

'He ain't looking for nothing, love.'

Finally. Someone who knew something. Jon drank and pretended to be only mildly interested. 'What do you mean?'

'He's dead, isn't he? You hear about the Bin Bag Killer?'

'Uh ...'

'Slaughters people and cuts them up in bin bags,' said the bouncer, with relish. 'The boss was only found in one of them.'

'No!' Saffy recoiled. 'Oh, that's so gross.'

'Oh yeah. I was one of the last people to see him alive. He walked out of here one night, said "See you tomorrow, mate" and disappeared, like that.' He snapped his meaty fingers. 'Next time anyone seen him he was missing his head.'

'Ugh.' Saffy shuddered attractively. 'Don't.'

'What for?' said Jon. 'Like a gang thing?'

The bouncer took a swig of beer and then a drag of his cigarette. He was clearly enjoying his audience. 'Big F wasn't in no gang,' he said. 'These places might have done better if he was, you know what I mean? He didn't have no head for business, but I sort of figure that was the point.'

'What do you mean?'

'This was his fourth club he owned. The other three all burned down. Mysteriously. Makes you think, don't it.' He tapped his shaved head. 'And Big F loved his insurance. He had insurance on everything, up to the hilt. Now that he's dead, his wife's rolling in it.'

'You think his wife killed him?' Saffy piped up.

'Nah. I told you, it was the Bin Bag Killer. That serial killer they banged up, it's been all over the news. And you know what's funny, this is the second person I know who was killed by a serial killer. My aunt, right, the Yorkshire Ripper got her. Peter Sutcliffe.' He spat on the ground, then dragged deep on his fag. 'When Big F disappeared, I thought he'd fucked the wrong girl. Sorry, love, no offence.'

'None taken.'

'So he was sleeping around?' Jon asked.

'That's one way of putting it. He was making his way through every girl who worked here, and punters as well. Used to ask me to watch out for the good-looking ones for him. He'd have had his eye on you, love.'

'Oh, well, my boyfriend can protect me,' said Saffy serenely, and Jon nearly choked on his beer.

When they went back into the club, the hen party were shrieking louder than the music and spraying sparkling wine all over each other. That quashed any hopes Jon might have had for continuing their dancing.

'I think we got what we came for,' he murmured to Saffy, and she nodded.

'Uh-huh. No gangs, dodgy insurance scams, lots of extra-curricular sex, big motive for wife. She's looking like the best bet right now.'

'You think a woman could do that?' he asked. 'Dismember a man and carry his corpse around in a bin bag? Cyril was a big guy, which is how he did it.'

'Don't be a sexist pig. Anyway, I think I should try to talk to her, and not you. You're too close, and besides, she might recognise you as the person who found her husband's body. I'll try tomorrow.' Saffy took a tiny mirror out of her handbag and inspected her face. 'I'm going to freshen up, and then we can go.'

While she was in the ladies', Jon went back to the bar, where the female bartender was filling the glass washer. 'Hey,' he said.

'Hey, another beer?'

'I'm good, thanks. Listen, do you mind me asking – how long have you worked here?'

She looked wary. 'About a year and a half.'

'I guess you've heard what happened to the owner, Francesco Fanducci.'

'Yeah, I heard.'

'I'm looking into a few things for the insurance company. Obviously if Mrs Fanducci had anything to do with his death, they can't make a payment. I was wondering if you might have observed anything that would give us insight into their relationship.'

'I thought that serial killer got Frank.'

'Yes, as far as I'm aware that's the police theory, but insurance companies. You know.' He gave her a conspiratorial smile, which he hoped wasn't too creepy. Maybe he should've got Saffy to do this.

'I don't know anything,' she said, and turned away quickly. Maybe a little bit too quickly. He took a pen out of his pocket and scribbled his phone number on a cocktail napkin.

'If you remember anything, please get in touch? Any time. My name's Jon. We really want to settle things for Mrs Fanducci.' He walked away without watching to see if she took the napkin.

Saffy met him by the door, where their friend the bouncer was back at work. 'Have a good evening,' he called to them cheerfully. 'Get in touch with me if you want to dump this loser, love.'

Jon put his arm around Saffy's shoulders as he flagged down a cab. It was a gesture of protection, but it reminded him of their dance. How she'd felt close to his body. How close he'd come to kissing her.

He took a chance. 'Do you want to come back to – well. To your place?'

It was a clumsy proposition, but he saw that she understood it from the small smile that touched her newly lipsticked mouth.

'So we can keep dancing?' she asked.

'That. And . . . other things.'

'Hmm. I'd like to explore what you mean by "other things".'

'So you'll come with me?'

She raised her eyebrows. 'Answer me honestly. When we were dancing, did you think about Amy?'

'Um. I . . .'

The cab pulled up and the driver rolled down the window. 'Where to?' he asked.

'I'll take this one,' she said to Jon, and stepped away from him, leaning into the window. He heard her give the driver her sister's address.

'Goodnight,' she said, and kissed him swiftly on the cheek. 'I had a lot of fun. I'll let you know what I find out tomorrow.'

He stood on the pavement watching her cab go, cursing himself for being such a terrible liar.

28

I N HIS OWN CAB, ALONE, he checked his phone again. There were several more messages on his Instagram account, all from accounts with blank profile pictures and names like Andy666 or CrazyHo420. It was a kid, with too much time on their hands. Some of the messages looked the same as the previous ones, more or less cut and pasted, all in capital letters. But the one on the top was different. It was from MelB6969 and it said, I KNOW WHERE YOU LIVE.

He frowned. He screenshotted the messages, in case he needed evidence in the investigation about Fanducci, and tapped on his email account. There was a message from MelB6969 there too. Subject line: YOUR WIFE IS SO PRETTY. No message, only an attachment.

He shouldn't look. It could be a virus of some sort. But . . .

He looked. It was a photograph of Amy, taken in what had once been their local coffee shop. She was sitting in a window seat, one of the upholstered ones that they always tried to grab when they went there together. The photograph looked as if it had been taken from one of the tables at the back near the till. Amy was wearing a new leather jacket, looking at her watch. She looked as if she were waiting for someone.

Whoever had sent this message had been in the same room as her. Maybe even today.

He called her. Her number wasn't in his new phone, on purpose, but he knew it from memory. It rang and rang, every ring making his heart beat more quickly, and then, finally, a sleepy: 'Hello?'

'Amy? It's Jon.'

'Jon? What are you – it's the middle of the night.'

'I'm sorry. Thanks for picking up.'

'It's not your number. I nearly didn't.'

'Yeah, I got a new phone. Listen, I'm sorry to disturb you. But I have to know – are you OK?'

He heard small noises, and pictured her sitting up in bed. Pictured her in the striped pyjamas she liked to wear. Or maybe she wasn't alone, and she was naked, holding the sheet to her chest. 'Yes, I'm fine,' she said, sounding annoyed. 'How else would I be?'

'Have you noticed anything strange lately?' he asked. 'Anyone hanging around the house, or following you? Taking your picture?'

'Jon, this is weird. Are you drunk?'

'No. I'm just ... concerned.'

'Because I haven't heard from you in months, you haven't even signed and returned those papers yet, and now suddenly you call me in the middle of the night saying you're *concerned*?'

'I've – some stuff has happened.'

'But nothing has happened to me, Jon. Nothing. It's been quiet and peaceful, and I'm getting on with my life. I've put all of that stuff behind me. I'm trying to be normal.'

He heard another sound, a low voice raised in a question. She wasn't alone. Maybe that was a good thing, he told himself. It was safer.

'Just be careful, OK?' he said. 'Be aware of your surroundings. Keep the doors and windows locked. Draw your curtains at night.'

She sighed. 'Are you going to sign the papers, Jon?'

'Yes. I'll sign them.'

'OK. Listen: I have no problem with talking to you. I want to keep this as amicable as it can be. But if you want to call, please call at a normal hour, all right?'

'Goodnight.' He resisted adding the words 'I'm sorry.' He'd said those words enough times, and they never seemed to make any difference anyway.

* * *

When he unlocked the door to Saffy's house, he half-expected Girl to come bounding up to him, tail wagging. Then he remembered he'd shut her in the kitchen so she wouldn't climb all over Saffy's white furniture. Saffy, to her credit, hadn't asked him what he'd done with the dog or anything about the state of her flat. She trusted his judgement, seemingly. Unlike the woman he'd been married to for seven years.

But when he got to the kitchen, the door was ajar and Girl wasn't in there. The light was on, as he'd left it, but her blanket-bed was abandoned. But if she'd escaped, why hadn't she greeted him? 'Girl?' he called, testing the doors to the outside. They were locked.

'Girl, I've got a treat!' he called. She didn't appear. He checked the living room, which seemed undisturbed, and tested the door into the garage. Locked. He thought about the Instagram message: I KNOW WHERE YOU LIVE. He'd assumed it meant the house he'd shared with Amy ... but what if it meant this one? What if someone had done something to his dog? What if someone was inside the house with him, right now?

He looked around for a weapon and saw nothing except for a tall cylindrical glass vase. When he picked it up, it had a heft to it. He turned it around so that the heavy bottom was foremost, and walking quietly, surveyed the rest of the house. His bedroom was dark and empty; he used the torch on his phone to check under the bed and in the wardrobe, and in the en suite. He listened, and then went up the stairs. The door to Saffy's bedroom was half-closed. Had it been closed before? Or open? He couldn't remember; he didn't go up here.

He gripped the vase and pushed the door open with his foot. Inside the room was dark. In the light of the torch as he swept the room, he saw a small huddled shape and a pair of reflective eyes, and heard a quiet whine.

'Girl,' he said with more relief than he'd expected. He put down the vase and turned on the light. The little dog was crouched against the far wall. Her expression was entirely sheepish. The very tip of her tail wagged as if of its own accord.

'What did you do?' he asked, with visions of dogshit on the white carpet, chewed-up Manolo Blahniks and Chanel suits. The dog snuffled a little bit, the very embodiment of the word 'hangdog'.

The walk-in wardrobe door was open. 'I hope you chose something cheap to ruin,' he said, 'because I don't think I can afford to pay her back for most of what's in here.' He flicked on the light and gazed with dismay. It was more of a dressing room than a wardrobe, and Girl had definitely been rooting around in it. Several pairs of shoes lay upended on the floor; handbags had been tipped over. A box spilled bright silken scarves. He kneeled on the floor and started putting things in order, checking for tooth marks, tears, slobber trails, and wet patches. It was huge in here, with units lining the walls, clothes arranged neatly on hangers and shelves, a large mirror at the far end. It was pristinely organised, where Girl hadn't been, but he couldn't help wondering how many clothes did one woman need? How many *handbags*?

He heard panting behind him and glanced at Girl, who was standing at the door, watching. 'If I put my hand into dogshit, I swear to God,' he muttered, and crawled a little deeper into the space. Girl had been chewing on something here, right in the back of the wardrobe, under a chair: a soft-sided box lined with fabric, one of those things you saw briefly on television shows about 'organising your space' before you thumbed straight past them to watch a good true crime documentary. The dog had destroyed the lid and pulled out the contents onto the floor: more clothes, several belts, and half-buried under fabric, something else. Something so unexpected that for a full minute, even though the object was entirely familiar, so familiar that he froze while reaching for it, staring, he didn't understand what it meant.

And then he did. He knew exactly what this object meant. It meant that Saffy had been lying to him all along.

29

I'M IN SOUTH CROYDON, SIPPING a coconut latte and casually scrolling the *Wall Street Journal*. The car is my sister's, a frankly embarrassing Fiat Uno, but it actually fits in quite well around here. I'm wearing Accessorize sunglasses (I know) and if anyone notices me, which they won't, they'll think I'm a desperate housewife waiting for it to be time to pick up the kids from school.

Once upon a time, when I was quite young, before Harold died, I longed to live in the suburbs. From what I saw on it during lonely mornings watching TV while the nanny talked on the phone, it seemed like heaven. All the families had both a mother and a father. There was usually at least one grandparent somewhere in the picture, and the neighbours were always up for cookouts or holiday celebrations. If they had staff, like a housekeeper or a cook, they were wise and pithy, and part of the family. Sometimes they had dogs. I didn't really like dogs, but mostly I'd only encountered little purebred things that yapped and shivered. Suburban dogs were real dogs. They were large and goofy. In the suburbs, people ate normal things like macaroni and cheese and chicken nuggets and spaghetti. The kids went to school in happy gangs with all the other neighbourhood kids, they rode bikes all over the place and had terrible teachers except for the one teacher who just got it and was totally inspirational. There were jocks and nerds and cheerleaders and the people who ran the yearbook who nobody ever really liked. I would be a cheerleader, I decided, and a homecoming queen. I would be kind to all of the nerds and the yearbook outcasts. I would be popular with everyone, and I would use my popularity for good. Compared to the tedium of private tutors or the cut-throat world of boarding school, suburban high school would be perfection itself. You could be both special and entirely normal. Apparently most of my generation dreamed of being in *Harry Potter*, I dreamed about living in *My So-Called Life*.

Of course, I grew up and realised that the suburbs are just as full of bigotry, misogyny, addiction, avarice, narcissism and misery as anywhere else. Maybe even worse. Only everyone wears high-street clothes and their houses are plastered with slogans like LIVE LOVE LAUGH.

Fatima Fanducci's house looks almost exactly like every other house on her street. It's semi-detached, and while the house attached to it has succumbed to the baffling trend of grey UPVC windows, grey pebble-dash and fake grass on the lawn, the Fanduccis' sports real grass, white double glazing and the original 1960s brickwork. It has a magnolia tree in front and some bedding plants blooming along the path. There's a child's scooter outside the front door and a Chelsea Football Club sticker in one of the upper windows.

There's also a panda car parked right in front of it, with two bored-looking PCs. The news about Francesco's death hasn't hit the papers yet, so there's no media presence, but there will be. With the police keeping a watchful eye on the property, I can't even pretend to be a friendly neighbourhood Avon lady. So I'm reduced to good old-fashioned stalking.

The thing is that, believe it or not, Fatima Fanducci has absolutely zero online presence. How has she managed that in this day and age? Has her husband actually confined her to the house?

Susie WhatsApps me. *When do I get my car back?*

When I've finished my intel-gathering mission.

OMG you are so fucking lame. Send me a selfie in my car.

I do.

What are those things on your face?

Accessorize, £15.99

NOOOOOOOOOOOOOOOOOOOOOOOOOOOO

I'm undercover.

You're enjoying this way too much, she types. *I'd be worried about you if I didn't know you were literally the most boring person alive.*

Thanks, Sis. Then again, it's exactly what I want her to think, right? *Did you message me just to insult me?*

Nooo, F and I are going to Goa this afternoon.

This afternoon? You didn't tell me?

We just decided, spur of the moment! So romantic <3

It's your birthday tomorrow! I made plans!

I knooooooooow Saffy-san but Finlay wanted to give me this amazing cleansing retreat.

Who's paying for it?

She doesn't reply for a few minutes. That's all the answer I need.

Susie and I have spent every single one of her birthdays together, since the day she was born. One year when we were at different schools I had to fake an appendectomy just so I could drive from New York to New England, stopping on the way to pick up her favourite chocolate cake from a bakery in Boston. We have rituals and private jokes and no matter what, even if I'm in the middle of something really important, I plan my week so that I can wake her up, first thing on her birthday morning, with a bowl of ice cream with sparklers stuck into the extra whipped cream on top. Susie's birthdays are my normal. They are my special. They are my suburbia.

I'll make it up to you, she messages finally.

Of course! I reply. *It's your birthday, you should do what you want and have fun! Please wear sunscreen.*

I hope Finlay gets third-degree sunburn. I hope he chokes on a vegan curry.

It's just as I'm imagining Finlay's face turning a satisfying colour of blue, that the door to the Fanducci house opens and a woman comes out. From here I have a pretty good view of her: she's a slight woman, probably about five feet tall if that, maybe a hundred pounds soaking wet. She has dark circles under her eyes and her hair is lank, though her outfit is cute in a mumsy way: a pretty A-line skirt and a lace-edged blouse. She's got a young child with her, holding a fluffy stuffed bunny. A toddler and a preschooler hold onto her skirt, and a baby car seat dangles from each hand. The poor woman has five children under the age of seven, two of them infants. I lift my phone and take pictures of her as she makes her burdened way to the minivan that's parked on the drive. It takes her an age to strap all of that lot into the back of the van, and hoist the car seats into place. Before she climbs into the driver's seat she wipes her forehead with the back of her hand, exhausted.

Imagine doing all of that every time you need a pint of milk! I feel like giving this woman the password to my Ocado account.

Well, that explains it, I think as she drives off. No wonder the police aren't holding her on suspicion of her husband's murder, even if she is the beneficiary of a large insurance policy. It would be a heroic undertaking just to get a babysitter for that lot for the length of a quick cut and blow-dry, let alone for long enough to kill a large man, dismember and decapitate him, and plant his remains somewhere across the city. Plus – how old were those babies? Only a few months at most, which means that when Francesco was meeting his death, the tiny Fatima was wobbling around pregnant to the brim with twins.

That said, in my opinion, a woman who can squeeze five whole human beings out of her vagina is capable of just about anything. Killing is much easier and less painful than giving birth, and a woman who's had that many babies is guaranteed to be strong, resilient and resourceful.

The Met might think that Fatima Fanducci couldn't be guilty of murdering her husband. Me, I think she'd do just fine. If she had a childminder.

I wonder if she knows that he was fucking around on her. She definitely knew that he spent all his spare time at a poxy nightclub instead of at home with her, helping her with enough kids to make up half a football team. He probably only spent enough time at home to impregnate her, and then he was off to shag any other poor girl he could find. What an asshole. Now there's a guy who deserved to die: not for any major villainy, not because he was a serial killer or a warmonger.

Just your average run-of-the-mill entitled foot soldier of the patriarchy.

What a dick. I hope Fatima's life insurance payout is enormous.

* * *

Even London traffic can't soothe me. I'm still fuming as I pull up outside my mews house, thinking about loyalty. You can call me many things, many of them punishable by life imprisonment and/or death: I am a killer, a stalker, a blackmailer, a desecrator of corpses, a burglar, a thief, a liar, a narcissist, a sociopath, and I have a low-key shopping addiction that is harmful to Planet Earth, but I have never in my life done two things: dyed my hair out of a box, or been disloyal. If I am on your side, I'm *on your side*. One hundred per cent. Would kill or die for you without a moment's thought.

That is, when it comes to Susie, I would. She's the only one who's proven good enough for my complete loyalty. But now she's spending her birthday on a beach with that waste of moisturiser.

It's men again. Men like Finlay and Francesco who just take whatever they want, with no thought about the feelings of women. It's not only entitlement, it's a lack of loyalty or values. They think that just because they've got a dick between their legs they can do anything.

I'm actually muttering under my breath when I get out of the car, so before I walk to my front door, I stop, close my eyes, and breathe. I think of green, perfectly mown lawns. I think of clouds scudding across a blue sky. I think of myself, age twelve, neatly eliminating Harold from our lives.

I think of the sexy man waiting for me in my house.

244

And when I open my eyes again, my fists are unclenched, my eyes are clear, my face is frown-free. People are disloyal sometimes, sure. Yes. But if there is one thing that I've proven, is that I can handle it.

I knock briefly on the door before I use my key to open it a little and call, 'Hi, honey, I'm home!'

Nobody answers, and my smile slips a little, but that's OK. I have time for a coffee and a freshen-up, and maybe even enough time to change my underwear just in case he's come to his senses and he's ready to forget about his ex. I go in and call again, 'Jon?'

'I'm in the kitchen,' he says, and I frown. Why didn't he answer me before?

'Well,' I say as I head for the kitchen, 'I can see why the police haven't arrested Fatima Fanducci. She was massively pregnant when her husband was killed. I guess she could have hired someone, though. What do you know about contract kil—'

I stop. Jon's sitting at the kitchen island, facing the door. Girl's at his feet, pressed up against his legs, eyeing me. He has several empty coffee cups at his elbow, he hasn't shaved or possibly slept, and in front of him on the island is something that I really, really didn't want him to see. Right there, in black and white and red.

'Oh,' I say.

'Yes. Oh.'

I thought he looked tired, but now I can see that he's poised to move. Instinctively I trace the path between where I stand and the knife block next to the cooker. I do it without looking, from memory. Not that I'm planning to stab Jon, not that I want to. But ... it always pays to be safe.

'Saffy,' he says. 'I think you owe me an explanation.'

30

I T WAS HIS OWN BOOK, *Without Mercy*, in hardback. As Saffy watched, he opened the cover to reveal the dedication that they both knew was there:

To Seraphina:
Happy clue-hunting!
Best wishes,
Jonathan Desrosiers

'Who's Seraphina?' he asked.

'Me,' said Saffy. 'It's my real name. I hate it.'

'I always date the books I sign. You were at my last reading. The one on the night that this all started. Or did someone else get the book for you?'

'I was there.' Her voice was quiet.

'You lied to me. You pretended not to know who I was or what I did for a living. You acted surprised when I told you.'

'Well, I didn't want it to be weird.'

He stared at her. 'You think it's less weird to lie to me than to tell me the truth?'

'In some ways, yes. It's ... easier.'

After the initial surprise, she was acting her usual breezy self. But there had been that split second of surprise. That single 'Oh' that told Jon that Saffy knew she had something to feel guilty about.

'Did you recognise me?' he asked her. 'When we first met, up in Scotland?'

'Well. You'd changed quite a bit since your book signing. No offence.'

'Did you follow me up to Scotland?'

'What? Why would I do that? Do you want some more coffee?' She went to the machine.

'No. I'm just trying to figure out the timeline here. So you came to my book signing. And then totally by chance, your path crossed mine in the depths of the Highlands.'

'I know, isn't it crazy?'

'And you didn't recognise me, even though I told you my name.'

'You told me your first name, and not even Jonathan but Jon, which is the most generic name you can get. And also, you didn't recognise me either, so maybe I should be the one taking offence. I thought I was pretty memorable.'

Her flippant tone made him grind his teeth.

'When did you figure it out?'

'When I saw you again on the train, I knew. But by then we were talking, and I didn't want to be a fangirl or anything, and you didn't want to discuss it, so I just . . .'

'. . . Lied.'

'I kept it on the down-low. I played it cool.' She snapped a canister into the machine, and pressed the button. Even the scent of the coffee made him tense.

'You didn't play it cool when I explained my job to you, days later. You got all excited, as if it were new information.'

'Well, I mean, that is playing it cool for me.'

'Had you listened to my podcast?'

'Yeah, sometimes. You know. I enjoyed it. So I went to your talk and bought a book, got it signed.'

'And then you totally by chance bumped into me in Scotland. You had no idea I was there, or who I was.'

She frowned at him, prettily. 'You keep on repeating this fact, as if it's unbelievable.'

'Because it is.'

'It seems pretty natural to me. Why would I follow you up to Scotland?'

'You tell me.' He folded his arms.

'I have a flat in Edinburgh. Usually I rent it out, but it was empty, so I went up and used it as a base for hiking.'

'Edinburgh is hours away from my cottage.'

'I was staying in a hotel for a few nights. Do you want to see the receipts?'

Her voice, for the first time, was testy. And she could be telling the truth, but from Jon's experience, good liars often believed their own words so much that they got angry when they were challenged.

'It's quite a coincidence.'

'Coincidences happen. But in my defence, this year I also went to book signings by Stephen Fry, Chimamanda Ngozi Adichie and Ali Smith, and I never ran into them in the Highlands.'

'Did you also hide their books in the back of your wardrobe?'

'Is that where it was?' She narrowed her eyes. 'Why were you in the back of my wardrobe, by the way?'

'Girl got loose while I was out.'

She looked between him and Girl.

'She didn't damage any of your stuff. I checked it all over. But if she did, I'll pay for it. Anyway, that's not really the point.'

'I think it is the point. You're a guest and you snooped.'

'No, the larger point is that you hid my book, and not any of the other books that you happened to have signed this year.'

'So your ego is hurt because I don't have you in pride of place on my shelf?'

'No. But I would like to know why you hid my book. Nothing else, just my book.'

She shrugged. 'I must have misplaced it.'

'In the back of your wardrobe? Saffy, I've been in that wardrobe. Your shoes are arranged according to style and colour. I don't know enough about clothes to understand, but I'd be willing to bet that they're stored according to a strict and elaborate system.'

'Alphabetically by designer,' she admitted, reluctantly.

'The jumpers in that box were folded up in tissue paper. You pretend to be a little ditzy, but you are in fact one of the most organised people I've ever met. You didn't misplace that book. You deliberately hid it in a place where I would be the least likely to look.'

'Again: why would I do that? I didn't know you were going to be staying in my house until I invited you, on the spur of the moment.'

'Yes. But it wasn't on your shelves when I got here. Which means you hid it before you went to Scotland. Which makes it at least possible that you hid it because you knew you were going to be meeting me, and you didn't want me or anyone else to know that you were familiar with my work.'

'Maybe I just didn't want anyone to know that I like true crime. It's a weird thing to like, when you look at it objectively. No offence.'

'Along with being one of the most organised people I've ever met, you're also hands down the most confident. Why would you care whether people know what you read?'

'You obviously have no idea what it's like to be a woman, do you?' She abandoned her coffee and headed for the door.

'Where are you going?'

'I'm going to check my shoes for tooth marks!'

Against his better instincts, he followed her. Girl followed him, but he stopped and told her to stay, and wouldn't leave her until she'd lain down on the kitchen mat. No point throwing petrol on a fire.

When he got to her room, Saffy was in the wardrobe already. He heard her moving around, muttering under her breath. He stood in the doorway and watched as she picked up individual shoes and examined them minutely.

'You've completely messed up my system,' she said. 'Apart from anything else.'

'I'm sorry about that. I should have got a dog-sitter.'

She ignored him, rearranging the pairs of shoes and placing them precisely on the shelves. Then she started on the scarves.

'You're angry, aren't you?' he asked, finally.

'I'm tempted not to say anything,' she said, not looking at him. 'Because I like you, and you're a man, and we all know what straight men want. They want laid-back women, women who are cool, who are fun, who are low-maintenance, who never get angry or annoyed or bored, who never nag and who love to listen to men and forgive them for everything. Straight girls learn this practically as soon as we're born and every relationship we have only makes us learn it more.'

'I don't—'

'So really if I like you, I should pretend to be OK with this. Being angry with you is liable to do me zero favours. You might decide that even though I'm hot, I'm too much work. It's in my interest to be breezy and sexy, and hide how I really feel and who I really am.'

'I don't want you to—'

'And yes, you might say that you don't want me to hide my true self, but believe me, all men say that. They think they can handle it, until it gets too hard, and then they can't. And I get it, I really do, we all want an easy life where we have lots of fun without any consequences, but the point is, Jonathan, is *loyalty.*'

'I'm not—'

She'd moved on to the clothes on the rails, and she held up a red dress. 'There's a tear in the hem of this one.'

'I'm so sorry. I'll replace the dress.'

'It's vintage Valentino.'

'Can ... I buy vintage Valentino somewhere? eBay?'

Her look was so withering that he couldn't help stepping back.

She replaced the dress on the rail and sighed.

'It's not about the dress,' she said. 'It's not about material things, or your dog, who's only a dog. It's about hypocrisy. You've made up this entire nutjob theory about me hiding things from you and following you around, when the ironic thing is, you are *actually* hiding things from me. You have been since the moment we met.'

'This might be true, but it's also not fair. I wasn't hiding my old job, so much as I just didn't want to talk about it. And you knew anyway, it turns out.'

'I wasn't talking about your job.' She walked out of the wardrobe, and he backed off a little more. 'I was talking about, for example, when I met you yesterday night and you were so busy looking at something on your phone that you didn't even notice me arriving. And then you hid what it was. Is *that* fair?'

'It wasn't anything you need to know about, and it had nothing to do with you.'

'Didn't it?' She took another step towards him, and he took another step back. 'Well, here's something that does have something to do with me, especially because you wanted to come home with me last night. When's the last time you had contact with your ex-wife?'

He stepped back again, and then realised that he was backed up against a wall.

'Last night,' he admitted.

'Last night when? Before you asked me to have sex with you, or after?'

She was angry. Not you-tore-my-dress angry, or you-looked-at-my-private-stuff angry. She was furious angry, more angry than he had maybe ever seen a woman, more like the way his dad used to get angry when he had too much to drink and wanted to teach his only son some respect – except his father had been sloppy and brutal and this was cold anger, controlled anger, precise anger that didn't even make Saffy clench her fists but burned in her eyes and in the edge of her voice.

'... After. In the cab home. But—'

Her jaw clenched and her eyes narrowed, steady on him. His words died in his throat. For a moment he thought she was going to . . . he didn't know. Slap him, maybe. Throw something. Start screaming at the very least. Do something to shatter the heavy air between them.

A tendril of something cold crept into his chest. Made his stab wound throb.

'I wish I could say that I was surprised,' Saffy said. For a moment, she did clench her hands.

Then she walked past him out of the room. While he was catching his breath, he heard the front door of the house slam.

31

I'M SITTING IN A CAFE in Shepherd's Bush, sipping on quite a decent double espresso, watching Amy Desrosiers as she sits at the table by the window, wearing yoga pants and reading something on her phone. As I watch, she smiles at something and curls up in her armchair, texting. I can see the look of happy anticipation as she waits for a reply.

I know flirting when I see it, and I can't help it: I wonder if she's texting Jon. Even sexting him, maybe.

I'm not really sure what's happening to me. I've never been jealous in any of my romantic relationships. Never. I've always thought that was partly because I purposely chose men who were a) too boring to stray or b) totally in awe of me anyway. But when I think that through now, that's total bollocks. First, a) boring men stray all the time. Infidelity doesn't make someone exciting; it's infinitely predictable. And b) lots of men have this madonna/whore thing going on, so it's a well-known phenomenon that men who adore their wives and put them on a pedestal, look for mistresses they can get down and dirty with.

The most compelling reason why I thought I was never jealous, was because I knew that if a boyfriend played away, I could just kill him. I've never done this yet, because close contacts are usually prime suspects, and besides funerals are so boring, but knowing that I *could* gave me the upper hand in all of my relationships.

This is all bullshit.

I am consumingly, incandescently jealous of Jon's love for Amy and her love for him. I'm jealous that they met and dated and married. I'm jealous that she wore a white dress and he wore a morning suit and they were surrounded by friends and family in terrible hats. I'm jealous that they lived together for years, had conversations about who snored and petty arguments about whose turn it was to do the hoovering and laid their toothbrushes together, side by side, every evening. I'm jealous that they had idealised, impossible images of each other that slowly wore away over time, or which crashed down all at once and ruined everything. I'm jealous that they broke each other's hearts.

This jealousy means that I'm out of control. It means that there's a problem in my life that I cannot solve with charm or money or murder.

Or maybe ... it means that I'm in love.

Last night, an hour after I left him in my house, Jonathan texted me. *I've found a hotel.* That was it. No apologies, no further accusations of stalking him or lying to him. Nothing. I didn't reply.

Across the cafe, Amy giggles and taps out a message.

The thing is, I was *thrilled* that he figured out why I'd hidden his book, and why I met him in Scotland. Obviously I couldn't tell him that he was right. But I was proud, almost: *look at how clever my man is.* I strung him along with part-truths and questions. It was fun, a little battle of wits. I was waiting for him to call me out on not answering his questions and turning the situation to attack him instead.

If he hadn't admitted about Amy, I would've forgiven him in a heartbeat. But Amy made me angry.

I'm not in love, though. I can't love anyone, except for Susie, obviously. That capacity has been numbed and deadened by all the things I've done and all the things that have been done to me. Or maybe I was born an unfeeling sociopath – apparently that's how sociopathy works, you're just born with something missing, though sociopaths are supposed to lack empathy and I have a lot of empathy, though only for approximately half the population.

I just get lonely sometimes. And I wonder what it would be like.

Amy's squirming in her chair. She's pretty, in a basic sort of way. She has dark hair in a bob and though I'm not close enough to be sure, I think she's got freckles. Who is she texting like that? Is it her new man? Or is it Jon – alone in his hotel room with Girl for company, lying on his bed, thinking about rekindling his marriage?

He called her minutes after asking me to come home with him. From the cab.

My chest burns. When I put my hand to it, my heart is beating very fast. I hate this feeling. I want to make it stop. I have a knife in my pocket, a big folding hunting knife, the blade polished to a lethal silver: it used to be Harold's. He used it on his big-game hunting trips, to rip out the throats of helpless antelopes and drugged tigers, so he could mount their heads on the wall of his lodge in the Adirondacks. When I came of age, I sold the lodge and all its contents, and donated the proceeds to the World Wildlife Fund.

Amy puts her phone in her bag, stands up and leaves the cafe. I want to follow her. I want to sneak up behind her and when no one is looking, I want to wrap my arm around her neck and drag her into a secluded alley. I want to rest the edge of the knife on her throat and press just hard enough for a trickle of blood to run down her freckly skin. I want to hear her beg, tell me that she'll release Jonathan from whatever tangle of love she holds him in, tell me that she'll delete his number, stop taking his calls, tell me that he's mine. All mine.

But I don't do that. I don't kill women. There are too many people out there killing women already. Even if I am a sociopath, incapable of love, I have ethics. I have standards.

So I take a deep breath and I let Amy go. Off to her yoga class, into her life, not knowing what a close escape she's had. She has no idea that she's been sitting in the same room as a predator who has watched her every move and weighed her life against her death.

I have other plans to make myself feel better.

32

HIS ROOM WAS IN A hotel near Earl's Court, and despite the purple cushions and throw on the bed, and the large flower painting on the wall, it resembled nothing so much as the inside of the prison where he'd visited Cyril. Girl sniffed every inch of the carpet. Jon tried not to think about what she was smelling. Comfort-wise, this room was several steps down from Saffy's Kensington mews house.

But he didn't have a lot of choice. It wasn't easy to find a dog-friendly hotel at the last minute, and he'd been told not to leave London. At least this room, unlike his Scottish cottage, didn't have mildew on the walls or leaks in the ceiling. To think: he'd felt he deserved that, to be damp and cold and miserable, to do nothing but drink whisky and brood. And then he'd met Saffy – by chance, or not – and everything had changed.

Jon lay on the bed and stared at the ceiling, contemplating his situation. Girl jumped up and curled next to him. Yes, Saffy had lied to him. And while she'd acted affronted at his accusations, she had never outright denied them. Maybe she thought he hadn't noticed, but he'd spent way too many years interviewing people. Parsing every word was second nature. She'd dodged his questions, answered them with hypotheticals or with questions of her own, and then, before he could pin her down, she'd gone on the attack. About her privacy, about her dress, about her gender, about his ex-wife. Deliberately or not, she'd worked herself up into a temper so that he couldn't ask any more questions about what she'd done, or explain his own actions.

And yes: maybe he was paranoid. It tended to happen, when you spent so much time around crime. Amy always said he was, too. But sometimes, paranoia was justified.

But had he overreacted? She had admitted that she had a crush on him; that could be why she'd tried to find him. She'd been shameless enough about flirting. The fact was, that whatever reason she was in Scotland, they'd met to save Girl's life. And maybe he was extra sensitive, because of all of the threatening messages, and oh yeah, the whole corpse on his doorstep thing.

She'd lied to him, and she was still trying to deceive him, for whatever reason. But the fact was, that twenty-four hours ago he'd been happier than he'd been in a long time. And now, he was not.

He sighed and checked his phone again, for a message from Saffy, or Atherton, or Amy, or maybe even Cyril or the bartender at Majicks. Nothing.

The windows were shut tight, but he could hear the early morning traffic below anyway. The day stretched in front of him, with nothing useful or interesting to do. He tried to think of who else he could call or visit to investigate Fanducci's death. But his heart wasn't really in it today. He called Atherton's number and left a message, with his new hotel details, as per instructions. He realised that he owed Edie an update, so he dialled her number.

She answered after half a ring, breathless and hoarse. 'Jonathan? How did you know?'

* * *

Edie's agency was based on the ground floor of her cheerfully pink Georgian Notting Hill house, while she lived upstairs in the top two storeys. Jon had always liked visiting her professionally; it felt much friendlier and cosier than visiting a corporate office, with walls lined with books, and squishy sofas and worn Turkish rugs and houseplants scattered in between paper, laptops and more books. Edie's own desk was a huge mahogany affair placed stolidly in the front bay window of what had once been the house's main reception room, while her assistants had smaller offices in the former dining room, study, kitchen and scullery. Sometimes one or another of Edie's three cats would wander downstairs to demand food or attention, or just to snooze on a visiting author's lap. As an agent and businesswoman, Edie was razor-sharp, but her office was more like the sitting room of a favourite aunt.

Now the pink paint was peeling and blackened, and the majestic bay window where Edie gazed out as she did deals had been smashed. Jon had been able to smell the smoke as soon as he stepped out of the Underground station; even if he hadn't known where Edie lived, Girl and he would have been able to follow their noses. The road had been taped off and a fire engine and police car were still parked in the middle of it; several firefighters and police officers stood around the property discussing something, though the flames appeared to be long gone.

Edie was standing in the road gazing up at her house. She wore trainers, a long chunky cardigan and pyjama bottoms with ducks on them, and she had a lit cigarette in her hand.

'Edie,' he said, and she turned towards him. Jon had never seen Edie anything less than perfectly groomed, but this morning her face was naked of makeup and dull with soot or exhaustion. Even though they had only exchanged air kisses in the past, Jon held out his arms and Edie walked into them, holding her cigarette out to the side. They hugged for a long time. She felt delicate and much older than he'd ever thought of her, and she smelled strongly of smoke.

'What happened?' he asked when they broke apart, though it was bloody obvious exactly what had happened.

'The smoke detectors went off at about three this morning,' she said. 'Thank God the cats sleep with us. And thank God that Marj insisted on that fire door on the back staircase.'

'Is Marj OK? And the cats?'

'Yes. All fine. The cats are with our neighbour now.'

'What caused it?'

Edie laughed, without humour. 'Marj has told me for years that I was going to set us alight in bed with my smoking, but no. It started in the front room, in my office. The firefighters contained the flames to the ground floor, thankfully, but the whole house has smoke and water damage.'

'Shit. Do you have good insurance?'

'Darling, I have *great* insurance.'

Edie's wife, Marj, came up with two takeout coffee cups. She was wearing a grey tracksuit and had an apple-green pashmina around her shoulders. 'Jonny,' she said, handing a cup to Edie and enveloping Jon in a one-armed hug. 'What a shitshow, eh?'

'I'm just glad you're safe.'

'Did Ed tell you that they think it was set? Well, hello there, you beauty.' Marj got on her knees to fuss Girl, as if she hadn't just dropped a bombshell.

'It was arson?' Jon asked.

Edie took a long drink of coffee and then lit another cigarette. 'It looks like someone broke into the office through the back door.'

'Was anything stolen?'

'Who knows. Everything's burned. I had so many books; they went up like tinder. We might know more in a few days, after they've done some investigations.' Edie winced. 'My laptop's encrypted, but if they stole it, they might be able to get my clients' contact details. Sorry. I've informed the bank, though, and they won't be able to access your financial records.'

'Typical Edie,' Jon said. 'Your house has been set on fire and your main concern is for your clients.'

'Her main concern was for me,' said Marj, still kneeling. Girl had flopped deliriously on her back so Marj could rub her belly. 'And then the cats. And then, her clients.'

'Actually the cats were number one,' said Edie, and the couple stuck their tongues out at each other. At least they'd kept some of their sense of humour.

'Please be careful,' he said to them. 'You could have been killed. Whoever did this must have known that someone was living upstairs.'

'You've got murder on your mind, as always.' Edie dismissed his warning with a flutter of her cigarette.

'I've been getting threatening messages,' he said. 'I really hope they have nothing to do with this.'

'Darling! Have you told the police?'

'The police think I murdered the man I found on my doorstep. So: no.'

At this news, Marj stood up. 'Mate. Are you OK?'

'I'm absolutely fine. All of this is going to blow over, it's nothing. I'm much more concerned for you two. Have you lost everything?'

'Mere possessions,' said Edie, while Marj replied, more practically, 'We'll go live in the house in France for a few months while it's all sorted.'

He gazed at the house. It looked dead, somehow: as if the pink paint were flesh, as if the windows were empty eye sockets. Another corpse in his life. Francesco Fanducci was a rumoured arsonist, too. Was this crime somehow linked to Fanducci? Was the common denominator Jon himself?

He was suddenly fiercely glad that he was living in a bland hotel room in London, and not in the leaky cottage that was his latest address in Edie's records. And he was just as fiercely aware that this woman, who had cajoled him and supported him and built him the career he'd once loved so much, could easily have died. Maybe because of him, and because of the career she'd helped to build.

'If you really want to help,' Edie told him, 'you could write this book about Walker so I can sell it for a squillion pounds. Mama's got to buy new cat beds.'

He hugged her again, as hard as he could. 'Please, never change.'

33

L ET ME INTRODUCE YOU TO Rupert Huntington-
Hogg, the Honourable Member for Swinley. Rupert
H-H voted twice against gay marriage. He is in favour
of putting migrants in jail and/or sending them to countries
with known records of human rights abuses. He thinks rich
people should pay little to no tax, and has gone on record saying
that food banks are a good thing and that council estates breed
'wastrels and addicts'. He has pledged to reduce environmental
standards, to cut salaries of healthcare workers, to slash funding
for libraries, and make all those terrible 'woke' university
students start paying proper tuition fees so they'll know the
value of a hard day's work. Three years ago he spearheaded a
campaign in his constituency to have a battered women's shelter
razed so that one of the many private companies for which he
is a shareholder could construct a block of luxury flats for urban
professionals. Currently the flats are half-empty (before it was
destroyed, the shelter was invariably full).

And at this very moment, he is sitting on my sofa, enjoying
a glass of aged single malt, and waiting to be killed.

I think you can guess which side of Parliament he sits on.
But I hasten to assure you that I am not politically partisan

in my choice of victims. Misogyny comes in all flavours, and regardless of his party affiliations, Rupert H-H is also a complete pig. Among select circles, it's well known that while at Oxford he curated a members-only database of 'upskirt' photos. He regularly calls female MPs 'fillies' and publicly asked the Deputy Shadow Chancellor, when she vehemently opposed a bill he had sponsored, if she 'had the painters in'. He has been quoted in *The Spectator* saying that Muslim women who wear hijabs are 'asking for abuse'. He refuses to tell the press how many children he has or how many of those he is financially supporting, though he has been divorced three times and is currently married to the mistress he was seeing during marriage number two, who is twenty years younger than he is. The mistress he was seeing during marriage number three, filed charges of sexual harassment and then promptly dropped them when she was offered an out-of-court settlement. I've spoken with her; the money was not worth what she had to put up with.

I've also spoken with the intern he raped five years ago, when he was fifty and she was just twenty-three. Ever since she was a little girl, she'd wanted to work in politics. She doesn't anymore.

Rupert H-H has been slobberingly eager to take me to bed for months now, since I met him at a gala for one of the charities I support (yes, it was the donkey one). I knew who he was, of course – both his public and his private profile. I'm meticulous about my research, even when it makes me feel sick to my stomach. I flirted outrageously while letting slip certain interests that I pretended to share with him. Since then I've been breadcrumbing him, keeping in touch just enough to pique his interest, waiting for the time to be right.

This morning, instead of stalking and killing Amy Desrosiers, I used a burner phone to send a message to Rupert. We'd set up a system via a webmail account for which we both had the password; I wrote a draft email, which he read and edited to accept what I'd proposed. I knew he'd be discreet and cover his tracks, both online and in real life. His current wife knows all the tricks, because she played them with Rupert before they were married. And as Teflon as he is, even Rupert's career might not survive yet another scandal in this age of #MeToo, especially if his wife turns against him.

The Honourable Member for Swinley turned up at my door promptly at five o'clock, wearing casual nondescript clothes. Normally I don't shit where I live, but inviting him to my house meant that I had one hundred per cent control of the environment, and my victim had every motivation to hide where he was going, so the pros outweighed the cons in this instance. I answered the door before he could knock and led him wordlessly to my living room, where I'd drawn the curtains.

I waited until I had his full attention before I untied my silk dressing gown and let it slither to the floor, revealing that I was dressed head-to-toe in a black PVC catsuit, complete with PVC gloves and thigh-high boots, my hair sleeked back in a high ponytail. Hardly original, but ... as I've said, Rupert has his proclivities, and I prefer wipe-clean clothing.

I poured him a double single malt on ice, and he's been sitting on my sofa sweating and trying not to drool ever since.

'I was beginning to think that you'd never meet with me,' he says. I pluck his glass from his hand and pour him another drink. 'I've been walking around with a permanent stiffy since I got your message. Thought I'd get arrested.'

'Anticipation is half the pleasure,' I tell him. Since he's come into my house I've stood at least two metres away from him and not allowed him to touch me. I hand him the glass. He paws at me but I step back, out of arm's reach.

'You're killing me,' he groans.

'Oh, you haven't seen anything yet.' I lightly trail my gloved hand down my neck, and between my latex-clad breasts. His gaze follows every move. 'Go ahead, drink up like a good boy.'

He tosses down the second Scotch, stands up and reaches for me. I back off. 'No, no, no. Be patient.'

'I have been patient,' he pouts.

Does this petulant horny man-child act usually work for him, I wonder? Presumably some of his sex has been consensual, so it must. He has indeed got a stiffy – not exactly an impressive one from this angle – and his cheeks and neck are flushed pink, his forehead agleam with perspiration.

I should wait a little longer for the bennie that I crumbled into his first drink to take effect. I know he's no stranger to recreational prescription drugs, so maybe he's got a tolerance. Again, it's a balance: I don't want to drug him so much that it would turn up anything unusual if there's enough left of him for an autopsy, but also, I need him at least a little incapacitated if possible. I'm considerably more fit, agile and skilled than he is, but he also outweighs me by a good nine stone. Rupert H-H likes a boozy lunch.

I pour more whisky in his glass. 'Come on, then, big boy. Let me show you my bedroom.'

'Your evil lair,' he chuckles, and he sounds drunk, so maybe the bennie is working. He follows me upstairs to my bedroom.

I can feel him staring at my ass the entire way. For a man who's apparently dead set against using condoms, he does like latex.

'Is that crotchless?' he asks me, pointing at my catsuit.

'No.'

'I want you to keep it on. Has it got a zipper or something?'

Well, this is handy. I open my bedside drawer and take out Harold's hunting knife. 'I've got a better idea.'

I've been planning this murder for a long time, and in my original plans it was supposed to go differently. I had plans of a suite at the Dorchester, questionable pornography, far too many recreational drugs. It was going to leave no evidence of my involvement, and the discovery of the body and the subsequent news headlines were going to be deliciously fitting of the way that Rupert H-H had lived his life. I'd been looking forward to those headlines a lot.

But I've had a change of mood. Pharmaceuticals and scene-setting aren't enough for me right now. I need a more hands-on approach.

The knife gleams, perfectly sharp and silver. Rupert's eyes widen with surprise and heightened lust.

In this moment, he thinks that we understand each other perfectly.

He holds out his hand for the knife so he can utterly ruin my outfit, which I'm starting to like in a sort of ultra-villain way, but I shake my head. 'Not yet,' I say. 'You didn't come here so that you could call the shots, did you?'

'No,' he pants. 'You're calling the shots.'

'Did you bring what I asked you to?'

From the pocket of his jacket, he pulls his old school tie. Eton, of course.

'Take off your clothes,' I tell him, taking the tie and reaching in the drawer for something else.

The ensuing visual is, sadly, something I have to endure. While he undresses, I picture Keanu Reeves.

'Good boy,' I say. 'Now, open your mouth.'

Ever willing to please, Rupert obeys. I sashay closer and stuff his tie inside his mouth. While he's still surprised, I use a length of silver gaffer tape around his head to secure the gag in place. 'Still OK?' I ask. Because, let's say it once more for the idiots in the back: the sexy stuff is never any fun without consent.

He nods and makes a muffled 'mmph' sound. I reward him with a little chuck on the chin.

'Now, I like my sex dirty, but my men clean, so why don't you go to the bathroom and freshen up a little bit, and I'll join you in a second.'

Off he trots, bum, balls and belly bobbing, to the en suite. As soon as his back is turned I'm pulling on a surgical hairnet and mask. I considered wearing PVC headgear, too, but that stuff takes ages to get on and off and I'd already used half a packet of talcum powder just for the catsuit. Yet another reason why Michelle Pfeiffer and Halle Berry have my undying respect.

There's a 'mmph' of surprise from the bathroom and I know that he's noticed the fact that every square centimetre of the room is covered in clear plastic sheeting, like something out of *Dexter*.

'Just doing a little bit of renovation,' I sing to him, and, raising the knife, I follow him into my own private murder salon. 'Have you ever seen *Psycho*? Classic.'

The Eton tie muffles his scream. He's actually quicker on the uptake than I expected – maybe the mask tipped him off.

He stumbles away from me, catches his leg on the back of the bath, and falls backwards into it, a pale sprawling flabby starfish. He scrabbles to get up, but by now I'm kneeling on the edge of the bath, the knife held to his throat.

'Are you wondering why I'm doing this?' I croon.

'Mmmp-mmp!'

I smile at him. My mouth is covered, but he can surely see my eyes. His own eyes are panicked, slightly bloodshot, darting around looking for an escape that doesn't exist.

I mention a woman's name to him, and then another one, and relief floods his face. He thinks that this is virtue signalling, some sort of empty #MeToo protest gesture. He thinks this is the drama of a hysterical woman, that I'm some crazed woke bitch, and he's already picturing the anecdote he's going to tell in the bar among colleagues, among men who never call him on his bullshit because they're just the same as him, drunk on power and privilege and patriarchy, man after man after man after man, all of them for so many years, and nothing ever changes.

I take the knife away from his throat. He relaxes, just a little. He pulls in a breath through his nose and gabbles through his stuffed mouth.

Then I sink my knife into his stomach. It parts the soft flesh like butter. He doesn't feel the pain for a moment.

And then he does.

*　*　*

I'm quite absorbed in my little project, so I don't hear it the first time the doorbell goes. The second time, I raise my head, but I figure it's a canvasser or a delivery person or a religious nut, so I ignore it and get back to work.

271

Then I hear a voice. 'Hello? Anyone home? Saffy?'

It's Jon. He's in the house.

Fuck.

I jump to my feet. My gloves are black, but it's pretty clear that this stuff on them is not Fairy Liquid. I pull them off, hurriedly, and drop them on the plastic-lined floor. I unzip my boots, abandon my mask and hairnet, close the bathroom door behind me.

'Just a minute!' I call.

There's a fluffy dressing gown hanging in my wardrobe, something I only wear when I've got flu. I pull it on over the catsuit. It's going to be stained on the inside with politician blood, but a quick check in the mirror shows me that it's covering most of everything.

'Sorry to interrupt you,' Jon calls up the stairs. 'I didn't think you were home, and I just needed to pick up a couple of things I'd forgotten. The dog's things.'

'No worries! It's all fine! Everything's good!' A quick roll up of the ankles and wrists of the catsuit to hide them, I tie the dressing gown tighter, and rub off my lipstick with a tissue I find in the pocket. Then I go downstairs.

Jon's standing near the front door, evidently having gone no further as soon as he heard my voice. He's looking quite rumpled, as if he's been sleeping in his clothes again, and even before I reach the bottom of the stairs I can smell the scent of smoke coming off him. Not cigarette, but something like woodsmoke, like campfires and nature.

'Sorry,' he says. 'I didn't mean to intrude. I wouldn't have come in if I'd known you were home. I realised I forgot to post your keys back through the door. I was going to leave them for you.' He holds them up. I take them and put them in my pocket, with the tissue.

'It's not a problem. I was just filling a bath.'

'I'll only be a minute. Girl's grown attached to this one toy.'

'Where is Girl?' Dogs are far too good at sniffing out blood.

'She's with Edie, my agent. I told her I'd only be a little while.'

But he doesn't move, and neither do I. The thing is, I got a little carried away with the enjoyment of my work, so I'm not one hundred per cent certain whether the MP in my bathroom is dead.

It seems wise to stand in front of the staircase right now, to block the way up. Or maybe it's wiser to get Jonathan the hell out of the house. But he's gazing at me, and he looks so good and decent and tired and wholesome and worried. Like the exact opposite of the man upstairs.

And God, I feel guilty about the man upstairs. Not about Rupert as such – he had it coming – but for letting my focus slip from Jonathan. I'd promised myself that I'd put killing aside until I'd got my man. Now I've messed that all up, just because I got a little testy and wanted to release some tension.

'The thing is,' he says, 'I haven't been honest with you. Not about everything.'

'What's wrong?'

'My agent's house burned down.'

'What? When?' And what does this have to do with me?

'Last night. Well, the early hours of this morning. Someone broke in and set a fire. They don't know if anything was stolen.'

'Are they OK?'

'Yeah. Yeah, they're fine. But . . . Edie means a lot to me. She could have easily been killed. She lives right above the office, and she was asleep. She only got out because her wife did a fire safety course at work. And that made me think.'

'. . . That you need a fire safety course?'

'Maybe, but also, life is short, you know?'

Rupert H-H could tell us something about that. If he could speak. Actually – is that a noise upstairs? Sort of a gurgle?

I cough to cover it up.

'Are you OK?' Jon asks.

'Fine. Allergies, I think. Anyway, you were saying . . . life is short.'

'Right. Which means there's no reason to keep hiding things from you. Especially if I've been accusing you of hiding the fact that you knew me. It makes me a hypocrite.'

'What are you hiding?' I resist the temptation to scream it. Does he know about my hobby? Does he know I've broken my promise to abstain from killing – like someone on a diet who's just eaten a whole sharing box of Maltesers?

He puts his hands in his pockets and looks embarrassed. 'I've been getting threats.'

'What? In person?'

'Online. I mean, part of that is just normal for being a person with a bit of a following on the internet. But it seems to have stepped up in the last few weeks, or even months. It's different accounts, all of them seemingly new, with very few if any followers and posts. So someone's making them to troll me.'

'What kind of threats?'

'You can see for yourself, if you like.' He unlocks his phone and gives it to me, his Instagram DMs open. I scroll down.

There are dozens and dozens of them: crude and tasteless and unimaginative. All threatening the man I fancy. How dare they.

'This is awful,' I say, giving back the phone. 'People are dicks.'

'Yeah. So, that was what I was looking at on my phone when we met. And I didn't tell you because ... well, I guess I was embarrassed. I wasn't really worried about it at the time. People who make threats like this aren't generally a real-life danger. They're braver behind their keyboard.'

As a rule, I'd agree, but I have a certain insight into the dangerous-person psychology. Maybe someone who sends DM threats is a coward, which means they might not track you down and confront you, but there are sneakier, more cowardly ways of hurting someone. Poison. Sabotage. Arson.

'Do you think the person who burned down your agent's office is behind this?'

'No reason to think they're connected. Though I did wonder ... Fanducci was involved with arson. Anyway, it's probably a good idea that I'm staying in a hotel now, for your safety's sake.'

That is definitely a noise upstairs. Not a gurgle this time, but a scrabbling sound. Like a nearly dead man trying to get out of a blood-slicked, plastic-wrapped bath.

'Is there someone upstairs?' Jon asks.

'No,' I say quickly. 'It's Gaye next door. Did you meet Gaye? She has her whole upstairs converted into a hot yoga studio. She grows marijuana in it too, for personal use, though she's happy to share. Anyway, she gets a little energetic some afternoons. Did you ever hear her?'

'No.'

'She's eighty-four but in great shape.'

Jon nods. 'So I've been feeling bad that I didn't tell you about the threats, because if they're serious, they could potentially affect you too. But also, it explains something. Because I got this.' He scrolls, and shows me an email with an image attached. The image is strikingly familiar: Amy, sitting in the same seat she was in this morning, while I was watching her flirt via text. For a split second I wonder if he's going to confess that he was the person she was texting, but then how would he have taken the photo? And then I see that she's wearing a completely different outfit in this picture.

'Someone's been watching Amy,' he tells me (like this is news). 'I got this photo right after we left the club, and it freaked me out. So I called Amy to check if she was OK. That was the only reason.'

A shuffle, a crinkle of plastic.

'Why didn't you tell me this?' I ask, maybe a little louder than necessary.

'I was on the back foot. You were really angry. I'd found the book, and Girl had been in your clothes, and to be honest, Saffy, you're a little scary when you're cross.'

If only he knew.

'I didn't call her to try to hook up with her. Or to rekindle our relationship. That night, I couldn't possibly have thought about anyone else other than you.'

Oh wow. Is it hot in here, or am I wearing head-to-toe PVC and a thick fluffy dressing gown?

'I know you're hiding stuff too,' Jon continues. 'But that's OK. I need to earn your trust, obviously. I can't be so scared of getting close to someone else that I wait for everything to be perfect. Life's too short. So I was wondering ... do you want to go on a date with me? A real date?'

I consider for a moment. 'Because we've had communication issues in the past, I want to lock you down on your definition of this. A real date as in ...'

'... Drinks, dinner, maybe dancing.'

'Maybe kissing?'

'It's on the table.'

'Then that will be a big yes.'

We grin crazily at each other, like we've both just won the lottery. Upstairs, Rupert is quiet. Maybe he's bled out, or maybe he's been finished off by the glorious power of burgeoning romance.

'I'll find a dog-sitter,' Jon says. 'And I'll make a reservation.'

I shake my head. 'I'll make a reservation.'

'I'll arrange an overdraft.'

I'd like to kiss him now, but I can't risk him finding out what I've got on underneath this robe. Like I told Rupert: anticipation is half the pleasure. Hoist by my own petard, etc., etc.

'Oh, and Saffy?'

'Mm?'

He reaches for me, as if to cup my cheek in his hand. Fuck it. Fuck it! One kiss has got to be worth even the risk of being discovered. My lips open of their own accord.

But he brushes a finger across the top of my cheek instead, underneath my eye, where the surgical mask didn't cover. 'You've got something on your face,' he says. 'It looks like blood.'

Spell broken. 'Oh. Oh yeah, I had a nosebleed earlier and it got everywhere. That's why I was running a bath.'

'Glamorous,' he says, and wipes his finger on his jeans. 'OK, I've got to get back to pick up Girl. But ... I'll call you.'

'You'd better,' I say.

I watch him leave. My guilt has dissolved into that fizzy feeling of triumph, but this is a reminder to me: keep my eyes on the prize.

But first, I've got to go back upstairs and finish off Rupert.

34

THE NUMBER WAS ONE HE didn't recognise. A week ago he wouldn't have picked it up, but this time he took the call without any hesitation. Was this the old Jonathan Desrosiers coming back? Maybe even improved?

'Hi, it's Trina?' said a voice on the other end. 'I work at Majicks?'

The happy pique of interest, the sense of being on the hunt, felt like the best part of his old life.

The bartender and he arranged to meet in a Costa in Waterloo Station. He considered calling Saffy to ask her to come with him – a female presence might be useful to make him seem less threatening, and Saffy loved the hunt as much as he did. But he decided against it, because he wanted the next time he saw her to be on their date. Maybe he was turning into a romantic.

Girl didn't like the crowds at Waterloo but she settled under Jon's chair, lying down with her head on her front paws. Trina turned up ten minutes late. He bought her a triple espresso and watched as she poured sugar into it. Behind the bar, she'd looked tough and capable, but today she was tired. Woven bracelets hung loose on thin wrists.

'How is Fatima?' she asked him. 'Have you spoken with her? I don't have her number.'

'I haven't spoken with Mrs Fanducci personally, but I've heard she's doing as well as can be expected. Do you know her well?'

'No. I just saw her around sometimes, you know. I talked with her a few times. I liked her and I felt bad for her. Frank left her at home with all those kids. He never helped her and he wouldn't let her get a job – she used to work as a teacher, before they had kids. I think she liked it. And then there was . . .' She seemed to think better of what she was going to say, and stirred her espresso.

'We know he saw other women,' Jon said gently.

'Well, I don't want to talk about that. Because you're with the insurance company. And I don't want you to think that Fatima had a good reason for getting rid of him or anything, you know? She's a decent person. Even Frank talked all the time about what a good mother she was. *Is.* She wanted him around more, not less. When he disappeared, she came in to talk to people in the club. She was scared. Really scared.'

'As if she thought she and the children were in danger?'

'She was scared that he might have been hurt. Or that he'd left her, alone and with no income. Which is what most of us thought had happened. We figured he'd picked up with another woman. Some of us thought maybe he'd picked up with the wrong one.'

Trina was the second person to say this. 'What do you mean by the wrong woman?'

'Someone who had a jealous boyfriend. Or someone who wouldn't put up with his bullshit.'

'You mean – the fact that he wouldn't leave his wife?'

'Or other stuff. Whatever. He had a lot of bullshit.' She averted her gaze. 'People talk a lot of crap, especially in a club.'

Jon leaned back in his chair and tried to hit the right balance of friendly, professional. 'Let me change the topic for a minute. Do you know what happened to the clubs Fanducci ran before Majicks?'

'You're the one who should know about that.' She smirked into her coffee.

'I only know rumours. Nothing proven. Do you know any facts? Anyone I could talk to?'

She shook her head. 'Are there dodgy characters hanging around nightclubs? Sure. I've seen them all. But I don't get involved.'

'Fanducci or his friends never said anything to you about arson?'

'Nope.'

'Even with all the crap that you said people talked? No names or anything?'

'Look, thanks for the coffee. I've gotta go.'

She was spooked. He tried changing the topic again. 'Did you ever date Frank?' he asked, quickly before she could stand up.

'Me? Do I look like a hypocrite? Didn't I just tell you that I like his wife?'

'I'm not being judgemental. I'm just trying to collect evidence about what sort of a man he was.'

'He was a bastard.' It came out fast and vehemently, and Trina looked surprised that she'd said it.

'Why do you say that?'

She narrowed her eyes, her fingers tapping the table. 'He had an affair with one of my friends, OK? I'm not going to tell you her name. And I know what you're thinking, but it wasn't me. Believe me, he tried it on with me like he tried it on with everyone with a pair of tits, but I've got way too much self-esteem to get involved with someone like that, and like I said ...'

'You like his wife. Right. What happened with your friend?'

'He hit her. He was a jealous person. He slapped her around one night when she'd been out with a male friend. And then another time he punched her in the stomach. Nowhere that it would leave marks. She said it was because she'd made him angry, but who actually watches where they hit someone when they're angry? I've had to hit plenty of people, in self-defence, and I never once thought about whether the mark was going to be visible or not.' Her eye twitched. 'I wouldn't be surprised if he beat up Fatima, too.'

So much for Atherton's characterisation of Fanducci as a family man. But this was another way he didn't fit Cyril's profile. He was straight, not a drug user, not vulnerable, which took him out of Cyril's orbit – but Cyril killed people he wanted to possess, and Cyril wouldn't want to possess a bully, or have one in his home. It was part of Cyril's twisted morality.

'Do you think that the police are right?' he asked. 'Do you think he was killed by the Bin Bag Killer?'

'No clue, mate. I'm really not interested in how he died, to be honest. The only thing I want to happen, is I want Fatima to be able to get her insurance money. She needs it, and she deserves it. That's why I told you this.'

'What do you think is going to happen to the club?'

'I've been looking for another job, so I can't say that I care.'

'I spoke with a bouncer who was working the same night as you—'

'Christian? Yeah. He's a talker.'

'He seemed to be certain that Fanducci set the fires in his clubs on purpose. Or he had them set. Are you sure you don't know anything about that? Anything you can give me would be helpful. Money you saw change hands, people that Frank used to spend time with. Even a rumour.'

He was thinking about Edie when he said it, and it obviously came across as too keen, because Trina stood up. 'I gotta be somewhere.'

'Can I call you in a few days just to see if you've remembered anything else?'

'No. Just get Fatima her money. Cute dog, by the way.'

*   *   *

Girl sat down outside the entrance to Waterloo Underground Station and refused to budge another inch.

'It's not scary,' Jon said to her. 'It's just a big train, under the city.'

Oh.

'OK,' he said. 'I understand that the concept of "underground" might be traumatic for you. But this is completely different.'

People were streaming by. Jon felt them watching. He tugged on the lead. Girl stayed on her squat haunches, her forepaws braced on the floor.

'When we get back to the hotel, we'll get Deliveroo cheeseburgers,' he promised.

Someone walking by tsked. He glared at them and then turned back to the dog. 'You've been on the Underground before. You were fine.'

She wasn't having it. Her brown eyes were implacable. Jon sighed.

'We're going to have to walk all the way back to Earl's Court, aren't we?'

Her tail twitched at the word 'walk'. Jon's phone rang in his pocket and he seized it, glad for a few minutes' distraction from this battle of wills. He didn't recognise the number, but it could be Trina calling him with more information.

'Hello, Jonathan Desrosiers.'

'Hello? Who's this?'

'I am a friend. I know you. Like thousands of others, all over the world.' The voice was flat, automated – the same electronic voice you would hear from a GPS or a spam call. Yet it was clearly aimed at him.

'Who is this?'

'We are waiting for you. We are impatient. We are watching you.'

'*Watching* me? Are you the same person who's been sending me messages? I've reported you to the police.'

'We are many. We are all watching. The man on your doorstep was a message.'

'Who is this?'

'We know everything about you. You can't ignore us. We are waiting. We want justice to be done.'

The call disconnected.

35

W HEN I STEP OUT OF the cab at the restaurant, Jon is standing outside. He's wearing a suit, with no visible signs of dog hair. His phone is nowhere to be seen. My heart does an actual flip-flop at the sight of him.

'Wow,' he says. 'You look incredible.'

I do. You would never know that twenty-four hours ago, I was wrist-deep in the blood of the patriarchy. I've had a manicure, a pedicure, a tint, a blow-dry, and I've had the equivalent of a dozen candles' worth of hot wax applied and ripped off various parts of my body. I am wearing a deceptively simple Miyake little black dress and mock-crocodile stilettos which make my legs look about eighty miles long.

I have probably spent ten times as much money and time than any man has spent on his grooming ever, and this was just routine maintenance. But at the same time, my heart is going pitter-patter because my date has showered and used a lint brush. Women are our own worst enemies, I know this.

'*You* look incredible,' I say, because men really do need praise for every little bit of effort. But also because he does look incredible. His suit is a charcoal that makes his eyes look more green, and it emphasises that whole geek-with-muscles physique.

'Do I need a tie for this place?' he asks. 'I have one in my pocket, but I've never been able to carry off a tie with any conviction.'

His shirt is open at the collar and his neck looks astonishingly kissable. When was the last time I actually had sex? Maybe back in the Ice Age? Maybe we should skip dinner and just go straight home to my bedroom. Which has been meticulously scrubbed clean of all forensic evidence of Rupert. Speaking of which . . .

'No tie,' I decide, and we exchange a kiss on the cheek. Oh, he also smells good. Not expensive, but like soap and shaving lotion.

'Edie helped me pick out the suit,' he tells me, opening the restaurant door for me. 'She said to thank you for inspiring me to dress like a successful author and not like someone who runs a podcast from his spare room.'

'Your agent sounds like a woman after my own heart.'

'She's ruthless and driven.'

'Ah, well, maybe not so much.' I wink and he smiles and my heart flutters again, and never have I been so glad of my choice in very flimsy underwear.

On our way to the table, he rests his hand on the small of my back. He pulls out my chair for me. 'Is this OK?' he says. 'Or is it too old-fashioned, opening doors and pulling out chairs? Am I trying too hard? I know you're a feminist.'

'Everyone of every gender wants other people to be kind and considerate to them. It's only reply guys on the internet who reduce feminism to things like opening doors for women. And they should die in agony.'

'Noted.'

The waiter asks for our drinks order, and I order a single malt on the rocks. 'For old time's sake,' I say.

Jon does the same. 'It's quite a contrast to drinking out of paper cups on a train,' he says, looking around at the restaurant's understated decor, the potted plants and gleaming cutlery.

'It's the company that counts,' I say.

When the drinks come, we hold them up in a silent toast. I watch Jon sip, and savour, and then he puts his drink down and says, 'I said I'd try to be honest with you, so I'm going to do that now, before the evening gets started. I've had a threatening phone call.'

'A phone call now? From the same people?'

'I don't know. They used an automated voice, and they said they were watching me. It makes me wonder if we're getting close to something about Francesco Fanducci.'

I lean forward, because I'm interested and also because I know it makes my cleavage deeper. 'I thought the threats were all about your podcast.'

'This was more general. And if someone is watching ... I got the call right after I'd talked with Trina, the bartender at Majicks. She seemed jumpy about my questions about who'd set fire to Fanducci's clubs.'

'You've been doing sleuthing without me.'

'Yes, and I know you wanted to be involved, but I thought it would be less intimidating for her if it was just one to one. Also, I'd just asked you out on a date and I didn't want to blow it.'

His honesty is endearing. 'I forgive you. Mostly. So you think you're getting threats from Fanducci's arson crew, and not from your own personal Annie Wilkes?'

'It seems like the two might be connected. They say they're watching me, but all I've been doing is investigating Fanducci. By the way, I wonder if you might think about moving back in with your sister for a while? Because this is a step up from random threats on Instagram. They've been watching Amy. If they've been watching me, they know where you live. It could be dangerous.'

Oh Jon, you sweet summer child. 'It's OK. I can handle it.'

'We don't know who these people are. They might have killed and dismembered a big man. They might have burned Edie's house.'

'If it makes you happier, I'll stay at Susie's. She's still on holiday, anyway. But not tonight.'

'Why not tonight?'

'Why do you think?' I smoulder at him. A pink spot appears on each of his cheeks.

'That might put you even more in danger,' he says.

'Then you'd better make it worth it, hadn't you?'

'Seriously, Saffy, you're not used to dealing with murderers. If—'

I reach over the table and put my hand on his. 'Jon, if the person who is threatening you turns up at my house, I will kill them.'

'That's nice of you to say. But—'

The waiter appears to take our order, and we still haven't looked at the menus, so the pressing needs of restaurant dining distract Jon for a few moments. But it gets me thinking, so when we've ordered and the wine is on the way, I ask him: 'Would you ever kill someone?'

'Seeing as I'm under suspicion, shouldn't you be asking me if I ever have killed anyone?'

'I know you didn't kill Fanducci. I'm asking theoretically. You must have thought about it, given what you've done for a living.'

He finishes his whisky. 'I've seen what murder does to the victim's loved ones. I don't think I could inflict that on anyone.'

'What if the person really deserved it? Like, *really* deserved it?'

'In those cases, we have to rely on justice. It's slower than murder, but it's how a civilised society works.'

Civilised, schmivilised. No one knows better than I do that it's all a thin veneer.

'What if someone was trying to kill you?' I ask.

'Self-defence is different from murder.'

'So self-defence is justified. What if you're defending yourself against someone who represents the societal forces which are trying to kill you? So, for example, killing a dictator, or a person committing genocide?'

'That's assassination, not self-defence.'

But he's enjoying this discussion, I can tell, so I lean into it more. 'You said that Cyril killed his victims because he was lonely. That his fucked-up moral code made him believe he was killing these men out of love. Do you understand that? Can you sympathise with it?'

'Are you asking me if I'm going to try to kill my ex? Because that's off the table.'

'No, I'm just making conversation.'

'It's a pretty niche conversation.'

'You and I have pretty niche interests.'

The wine arrives. I chose the wine, so the waiter pours some for me to try instead of automatically assuming that the man will do it, so that's one less instance of everyday sexism I have to distract me from this dialogue. I've never discussed murder on a proper date before, and I feel as if I've been missing out.

'Do you think that anyone could justifiably kill out of love?' I ask, when the waiter has left.

'We're talking in an abstract sense here, right?'

About as abstract as what's going on in my knickers right now. 'Of course.'

'Hmm.' He sips his wine and he thinks. 'I believe that euthanasia is often performed out of love. People hate to see their loved ones in pain, so they want to help them end it.'

'I'm talking about something more vicious than euthanasia.'

'Most murder victims knew their killers, though I'm not sure you can say that therefore they were killed out of love. Abused spouses sometimes kill their abusers. If their abusers don't kill them first. You could argue that's because of love, in that the love traps them there so they have no other escape. Though it's a very destructive form of love.'

I think about Mandy Brett, all those years ago in New York. I wonder, if I hadn't intervened, if one of those things would have happened on its own. If coked-up Chad would've gone too far one day – or if mild-mannered Mandy would have snapped.

'You could kill someone who was about to hurt someone you loved,' Jon suggests.

Harold, water glistening in his ginger chest pelt, in the swimming pool, waiting for my sister. I nod. 'Good reason. But I was thinking more about killing the person you love. Taking their life personally, intimately, with your own hands.'

The waiter arrives with our starters just at that moment. 'Don't worry,' I tell him. 'We're writing a book.'

He merely smiles and puts our plates on the table. It's a testament to his professionalism that he neither flees our table nor hangs around to eavesdrop some more, but walks away at a normal pace. I always tip service staff generously, because God knows they deserve it, but this guy is getting extra.

'In theory,' continues Jonathan, who I guess is used to having people hear him talking about murder, 'if someone you loved was being tortured, you might kill them quickly yourself to spare them the pain. I guess that's the euthanasia argument, in a different context. Parents have killed their children in wartime rather than let them be taken or tortured by the enemy. I don't think I would do that, but hope I'm never in the situation where I'd have to find out.'

'I hope not too.' I cut into my wild mushroom tart.

'What about you?' he asks. 'Can you imagine killing someone out of love?'

'I don't think I've ever loved anyone deeply enough to kill them.'

He hasn't been surprised by this conversation at all so far, but this time, he stops eating his starter and looks at me.

'Except Susie,' I add. 'But I would never kill her. She'd never forgive me.'

'You think that murder *could* come out of loving someone deeply?'

'No – most murder doesn't come out of loving the victim at all. It comes out of hatred or contempt or anger or indifference. Or if it's love, it's twisted love, not real love. But if I were going to kill someone I loved, I think I would have to love them very deeply indeed. Killing changes you forever. Taking their life could be seen as the ultimate sacrifice on their part, but also the ultimate dedication on yours.'

'When you phrase it that way, murder sounds more like marriage.'

'It's a lifelong commitment.'

'Which is longer for one person than the other,' says Jon.

'That's why it's not entered into lightly.' I hold up my fork. 'Taste this. It's delicious.'

And I watch as he eats out of my hand.

* * *

When we leave the restaurant, Jon takes my hand. And we walk along like this for a few minutes, silently side by side, without any plan of where to go. It's so natural, and so romantic.

I can't remember any time that I've had a better evening without someone ending up dead.

London can be beautiful at night. We turn into a little park, one of those pockets of green throughout the city, the size of a few trees and fewer benches, where the city sound is a velvet purr, and the street lamps' light is muted to a rosy glow, and shadows stripe the ground. There's a scent of orange blossom or jasmine. Jon stops, and without letting go of my hand, he faces me.

'Can I tell you something?' he asks.

'Anything you want.'

'I lost myself for a while there. After Amy left me, and Cyril stabbed me. When we met, I thought I didn't have anything left. But these past few days ... I've felt like myself again. Like the best parts of myself. And that's because of you.'

I smile gently up at him. 'It's like I told you when we first met, Jon: you're a good man.'

'Thank you for believing that,' he says, and his voice is both gentle and rough, and I know he's about to kiss me. It's the perfect place, and the perfect time. He tilts his head down and I lift my chin, lips opening, flowering, ready.

His phone rings. His mouth is a breath from mine. I clench his hand in a death grip.

'I have to look at that,' he murmurs. 'I'm sorry. It could be the police. Or Edie, about the dog.'

'Get rid of them fast,' I breathe.

In the darkness, his phone lights up his face. 'I don't recognise the number.'

'Maybe the police, then?'

'It's not Atherton. Maybe the person who's been threatening me.'

'Is it the same number as the last time?'

'No, that was a mobile number and this is a London landline. But the first one was fake, so this one could be too.'

The phone is still ringing. 'Answer it,' I say.

He puts it on speakerphone. I lean against him, close, to listen.

'Is this Jonathan Desrosiers?' says a voice. A man, but not an automated voice. This person is hoarse and sounds tired. Jon and I exchange a glance.

'Who is this?' Jon asks.

'My name is Colin, and I'm calling from the Whittington Hospital. You're listed as next of kin for Mrs Amy Desrosiers, is that right?'

My stomach sinks.

'Amy? What's happened? Is she in hospital?'

'Yes, she was admitted via ambulance this evening. She was unconscious and having convulsions. We suspect it's some form of toxin.'

'She's been poisoned?' Jon shouts it into the phone.

'We're awaiting tests obviously, but—'

'I'll be right there,' says Jon, and ends the call. He turns to me. He looks terrified. 'I'm so, so sorry, Saffy. I have to go. I really don't want to, and I know tonight was supposed to be special, but—'

'You think the person who threatened you has tried to hurt her.'

'Yes. I need to find out what happened and make sure she's OK.'

I sigh.

'This sucks,' I say. 'But I can't talk about what a good man you are, and then get angry when you do the right thing. You should go.'

He smiles, sadly, and kisses me on the forehead. 'I'm sorry.'

'Call me when you find out what's happened. And if you want ... come back to mine? Don't worry if it's late.'

'That's a promise,' he tells me.

36

HE'D HAD A WHISKY AND half a bottle of wine, he was drunk on his date and with worry, and the hospital was a maze of corridors and lobbies, lifts and staircases and signs that didn't make sense, like one of those dreams where you hear someone you love crying in the distance but the walls keep shifting and the landscape keeps moving and you can't get close enough to help.

Finally, after asking preoccupied nurses and talkative volunteers, he found the ward. 'I'm looking for Amy Desrosiers,' he panted at the woman behind the desk.

'Amy Desrosiers,' she repeated with maddening slowness. 'Who are you?'

'I'm her – well, I'm still her husband. Jon Desrosiers. I'm her next of kin. Colin rang me,' he added, craning his neck to peer into the ward rooms, looking for Amy in the beds.

'Colin?'

'Yes – actually she might be here under her maiden name, Amy Barbour?'

'Mm. She's in a side room, but she's already—'

He abandoned the conversation and went to check the side rooms. The first was occupied by an elderly man, the second by an entire family surrounding a bed, and the third—

He rushed to her side. She was attached to drips, her skin was grey, her eyes were closed. 'Amy?' he gasped, not expecting her to hear him.

Her eyes flew open, wide, instantly awake, and her face filled not with gladness, but horror. Her skin went from grey to ashen.

'Jon? What are you doing here?'

'I got a call. Are you OK? What happened?'

'You shouldn't – why did you—'

A hand seized his shoulder and pulled him roughly around. 'What the hell are you doing here?' growled a voice.

It was the man he'd seen with Amy through the window, the one she'd been kissing.

'Who are you?' Jon asked.

'None of your fucking business.'

'Marc—' said Amy from the bed.

'Amy's still my wife. I'm her next of kin. I need to know what happened.'

'You know what happened,' said the man, whose name was apparently Marc, who was still holding onto Jon's shoulder. Jon tried to shrug him off but he held on.

'No, I don't,' said Jon. 'I was told she had convulsions, she was in a coma. That she'd been poisoned.'

'Please leave,' Amy said. 'Please Jon, just go. Let's not do this here.'

'He's not going anywhere,' said Marc. He was taller than Jon. 'Not until he tells me why he did it.'

'Did what?'

Marc shook him by the shoulder. 'Stop playing stupid. I knew you were unhinged, with what you do and with calling Amy in the middle of the night, watching her from outside

her window, trying to scare her, but this is low. You could have
killed her!'

'What do you mean, I could have killed her?'

'Jon, please. Leave.'

'We called the police,' said Marc. 'They're on their way. So
no, Jon: stick around. Explain all of this to them.'

Jon grabbed Marc by both shoulders. '*What do you mean,
I could have killed her?*'

'You sent her poisoned chocolates! You're the reason why
she's here! If I hadn't found her, she could have died! What
the fuck were you playing at? Are you that jealous and twisted?'

'What makes you think I sent her poisoned chocolates?'

'Because you signed your name in the card, Jon,' said Amy.
She sounded sick and weary. 'We've rung DI Atherton.'

'You've spoken with Atherton?'

'He came by to ask some questions a few days ago. He said
you were already under suspicion for killing that man you found.
You need help, Jonny. You haven't been right for a long time,
but this ...'

'You need putting away,' growled Marc. 'Why did you come
here?'

'I got a call,' said Jon. There were more important questions
to answer, to ask, very important questions about poison and
the police, but this was the only one he could manage. 'I'm
next of kin—'

'You're not my next of kin,' said Amy. 'I changed it to my
mother.'

'You came here to finish the job.' Marc pushed Jon aside and
went to the door of the room, never taking his eyes off Jon.
'We need security in here!' he called.

'Please leave,' Amy said.

Jon looked at his ex-wife. She looked so frail, so sick. She thought that he could try to hurt her. She thought that he had killed Fanducci. All the years of their marriage, and it came to this.

'Don't worry,' he said. 'I'm going. Please get better quickly, and be careful.'

He pushed past Marc into the corridor and hadn't taken two steps before he saw the doors at the end of the ward open and DI Atherton and two uniformed constables coming through.

He didn't think. He turned and walked rapidly for the door at the other end of the ward. He was nearly there when he heard behind him, 'That's him!'

Jon pushed open the doors and bolted.

It was a bad idea to run. It was a stupid idea. It made him look guilty. It would make them chase him and that would make Atherton out of breath and angry. But his ex-wife had just accused him of attempted murder and the detective behind him thought that he had murdered and dismembered a man, and he wasn't going to wait to be caught.

He needed to figure this out, he had to solve it. There was something else going on, something that targeted him and the people he cared about.

He ran down the maze of corridors, dodging corners and bursting down the first set of fire stairs he came to. He hurtled down them, found himself in another corridor, recognised this one because of an abandoned newspaper on a windowsill, the headline MISSING MP. Down another set of stairs, into the open-plan lobby, past the booth with the receptionist and out of the glass doors into the night. He didn't see any police cars.

What should he do? Should he keep running, try to hail a cab, run to the Tube? He glanced behind him and saw no police through the glass, but they would be here any minute.

'Jonathan! Fancy meeting you here!'

Two things happened at once. He whipped his head round and saw the person who was speaking to him, someone close at hand, someone he knew from another life that seemed so long ago. And he felt a sharp stinging in his arm.

'Are you all right?' the person said, someone Jon knew, someone wearing a peaked hat that cast a shadow and glasses, and pushing an empty wheelchair, but his brain wasn't working correctly, he was running from the police, they wanted him for murder, he had to run right now but his legs weren't working correctly either. He stumbled.

'Here, let me help you,' said the person. Jon felt hands on his arms, felt himself lowered into the wheelchair. Jon tried to speak but his mouth didn't seem to want to open. Everything felt hazy and dizzy; his peripheral vision faded to black and he could only see flashes of what was directly in front of him: the street, a striped jumper, a hand.

Someone patted him on the shoulder. 'Don't worry, Jonathan,' the voice said. 'I'll get you where you're supposed to be.'

37

AT HOME, I TAKE OUT two champagne flutes for the bottle I've already got chilling, I spritz on a little more scent, I check my hair, makeup and bikini line. I debate putting on music: will it make me look literally like a terrible cliché of a 70s seducer, like Burt Reynolds in drag? I decide that silence is golden, and that I'd rather listen to the sound of Jon's jaw hitting the floor when he sees my underwear.

Then I wait.

And wait.

And wait.

It's tacky to text him when he's more or less at the deathbed of his poisoned ex-wife, right?

So I wait some more. At first it's a reasonable amount of time, then it's an unfeasibly long time. I think about Tube delays and traffic. I think about hospital bureaucracy and forms to fill in. I think about Amy hooked up to machines, surrounded by doctors, the sad decision to pull the plug. To be fair, my knowledge of medicine mostly revolves around the anatomy of murder, so I don't know how long someone would have to be in a coma before they switch everything off. Will I have to wait that long?

I get no message, no phone call. I check my phone every few minutes, like a desperate pathetic teenager.

Oh God. Has the unthinkable happened and I've been ghosted? Am I going to have to kill Jonathan Desrosiers after all?

I get up, kick off my heels, and walk round my flat. I don't want to kill Jon. I mean, I would much rather have sex with him, and I'm very definitely *not* a necrophiliac. I'm nothing like old Cyril Walker and his heads. Sex and murder are at the opposite ends of the spectrum for me, despite what Rupert H-H might have thought in his last moments. Killing Jon would be the ultimate cock block.

But what if he is ghosting me? Doesn't he have to be taught a lesson?

Ugh. I give up, pop the champagne, and pour myself a glass.

Somehow, murdering someone who can't even be bothered to sleep with me seems so undignified. It's not as if I have a shortage of would-be lovers. I'm a straight-up hottie. Brains, beauty, money, charm, skills: I've got it all. The only reason, aside from insanity, that Jonathan Desrosiers might decide not to have sex with me is that he's still in love with his ex-wife, but he has sworn to me that it's over with Amy, and Jon isn't a liar.

Well.

There could be another reason.

What if Jon's discovered my little hobby?

I stop my pacing and put my glass down on the table without even using a coaster.

He did walk in on me when I was finishing off old Rupert. But he didn't seem to notice anything at the time. No, wait …

he noticed the noise. Though he'd seemed to buy the Gaye hot yoga story. And then he asked me on a date. Would he ask me out if he knew I was a killer?

He would . . . if he were looking for more evidence.

I cast my mind back on our conversation over dinner. Admittedly, a lot of it was about murder and love. Which could have given him an inkling, I guess. I must choose my conversational subjects more wisely in future.

But if he thought I was a serial killer, why wouldn't he confront me about Amy being poisoned? Seeing as I'm the only one with an actual motive?

I abandon my self-esteem and text him, choosing my words carefully to convey a message of concern rather than outrage, thereby proving that my feminist principles are a pile of shit when dick is on the line.

Is Amy OK? Please let me know what's going on.

I send it. I'm disgusted with myself. But I still wait for an answer.

There's none.

Maybe I should get out some duct tape and Valium in preparation for if he ever does arrive. It's not ideal. I really prefer to plan these things more carefully.

And I *like* him.

Bollocks.

There's a knock on the door. Jon! Finally! I fly to it, forgetting murder plans, forgetting my last shreds of self-respect, forgetting everything except for utter joy that he's turned up finally, and I'm going to get to rip his clothes off him.

But when I open the door, it's not Jon. It's two uniformed police officers and one in civilian clothes, presumably a detective.

And everything within me goes still.

I've expected this day, of course. The odds were extraordinarily against me never being questioned for all of the murders I've committed. And I slipped up with Rupert, though I wasn't aware he'd been found yet.

The thing is, that for all my love of planning and detail, I've never really thought through what I would do if the police turned up on my doorstep. I've considered my options, of course. Play the wide-eyed innocent? Go out in a blaze of blood and glory? Run? Turn myself in and enjoy the publicity? They all have their pros and cons, and I've never been able to settle on which would be best.

Which is why I decide to wing it. I'll start with wide-eyed innocence.

'Oh my God,' I gasp. 'What's happened?'

The detective seems unmoved by my act. 'Are you Seraphina Huntley-Oliver?'

'I prefer Saffy. What's wrong?'

'Are you alone?'

'Why?'

'Can we come in?'

I'm not that stupid. 'I'd rather you didn't until I know what this is about.'

'We're looking for Jonathan Desrosiers.' Yeah, so join the club. 'Is he with you?'

'No.'

'Do you know where he might be?'

'I'd like to. What's this about?'

'When was the last time you saw Jonathan Desrosiers?'

'We had dinner together tonight. Are you DI Atherton?'

The detective, in his ill-fitting suit and rumpled half-mast tie, gives me a curt nod. 'And this is PC Cohen and PC Khan. Has Mr Desrosiers told you about me?'

'He says that you suspect him in the murder of the man he found on his doorstep in a bin bag, which is frankly ridiculous.'

'His wife has also been poisoned. Did he tell you that as well?'

'Yes.'

'Did he tell you that he'd sent the chocolates that poisoned her?'

I pause at this. Jon is *not* the type. Poisoners are sneaky and two-faced, and often inadequate in bed. And also, he likes his ex. 'He never would have done that.'

'The evidence is pretty overwhelming, especially since when he saw us at the hospital, he ran.'

I mean, who *wouldn't* run at the sight of that grey shiny suit? 'If I know Jon, he'll be trying to solve who did it.'

'So you know him well, eh?'

I give Atherton a sweet smile. 'My private life is literally none of your business, but thank you for asking. Why are you looking for him here?'

'Because he gave this as his last forwarding address.'

'I see. Actually he hasn't been staying here for a few days; he's been in a hotel somewhere. I suspect he already told you that, yes?'

'Can we come in and have a look?'

'Have you tried ringing his agent? It's literally her job to know where he is.'

'Yes. She doesn't know where he is. Can we come in and have a look?'

I sigh. 'Please take off your shoes, though.'

They plod through my pristine house, front to back, up and down, as thorough as a hygiene-shy teenager brushing his teeth, and conclude that I do not have a full-grown man lurking anywhere.

'He's been getting threats,' I tell Atherton, as he stands in the exact same spot in my bedroom where Rupert stood when I showed him the knife. 'Someone threatened both him and his ex-wife. Did you know about that?'

'No.'

'That's probably a good avenue to follow up. It's more likely than that Jon tried to poison Amy. He really cares about her, which is worse luck for me. His agent's house was burned down, too.'

'We'll do the detective work, Miss Huntley-Oliver.'

'Ms.'

He stomps down my stairs and pauses by my front door. 'If you speak to him, please encourage him to report to the nearest police station. And give me a ring. Here's my card.'

I take it and immediately drop it onto a console table. 'Aren't you worried that Jon might be in danger? Do you think he could be running because whoever tried to hurt Amy, whoever burned down his agent's house – maybe whoever left the corpse on his doorstep – might be after him too?'

'Like I said, we'll do the detective work. Just let us know if you hear from him.'

I close the door after them, unimpressed. With police work like that, it's no wonder that I keep on getting away with homicide. I watch out of the window until they've gone and then I ring Jon. It goes straight to voicemail.

'The police were just here looking for you,' I tell him. 'I'm going to go to my sister's house – you can meet me there, yeah? If you're OK. Are you OK? Call me.'

While I'm getting changed into more sensible clothing, I think through the clues that I've given to Atherton, and which he has ignored. I know that Jon didn't poison Amy. I also know that he didn't kill Fanducci. He's an innocent man, and so the most plausible reasons he would have disappeared would be because he's looking for the real poisoner, or because he's been distracted or detained by the person who's been threatening him.

Which means that if I want to find Jon, I have to find the person who's out to get him.

38

I T WAS DARK. HIS HEAD hurt. His tongue felt dry and
too big for his mouth. Jon tried to raise his hand to touch
his forehead but he couldn't move it. Again? Still? Wait.
What was happening?

He remembered running through the hospital, trying to get
away from Atherton, and then running into someone familiar
outside, and then a stinging pain, and he couldn't walk or speak.

He'd been drugged. And now ...

He tried to raise his arm again. It wasn't paralysed; it was
fastened at the wrist to something. And it wasn't dark; he had
a blindfold on. Chinks of yellow light seeped in through the
edges on top and bottom.

'Help,' he croaked, shocked at how broken his voice sounded.
It fell dead in the room. No echo. No reply.

He tried both arms, and his legs. He seemed to be strapped
into a chair. But the blindfold wasn't tied as tightly. He shook
his head, scrunched up his cheeks and forehead, and the blindfold slipped a little down his face. But then it was stuck on
the bridge of his nose. He tried the opposite direction, tilting
his head back. The chair seemed to be against a wall, and he
could use the wall behind him on the blindfold's knot for

friction. He waggled his eyebrows, rubbed his head against the wall, even blew upward until the blindfold was up above his eyes and loose enough to shake off his head.

He was bound with silver tape to a wheelchair. It was probably the same wheelchair he'd been helped into after being drugged. He was in a cellar, or something like a cellar. It was a large room. There were no windows, or if there were windows, they'd been boarded up. There was a single door opposite him, which was closed and, he assumed, locked. The walls had been covered with corrugated grey acoustic tiles – much the same as what he'd used to use in his home studio to record his podcast. There was a metal fold-out chair placed across from him, along with a collapsible table. There was a cot against one wall, made up with a pillow and sheets and a light blue blanket. Two plastic buckets, one yellow and one green, sat in the corner. The light came from a bulb in the ceiling which was covered, a little surreally, with a plain Japanese-style rice paper globe. However, none of that was the strangest thing about the room.

The strangest thing about the room was the cats.

They were clearly dead. Their eyes stared, sunken and glassy. Several taxidermy cats stood on a shelf to Jon's left, at what would be about eye level if Jon could stand. Others crouched on wooden plinths. A few lay as if asleep on the floor. They were striped, black, grey, tabby, ginger: all of their fur was scruffy. Some looked moth-bitten. And whoever had skinned them and stuffed them (and presumably killed them first) was not actually very good at it, so that the cats grinned and leered out of crooked faces, with single ears drooping, limbs twisted into grotesque parodies of life.

How long did it take to taxidermy a cat? Jon had no idea, but presumably it was hours and hours of toil over a corpse, only to produce these inept, misshapen collections of fur and teeth that looked very little like actual cats. For some reason, that made the killing even more disturbing.

Was that why he was here? Had he been found and drugged and strapped into a wheelchair and taken wherever this was so he could also be killed and stuffed and made into something that looked almost but not quite entirely unlike himself?

That idea made a weird kind of sense, when he considered who'd taken him. Someone he'd believed to be harmless. A little bit pathetic. Someone he'd dismissed, who had tried absolutely everything to get his attention, and who now, perforce, had it.

No. That was ridiculous.

He swallowed hard, tried to get up some moisture in his mouth and throat so he could yell. Was he still in London? He couldn't hear any traffic sounds outside, but that didn't mean anything, considering the soundproofing. Who knew how long he'd been unconscious. His body ached, as if it had been in one position for a long time. Was it better to yell now, and risk attracting his captor? Or should he keep quiet and suss out this room, try to wriggle out of this chair?

He wriggled. The tape cut into his wrists. Someone in a film would probably be able to rip through the tape. He couldn't. So he yelled: 'Help! Help me, someone help me!'

As before, his words fell dead in the room. He rocked his body from side to side so the wheels of his chair made thuds on the floor, and yelled again. And again. His voice a rough, painful scratch. And faintly, he heard someone beyond the door.

'Coming, coming,' said a voice, closer now, and then the sound of a key in a lock, and then the door opened and there he was, in his striped jumper, without the hat and glasses this time, looking just as Jon remembered him. He was holding a large black suitcase. He stepped in and put the bag on the cement floor. Something inside it clanked. Then he closed the door carefully after him, locked it, and then turned to Jon and said in a friendly tone, 'You really should preserve your voice, you know. You'll be needing it later.'

'Hi Simon,' croaked Jon. 'Nice cats.'

39

I ARRIVE AT SUSIE'S FLAT TO find the hallway full of suitcases. My sister and Love Rat Finlay are sprawled on the sofa with several empty beer bottles and *Love Island* on the TV.

'Saffy!' Susie bounces up when she sees me, and gives me a huge hug and a kiss on either cheek. She looks sun-kissed and healthy. 'Did you miss me? Did you bring me something back?'

'You're the one who's been away,' I point out.

'Oh yeah. I got a Toblerone, but Finn ate it.'

Finlay doesn't bother to get up. He gives me a shit-eating grin that I would like to carve, inch by inch, off his face.

But it's nearly one in the morning. Jon left me to go to the hospital about five hours ago, which by my calculation means he's been missing for at least three. I swallow my pride. It hurts going down.

'You're a tech bro, right?' I ask Finlay. 'You know all about software?'

'So?'

'Are you like a hacker? Or do you know how to hack into things?'

'I've done my share.'

'I need your help,' I tell him.

* * *

Unlike almost everyone I know, I don't have any social media profiles. I don't have the time for them, I don't really see the point except for stalking or being stalked, and more than any of that, I have enough asshole men in my life already, why would I ask for instant access to fifty million more of them? Or give fifty million of them instant access to me? I'm much more of a real-life, get-my-hands-dirty girl. I look at people's social media feeds, but I do not participate. The downside of this is that I'm not as au fait with the way they work as I possibly should be.

This is why I need Finlay.

He squints at my phone, scrolling through comment after comment on Jon's Instagram feed. 'These are all bots,' he says.

'Well, I didn't think they were Shakespeare. Can you find out who made them?'

'Hmm.'

'He's had threatening emails, too. Would those be easier to trace?'

'Maybe, if you could get into his email account? Do you know his password?' Finlay reaches for his laptop on the coffee table.

'Is this legal?' asks Susie, who's perched on the sofa arm looking over Finlay's shoulder.

'Susie-san,' I croon. 'Do you think you could make me a cup of tea?'

She pouts, but goes off to the kitchen. I say, quickly and quietly, 'I think Jon's in danger. This is why I'm asking. And I told the police, and they don't want to do anything about it. I need to know fast, and I also need Susie not to know why I'm asking, because she'll want to get involved, and I don't want her to be in any trouble or danger.'

'So you need not only for me to do you a favour, but you also need me to keep the reason a secret?'

'Yes. For Susie's sake.'

He pretends to think about this. I know he's pretending because he looks so infuriatingly pleased with himself.

'What happened about carving a bloody swathe through London?' he asks. 'Not so appealing now that you need my help?'

'Oh, it's still appealing. But this is a truce.'

'What do I get out of it?'

You get to keep your face, I think. 'What do you want?'

'A double date,' he says. 'Me and Susie, and you and whoever. This Jon guy. And you have to pretend it was your idea.'

'Why do you want that?'

'Because it will prove to Susan that you accept that she and I are a couple. It will make her happy.'

That *will* make Susie happy. Damn him.

'Deal,' I say.

By the time Susie brings me my cup of tea, Finlay has pulled up Jon's webmail login page and I've got the laptop, contemplating what Jon's password is likely to be. 'Of course, it won't work if he's turned on two-factor authentication,' Finlay says. 'Unless you've got his phone? But there are other things we can try.'

I think about Jon and how easy it was for me to find his secret cottage in Scotland, how he left his divorce papers around where I could take a casual look. How easy it was for someone to poison his wife or leave a corpse on his doorstep or break into his agent's office. 'I don't think he's crazy security-conscious,' I say.

I start with the basics: various combinations of Amy's name and birthdate. (I said I don't have social media profiles; I didn't say I didn't look at other people's. Amy has hidden nothing on hers.) When that doesn't work, I move on to Jon's main interest, which is murderers. I try all the usual suspects – Ted Bundy, Peter Sutcliffe, Fred West, Rosemary West, etc., etc., etc. – and none of them are any good.

'You can't know him very well if you don't know his passwords,' Susie yawns.

'It's not really something you ask on the first date, or even the second.'

'Yeah, but I bet you could guess my passwords. Just from being my sister.'

'It's not a good idea to have a password that someone can guess,' I tell Susie.

'You should be using a password keychain, babe?' says Finlay, back to that fake-Aussie upward inflection since he's talking to her. 'And different ones for every account?'

Susie ignores us both and says, 'Go on, Saffy. Try to guess mine.'

I squint. 'HarryStylesIsHot?'

'Oh my God Saff, you are so basic.'

'ILoveFinnDick,' suggests Finlay. Susie hits him with a cushion.

'SaffysSister01,' I try, typing in some more guesses into Jon's email.

She rolls her eyes. 'No.'

'What is it?'

'I can't believe you can't guess.'

'It's a little much to ask me to guess two passwords at the same time. And this one is more urgent.'

'It's Sofia,' she says, and that makes me look up from the laptop.

Sofia was our mother's name.

'I . . . didn't know you thought about her so much,' I say. 'You were so young when she died. I didn't even think you remembered her.'

'I think about her every day,' says Susie. 'I like to. That's why I use her name as a password.'

'But babe, you should still use a keychain?'

I think about our mother, holding a baby Susie. I remember the day after she was born, our mother in a hospital bed, Susie in her arms. Their hair was the same pale golden colour. I remember my mother saying, 'Now Seraphina, this is your baby sister, and she is precious. You are going to have to look after her, darling.'

Susie and I exchange a look of love and grief. Then my eyes widen.

'I've got it,' I say. And I type 'Alain' into the password box.

Nothing. So I try '83FH' instead.

'It doesn't seem to be working,' says Finlay.

'You, shut up.' I try 'Alain83FH' and when that doesn't work, I swap the name and number around.

Immediately the account opens up.

'What was it?' asks Susie.

'His father's name plus his badge number when he was a sergeant. He used to be in the Met.'

'You know that but you don't know his password?'

'Google and a photographic memory.'

'Is he close to his dad?'

'He hates him.' I start scrolling through Jon's messages, looking for the photo of Amy. 'Here,' I say to Finlay, handing him the laptop. 'It's this one.'

Finlay immediately gets to clicking and typing. Susie yawns, kisses us both on the cheek, and wanders off to bed. I check my watch. Time is ticking. And looking at these emails, I have a bad feeling about what's happening with Jon. The attack on Amy was obviously to draw him out, and there's been plenty of time for someone with a weapon and a bad attitude to do all sorts of terrible things to that body of his, the same body that I very much want alive and in my bed.

Before I realise it, I'm pacing the room.

'Stop it, you're distracting me,' says Finlay absently.

'No. Hurry up, please.'

Finlay looks up. 'If I find out who this person is and where they are, are you going to go there?'

'Maybe.'

'You should really tell the police.'

'I'll take your opinion into consideration.' I'm practically twitching with anxiety now. 'Have you found it yet?'

'I could tell the police, as soon as you left.'

'That would imply that you gave a toss about my wellbeing, which you do not. Also, if you do, I will kill you. Have you found it?'

'No.'

I want to scream with frustration. I want to strangle my sister's boyfriend. I want to make the whole world stop, right now, and hunt down whoever has got Jon. Failing all that, I want to get an advanced degree in online security systems, so I can stop relying on this tosser.

'Do you even have a general area?' I'll do a house-to-house search if I need to. I start planning the equipment I'll need to bring, the detours I'll have to take to pick up the necessaries.

'Well, I've narrowed it down to the UK.' Finlay says. 'Or possibly the Netherlands.'

'Have I mentioned to you that this whole thing is life or death?'

'Yeah, yeah.' He chews on his lip, and clicks a few more things, and types a little more. Then he sits back and laughs.

'What? This isn't funny.'

'You think whoever sent this photo is the person you're looking for?'

'That's what I said.'

'Then I might have good news for you.'

'What?'

He turns the laptop so I can see the screen. It's the photo of Amy in the cafe, sitting in that same seat in front of the window. As I watch, Finlay zooms in on the image at a spot beyond Amy's right shoulder. In the window. Where there's a reflection of a man holding a phone.

'I'll make it a little clearer,' he says, and clicks a couple more things, and the image gets sharper.

'Do you know who that is?' he asks.

In an instant, I go from desperation to joy. I know exactly who that is: the man holding the phone, taking a photograph of Jon's ex-wife.

Simon Simons, pronounced 'Simon Simmons', is apparently a very bad man.

40

'DO YOU REALLY LIKE THEM?' Simon glanced at his stuffed cats. 'I did them myself.'

'I can tell.'

Jon knew Simon. His superfan. The one who came to all of his readings and collected multiple copies of signed books. The one who always wanted to chat after public appearances. The totally harmless geeky guy, slight Simon with his weedy shoulders and his little belly, with his glasses and his balding head and the deeply unfashionable jumpers, who'd been writing actual letters to him via his agent as if it were 1955.

'Did you burn down Edie's house?' Jon asked.

Simon nodded. 'It wasn't my primary intention, of course. I needed your details. I noticed she had cats, too. Did she live?'

'Yes. But she could have been killed. She almost was.'

Simon shrugged, as if this information were irrelevant. 'It's good to see you again, Jonathan.'

'Why did you drug me? Why am I tied to a chair?'

'You're a difficult man to pin down.' Simon came further into the room. He went to one of the cats on a plinth, a ginger one with one small eye and one big one, and stroked imaginary dust off its fur. 'I like the cats better like this. Don't you? They're so noisy and smelly when they're alive. I told you about my neighbour with all of his cats, didn't I?'

'You asked if I thought he could be a serial killer.'

'Ah.' Simon giggled. Actually giggled, hand to mouth. 'That was a little bit of misdirection. Was it clever? Did it fool you?'

'Did you poison Amy?'

'Now. *That* was clever. You've got to admit it, Jonathan. You fell right into that trap.'

Jon bit his lip to stop from yelling. To have a moment to think.

He had never thought of Simon as any sort of a threat. He was a little obsessive, that was all. Even Edie had asked him to reply to Simon's letters. But the fire, the poison, the drugs, the gaffer tape . . . the cats. Simon, who had always seemed ill at ease with normal social interaction, seemed utterly comfortable with all of this.

No, not comfortable. Elated.

Up till now, Jon had felt more annoyed than frightened. Angry. Simon wasn't a frightening man; he was a nerd. But this elation made Jon . . . uneasy.

Simon stepped a little closer. He squatted down so he could be face to face with Jon, though in fact this made him a little shorter than Jon. He said, quietly, 'You can tell me. I won't tell a soul, absolutely no one. It's between you and me. Did you know it was me all along? Have you been playing a game of cat and mouse with me?'

'No,' said Jon, and seeing the little burst of hurt cross Simon's face, he added, 'Why would I play a game with you? Do you think I wanted my ex-wife to be poisoned? Do you think I like being drugged and tied to a chair?'

'Is Amy still alive? I didn't mean to kill her, but if it had to happen, the ends were worth the means. I had to get hold of you somehow, and I didn't know where you were staying.'

He'd never given Saffy's address to Edie, just the police. 'Were you the person who called me from the hospital?'

'Yes! Worked like a charm. And here you are.' Once again, Simon was wreathed in smiles.

'Why am I here, Simon?'

He clapped his hands. 'I thought you'd never ask. I have a special project for us!' He went to the black suitcase that he'd brought with him, kneeled on the floor and opened it, his back to Jon. He took out a laptop and a microphone and carefully set them up on the table in the centre of the room, then looked at Jon expectantly. The soundproofing made even more sense, now: it wasn't just to keep Jon from being heard, but it was to make the room more acoustically sound.

'You want me to record a podcast?'

'Not just any podcast. A *special edition*.' Simon said the words with relish. He reached into the suitcase again and took out a fat wodge of paper. 'I hope you don't mind, I didn't want to suggest that you weren't capable, but I've written a script.'

'About you.'

'About my career.'

Killing cats and poison chocolates? 'And you want me to release this podcast? Wouldn't that be problematic, seeing as you have me tied up in your basement?'

'No. I want it for myself. A very special edition, for an audience of one. Then, the real work will begin.'

'The real work?'

'Your book! About me.' Simon raised his eyes to the ceiling in ecstasy. 'I always dreamed I would be in one of your books. And now it's going to happen! This is so amazing. I'm so happy!' He raised himself on his tiptoes and did a little dance.

That was too much.

'No,' said Jon. 'I am not going to record a podcast about you. I am not going to write a book about you. I'm not a cat that you can steal and stuff for your own amusement. Your game is over. You've had my attention. Now let me go.'

Simon stopped dancing. Slowly, he sank down off his tiptoes. His hands hung beside him, limp. His face, which had been so gleeful, sobered.

'Oh dear,' he said.

'When you let me go, we can pretend this never happened,' Jon lied. 'No one's been seriously injured yet. But you need to stop now, before this goes too far.'

'I was hoping you wouldn't say that,' Simon said. Instead of moving towards Jon to unfasten him from the wheelchair, he turned away from him and went back to the open suitcase instead. He kneeled again, this time by the side of the suitcase so that Jon could see him in profile, and could see what he took out of it, object by object, one by one, as he lined them up on the floor, like a surgeon laying out his instruments.

A bottle of water.

A roll of silver tape.

A small packet of pills.

A plastic squirt bottle containing a dark liquid.

A long object wrapped in cloth.

A large packet of bandages.

A sledgehammer.

A pistol.

Jon felt all of the blood drain from his face. His hands and feet went cold.

'You're just trying to scare me,' he said through numb lips.

'Sadly not,' said Simon. 'I've given all of this a lot of thought.'

He stood and picked up the sledgehammer. That was, Jon realised, what had made the clank when he'd first set the suitcase down. The head of it was green and shiny. It looked as if it had never been used.

'I know what you're thinking,' said Simon. 'In fact, I almost always know what you think, Jonathan. I've listened to your podcasts over and over and over. Same with your books. And the audiobooks, too. You read those beautifully, by the way. I like to think that I catch things that others would miss. I really feel as if I know you.' He hefted the sledgehammer in his hands. 'That's how I know that you're thinking of *Misery* right now. That was a great film, wasn't it? I know you think that the book was even better. I agree with you, of course. There are a lot of parallels with the situation we're in now. You're a writer, and I'm your biggest fan.' Simon giggled. He was looking elated again. 'But in the book, Annie uses an axe to cut off Paul's foot. In the film, she uses a sledgehammer to shatter it. I approve of that choice. I think it's less gory, and at the same time even more brutal. It's literally blunter.'

'You wouldn't—' Jon's voice came out hoarse; he cleared his throat and tried to make himself sound rational. 'You wouldn't do that to me, Simon. That's not your style.'

'You're right! It's not. Good call, Jonathan. I'm much subtler than that. For example, the people I've chosen to kill. No one has even realised they've been murdered!'

'What ... what do you mean?'

Simon still held the sledgehammer. 'The trick is to choose victims who are expected to die. It's how Harold Shipman got away with his murders for so long, right? Old people, sick people. When I killed my mum, she'd been living with cancer for five years. People even said it was a blessing that she'd passed. Her funeral was so much fun. Everyone thought I was sad.'

'You ... murdered your mother?'

'Every great career starts at home, doesn't it? You recorded all your early podcasts from your attic, didn't you?'

Jon struggled to get control of this situation. Simon adored him. He could talk his way out of this, couldn't he? Create empathy?

'Your mother was abusive to you?' he tried.

'Oh no. She was fine. We were very close. But then she got older, and she kept on needing attention.' He wrinkled his nose. 'Also, she smelled.'

'How many other people have you killed, Simon?'

Simon nodded at the script he'd written. It was, Jon noticed, quite a thick script.

'Oh, it's all in there. They were mostly old people, but not all. Old people are horrible. Like cats.' He put down the sledgehammer, which was a small relief. 'Anyway, as I said: I'm subtle. And subtlety is wonderful if you want to get away with murder, but it means that for someone who's an aficionado, like me – like both of us, Jonathan – you feel ... lonely. There's no one to discuss your hobbies with. Your podcast made me feel seen. It gave me a community.'

'A community of killers.'

'Exactly. There's a family, almost. We're all connected with each other. You helped me see that. None of us who have taken even a single human life, are alone. And that's why I loved it so much. And why I was so desperately sad when you ended it. You don't have the right to take that away from us, Jonathan.'

'Are you monologuing at me, Simon? That's a very villainous thing to do. Do you see yourself as the villain?'

Simon laughed. 'I prefer the word "protagonist". Because villains and heroes are one and the same sometimes, aren't they? If I am monologuing, it's because I've been waiting for this moment for so long! But you'd never go for a drink with me, or meet me in private. You ignored all of my letters and my messages and my emails. You even ignored me when I took a photograph of your wife. We could have settled this in a more civilised way, if you'd only deigned to notice me.'

'You're crazy.' He knew he shouldn't antagonise Simon, but he couldn't help it.

'Well, that will remain to be seen. Once you've recorded my podcast and written my book. Shall we get started?'

'No. I'm not going to follow some script to glamorise the fact that you've killed people.'

'Do you think it's a good idea to refuse me, Jonathan?'

'You won't kill me. That's too blunt for you. And if you did, you would never get your podcast.'

'No, I won't kill you. Not unless it's necessary. But you forget ... I've given this whole thing a lot of thought.' Simon picked up the bottle of water and the box of tablets and brought it over to Jon. 'You're going to want to take one of these.'

'Are you drugging me?'

'What? No. This is co-codamol this time. Plain old paracetamol with codeine. I imagine you have a headache after what I gave you earlier. Also, you're going to be glad of the painkiller.' Simon smiled. 'See how much I've thought about your comfort, Jonathan?' He cracked open the seal of the bottle and Jon swallowed, his throat dry.

'How did you kill the old people?' he asked. 'Was it poison? Like you poisoned Amy?'

'I just gave Amy a whiff of it. It's not my fault if she's a pig and ate a whole box of chocolates at once. But yes. Poison, mostly. I like it. It's clever. The details are all in the script I wrote for you. You're going to love it; it's a good read. If I do say so myself.' He opened the box, took out a blister pack, and popped out a pill. 'I think you're going to need two of these, actually. They might make you dozy for a little while, but I'm not in a hurry for you to do any recording. I want you to be at your tip-top best. Open up.'

He held a pill up to Jon's mouth. Jon shook his head.

'Come on, Jonathan. You can see what these are, it's written on the foil. The seal hasn't been broken. And it's a brand-new bottle of water, too. Not tampered with at all. Have I ever lied to you?'

'You never mentioned that you were a serial killer.' He said it with his teeth clenched, in case Simon tried to shove the pill down his throat.

'Omission isn't the same as a blatant lie. I promise you, I swear on my mother's grave: this is just a painkiller and a bottle of water.'

'Not the best thing to swear on.'

'You haven't seen my mother's grave. I spared no expense. OK, I'll swear on *Without Mercy*. It's my favourite of your books.

I have twelve copies upstairs, and you signed seven of them. They're my most treasured possessions. I can't believe you asked me that time if I was selling them on eBay. As if! Though I guess I can imitate your signature well enough by now that even your wife can't tell the difference.'

Jon shook his head again, lips clamped shut.

'All right, your choice. If you change your mind, just let me know. Anyway, you're going to need to eat and drink eventually, so you're going to have to trust me. It makes sense to do it sooner.' Simon laid the bottle on the table with the pills next to it, and went back to his array of tools. Including the gun.

He wasn't having any luck persuading Simon to let him go. What should he do? Record the podcast, write the book? Hope that while he was doing it, someone would find him or he'd have a chance to escape? That was probably his best bet.

But what if no one came? What if he couldn't escape?

After he'd written the manuscript, Simon would have no further use for him. Then it would be poison. Or the gun.

The best thing he could do would be to hold out, delay recording and writing, and hope that Simon wouldn't get frustrated. He would stall for time. Maybe Simon would get careless.

'I'd hoped not to have to do this,' Simon said, stooping down. When he stood again, he was holding the object wrapped in cloth. As Jon watched, he unwrapped it. It was a bolt cutter.

'You don't have to do anything,' Jon said quickly. 'You can let me go. If you hurt me, the police will find you – all those messages you left me – the photograph of Amy—'

'Maybe,' said Simon. 'I left clues for you to find. I don't think you contacted the police about me, though.'

'How confident are you of that?' He didn't want to look scared. But he couldn't look away from the bolt cutter. That, too, was new-looking, a two-handed model with cruel shiny pincers and cheerful yellow handles.

'Fairly. Like I said, I know you pretty well. You didn't contact the police when you went looking for Cyril Walker, for example.'

'I might have learned my lesson.'

'Mm. I don't think so.' To Jon's surprise, Simon kneeled in front of the wheelchair. For a split second, Jon thought he might be unfastening his ankles, but instead, Simon untied Jon's left shoe and pulled if off.

'What are you doing?' Jon asked. Though he knew now. He felt sick.

'I considered taking one of your fingers,' said Simon, placing Jon's shoe neatly to one side. 'But then I realised, that might make it difficult for you to type. Are you a touch-typist, Jonathan?'

'Yes.'

'I thought so. Fortunately, while you're with me, though you are required to type, you're not required to walk. Forgive me, this is a little intimate, but it'll be over in a second.'

He rolled down Jon's sock and pulled it off. As Jon's ankles were still secured with tape, Simon must have intentionally made his sock accessible while he was tying him up. Simon carefully folded the sock and put it into Jon's shoe.

'Now. You'll be glad to know that I've done some research about this. Your big toe does between thirty to sixty per cent of the work, depending on whether you're standing, walking, running et cetera, and the percentage decreases as you go down the foot. So really, to cause the least damage, I should take the little toe of your left foot. You're right-footed, aren't you, Jon? I don't want you to be unable to kick a football.'

'You don't have to do this. Don't do this. I'll do the podcast.'

Simon rocked back on his heels. 'Here's the thing. We've been going through a process, here. I abducted you and brought you to a locked room, and you refused to do what I wanted. I showed you I had a gun, and you refused. Then I showed you a sledgehammer and talked about *Misery*. And you still refused. I don't think you take me seriously.'

'I take you seriously!'

'No you don't, Jonathan. You think I'm a sad little fanboy, a geek who lived in his mother's basement until he poisoned her and got to take over the whole house. You've never taken me seriously. You've glanced over my shoulder while you've spoken to me, looking for someone more interesting to talk to. You probably joke about me to your friends – the superfan who follows you everywhere. So my showing you things, telling you about the people I've murdered, is never going to make you believe that I mean business. It's never going to make you believe that I'm as good and important as you are, that I'm the protagonist here. I have to *show* you.'

As Jon watched, Simon reached over and picked up the plastic bottle. He flipped off the cap and squirted orange-red iodine all over Jon's foot, and especially on Jon's little toe.

'Don't worry,' Simon said. 'I sterilised the bolt cutters. And I've got some antibiotics, just in case. They were my mother's, but I'm sure they still work.'

He smiled up at Jon, a smile of pure joy. Then he took the cheery yellow handles of the bolt cutters in either hand and carefully positioned the cutting blades on either side of Jon's little toe.

They were strangely warm.

'Stop! Stop! I want the painkillers!' It was a cry, a squeal. Undignified. Jon didn't care.

'You can have them after,' said Simon. 'This will just take a moment.'

Then he snapped the bolt cutters shut.

Jon squeezed his eyes closed at the final moment, so he didn't see the loss of his little toe. But he felt a *crack*. A shattering. No pain for a split second: then a rush of warmth up his entire leg. A burning pain.

Then the thought: *that was part of me. Part of me is gone forever.*

He screamed, not so much in pain (there was a lot of pain now) but in loss.

His eyes wide open now, every nerve in his body telling him to run, get away, despite being trapped in this chair in this room, he looked at his foot and saw blood spurting out over the concrete floor. Simon, a smile still on his bland face, put down the bolt cutters and pressed bandages to the wound. He murmured something soothing and that was so bizarre – this whole thing was so bizarre – that Jon's feelings crossed the barrier over fear and all of a sudden, Jon was furious.

How dare Simon? This person who took the lives of helpless people, helpless creatures, who was so desperate for attention that he poisoned the innocent and chopped off body parts? What gave him the right? What gave any of them the right, the ones who ruined other people's lives?

Jon gritted his teeth to stop the scream that wanted to come out. He would not give Simon that. He clenched his fists and tensed every muscle. He willed the blood to stop pumping out of his foot, but in truth it was the pressure Simon was applying that would do it, and that made Jon even angrier.

Simon glanced up at him. 'There now,' he said. 'That wasn't so bad, was it? You'll be able to get to work recording very soon.'

Jon glared at him. Who did he hate more – Simon, or himself for being weak?

Simon wrapped bandages around Jon's foot, round and round until it was swollen and white, a grotesque football. He surveyed his work with evident satisfaction and then got up, wiping smears of blood from his hands on his beige trousers.

'I'm going to have to pop upstairs and get changed,' he said cheerfully, and went to the table. 'So, like I promised, here are your painki—'

He stopped. Frowned. Cocked his head to the ceiling. Appeared to be listening.

From above them came a crash, like splintering crockery, loud enough to be heard through the acoustic tiles.

Someone was in the house.

'Help!' Jon yelled, upward. 'Help me! I'm down here!'

'Shut up,' said Simon. He put down the drugs and picked up the gun from the floor. 'I'll be right back, don't go anywhere.'

And then he was gone, leaving the door open behind him.

Now was his chance. As soon as Simon turned his back, Jon was pulling at his wrists, wriggling his arms, trying to stretch the gaffer tape. He bent his head and chewed at the tape on his right wrist. He listened for a gunshot, listened for Simon coming back.

The tape was wound around and around, like the bandages on his foot. Good old safety-conscious Simon. He'd left the door open, even though Jon was yelling. Why? Because he was in a hurry, because he knew who was upstairs? Because he was confident that whoever it was, he would be able to shoot them? Because it was another victim?

He tugged hard at the tape with his teeth. He felt it give, a little, and that made him tug harder. So what if he lost his teeth? Teeth were replaceable. Unlike his toe. Or his life, because he was sure that when he was finished recording Simon's podcast, when he was finished writing Simon's book, Simon would kill his pet author just like he had killed all of his neighbour's cats. Maybe he would stuff Jon, too. Put him on a plinth, in an unnatural pose, one eye smaller than the other. A memento. A prize.

The tape loosened and tore, and at the same time, Jon pulled his arm back and managed to free his right hand. He immediately got to work on his left.

He could hear voices now, through the open door, though not the words they were saying. Simon's voice, and another, a quieter one, one that he strained to make out over his own breathing as he freed his left hand and bent to untape his ankles. A feminine voice. It was ...

Oh my God. It was Saffy.

41

JON RIPPED THE TAPE FROM his ankles and stood up, muscles stiff and protesting. With the sound of Saffy's voice he'd forgotten his toe but the bolt of pain reminded him, and he bit back an involuntary yelp. Then he limped, clumsy like a rag doll, to the suitcase. He picked up the sledgehammer.

'Get back in the chair, Jon,' said Simon from the doorway.

He had his arm around Saffy's neck from behind. The gun was pointed at her temple. She was wearing different clothes than she had on their date – jeans and sneakers and a sweatshirt – and her hair was piled up on top of her head.

'Jon,' she gasped. 'You're still alive.'

'But *you* won't be alive for much longer, unless Jonathan sits back in the chair. Who is this, Jon? Another one of your fans?'

'What happened to your foot?' she asked. 'Are you hurt?'

'Let her go, Simon.'

'Why do you call yourself Simon Simmons?' asked Saffy. 'It's spelled Simon Simons. Did your parents hate you?'

'Shut up, bitch.' He shook her and ground the point of the gun into her temple. 'You're not part of this story. You're a subplot that's about to end.'

'You are so rude,' said Saffy.

She was brave. So brave. Pretending she wasn't frightened, when she had found him somehow, tracked him down, come here alone and unarmed to help him. She was so beautiful and clever, better than a million Simons. She was another innocent person who this sociopath was prepared to toss aside.

She met his gaze with hers, and nodded almost imperceptibly.

'Get your hands off her!' Jon bellowed. He leapt forward, swinging the sledgehammer, aiming for Simon's shoulder. But his missing toe made him misbalance, misjudge; the sledgehammer headed straight for Saffy's face.

She ducked and twisted at the last moment, freeing herself from Simon as the sledgehammer hit the arm that held the gun and sent the weapon flying out across the room.

'You little bitch!' cried Simon, and he scrambled for the gun. Jon dropped the hammer and lunged for it as well. He was bleeding again; his foot slipped on the concrete floor. Saffy, on all fours, grabbed Simon's legs and pulled, toppling him down with her.

Jon heard a struggle behind him as he reached the gun and when he turned, weapon in hand, he saw that Simon was on top of Saffy, pushing her down, his hands at her throat.

Jon didn't hesitate. Pure anger, pure instinct to protect – whatever it was. Or instinct to hurt. Any or all of it. He pulled the trigger once, twice.

Simon's head snapped backwards. A spray of blood and matter, a flower-like shape in the air. Then he slumped on top of Saffy.

Jon dropped the gun. 'Saffy,' he gasped, and fell to his knees to push Simon off her. Her face was sheeted with blood, her hair matted with it. Simon's. Her blue eyes, a bright contrast with the red. 'Are you all right?'

'Yes,' she said. 'Yes.'

She kneeled. Gazed wide-eyed from what was left of Simon to Jon. They were both in a warm, slick puddle now.

'You shot him,' she said.

'He was hurting you.'

'You killed him. For me.'

'Yes.'

'Oh my God,' she murmured. 'I think I've fallen in love with you.'

He reached for her and pulled her up against him. Held her tight, felt her warm and alive and wonderful. They were safe.

His foot throbbed. They were in a room full of dead cats. He had just killed a man.

None of that mattered now. She'd come for him, she'd saved him. They'd saved each other.

He kissed her, and she wrapped her arms around his neck and kissed him back, and maybe this was wrong, considering where they were and what he'd just done, the blood on her lips – both their lips, now – and the ringing of gunshots in his ears. Maybe this was wrong.

But he hadn't felt this happy in a very long time.

42

... Of course I had my hunting jackknife in my pocket the whole time, and a detailed plan about how to insert it into Simon Simons' femoral artery. You knew that, right?

But this was *so* much better.

43

WHEN THE KISS FINISHED, SAFFY tenderly wiped the blood from his lips. 'Are you all right?' she asked.

'Yeah. Yeah, I'm fine.'

But she frowned, and held his face in her hands. 'Don't take this the wrong way, but you look like hell. What did he do to you?'

'He cut off my toe.'

'Holy shit! Does it hurt?'

'No.'

And it didn't. Maybe it was the shock. Maybe it was the kiss. He leaned in for another one.

She stopped him. 'Where's your toe?'

'I don't know.'

'We have to find it! They can reattach it. Which one was it?'

'Little toe, left foot. Simon said—'

Simon said. Simon says. The funny side of it struck him and he started to laugh. He laughed even more as he watched Saffy crawl over the concrete floor, through the blood and gore (that rhymed, even funnier), between the taxidermy cats and Simon's corpse and the remains of his carefully laid-out tools. She had blood all over her, like the last survivor in a horror film, the beautiful girl who somehow lives to feature in the sequel.

But this was real.

His laughter, close in the soundproof room, rang ghastly in his ears. *This was real.* He stopped.

He swallowed hard to stop himself from being sick.

'I found it!' Saffy cried in triumph, and held up a small and terrifyingly familiar piece of flesh. 'We need to get it on ice right away. Can you walk?'

'Yes.' He stood up, felt dizzy, reached for something to steady him but there was nothing except for a cat on a plinth. Saffy hurried over and put her arm around his waist. Slowly, she helped him to the door. As he'd thought, it led to the rest of the basement: incredibly tidy, with a workbench against one wall and concrete stairs going upward. Together they reached the stairs.

'Sit here for a minute,' she told him. 'I'll come back to get you. I just want to grab some ice for this toe.'

He nodded. He should maybe be ashamed that she was so much more competent than he was in this situation, but he wasn't. He was grateful. He sat down on the bottom step and tried not to look at the contents of Simon's workbench. He could hear sirens in the distance, getting closer, very close now. He could hear Saffy's footsteps going upstairs, crossing a room above him.

It was going to be OK. They were safe now. Help was coming.

And then above him, Saffy screamed.

It was Simon. He'd come back to life, like Annie Wilkes in *Misery*, like the final jump scare in the third act. Somehow he'd got upstairs. He was hurting Saffy.

342

Jon scrambled up the stairs. Saffy was still screaming. He lurched into a kitchen, a tidy kitchen with beige tiles and beige units, realising too late that he should have gone back for the gun.

But Simon wasn't in the kitchen. It was just Saffy. She stood in front of a fridge-freezer. It was one of those with the freezer below the fridge. She'd pulled out the top drawer, and even from across the room Jon could see what was inside it, why she was screaming. He could tell because he'd seen several of them already.

It was a frozen head.

44

H E DIDN'T HEAR THE FULL story until he was out of surgery, hours later, his throat and head sore from the anaesthesia but his foot whole again. He had a side room, at a different hospital from where he'd run from the police. It was, ironically, the same hospital he'd been in after Cyril stabbed him.

This time, Saffy sat by his bedside. She'd brought him grapes, chocolate, Evian, Lucozade and a contraband flask with a nip of Ben Nevis because, as she said, 'If you can't have a wee dram after having your toe amputated by a serial killer, when can you?'

She was wearing fresh clothes and she was clean and sweet-smelling and beautiful, though she had bruises on her throat from Simon's hands. She held his hand while DI Atherton took his preliminary statement. From Atherton's demeanour, it was clear that Jon was no longer suspected of murder.

'It was Fanducci's head in the freezer,' he confirmed. 'Along with his hands. And Simons considerately left us a full confession of his crimes, in the form of a podcast script. He admits to poisoning eighteen old-age pensioners. We found his cache of poison, and also some trophies from his victims.'

Jon found he didn't want to know what those were.

'He had dossiers upon dossiers on you,' Atherton told Jon. 'All the clippings about Cyril Walker's arrest. And, we found Edith Mayfair's laptop in his possession.'

'You were right,' Jon told him. 'My work encouraged him.'

'Don't you *dare* say that,' Saffy said, squeezing his hand. Her voice was gravelly from being strangled. He probably shouldn't find it sexy, but he did. 'That man was responsible for his own actions. He would have done what he did whether you had a podcast or not. He was the bad guy. Not you.'

'His confession goes back twelve years,' said Atherton. 'So he was at it before he ever heard of you. We've got a lot to look at, but preliminary enquiries suggest that many, if not all, of the cases weren't considered to be homicide at the time.'

Jon wasn't stupid. He knew that Atherton was offering him absolution from encouraging Simons, if Jon offered the Met absolution from missing a serial killer for a dozen years.

'Did he write about killing Fanducci?' Saffy asked.

'No. His script goes into great detail about the poisonings, but it stops before it gets to anything to do with Fanducci. The last words are, "I'll let Jonathan talk about how I got his attention." It's pretty clear what he meant.'

'He was saving it for dramatic effect,' said Jon.

'And people call me a drama queen,' said Saffy.

Atherton got up. He made as if to leave, and then hesitated. He shoved his hands in the pockets of his coat.

'So that's two serial killers you've caught on my watch,' he said. Reluctantly. 'Maybe when you're up and around, we can meet for a beer.'

'I'd like that,' said Jon.

Epilogue

Y OU KNOW THAT SAYING: *BEHIND every great man is a great woman*? What it really means is this. Behind every man, no matter what his merit, there is a perfectly normal woman working her ass off to make sure that everything works out the way it's supposed to, without getting any of the credit, while the man basks in the praise.

Still. In this case, it worked out pretty well for me, too.

Except that for the foreseeable, while Jon's healing from his surgery, I'm stuck with walking the dog.

It's not all bad. She doesn't like me much, but she'll consent to a ramble around Kensington Gardens so she can sniff the butt of every other dog in London. We've worked out a sort of truce: as long as I don't actually try to stroke her, she'll tolerate my conversation.

Which is good, because she's the perfect listener and I have a lot to say – stuff that I would love to share with Jon, but I have to share with the dog instead, because she can't tell anyone.

'It would be weird if I told him I was turned on by the sight of him covered in blood, wouldn't it?' I ask Girl as she's rooting around in a particularly smelly bush lining a less-than-popular path in the Gardens. She ignores me. 'Yes. I know it's a stupid question. He would think it was weird.' I sigh. 'But can you imagine a universe where he didn't? He says that he had terrible nightmares after Cyril, and panic attacks and everything, but he hasn't had a single one about Simon. He says it's because I'm there with him, which don't get me wrong, is incredibly sweet and makes my heart melt. But ... maybe it's because he's getting used to violence, in certain limited and controlled circumstances.'

Girl ignores me.

'Maybe ... maybe it's because he could get to like it.'

I know. But a girl can dream, can't she?

The headlines have been gratifying. It's a newspaper editor's wet dream: amateur podcaster catches not one, but two serial killers. While Jon's name has been all over the press (and I've had to spend a lot of time talking with him about his feelings about this – footnote: a man who talks about his feelings!!!), the Met was kind enough not to make my own name public. After all, according to them, I was just a victim: someone who stumbled upon the crime while looking for my man, and became a hostage. Not a main player.

The women in these cases are usually the victims, and they often don't have a name, or not one that the public remembers.

It suits me fine, of course. I have my own reasons for staying under the radar. And also, I have a brand-new relationship to enjoy. It's been so long since I had a boyfriend, and I've never had one that I have so much in common with.

And the police have actively been nice to us. Fatima Fanducci has even sent us a thank-you note. I sent her a hamper from Selfridge's full of baby and children's clothes, and a few pampering items for herself. If she ever gets time.

Girl and I move on to an open stretch of park, with no one within earshot.

'I don't mind Jon getting all of the praise,' I say to her. 'But it is a teensy bit galling that Simon is getting so much credit.'

It's my own fault, I know. And at least he's not still alive to deny it. But still.

For instance, Simon was a *terrible* burglar. He had to set Edie's office on fire to cover his traces. Whereas months ago, when I needed to know Jon's address in Scotland, I was in and out of Edie's office without anyone being the wiser. I doubt that even her cats noticed I'd been there.

If I were ever short of cash, that could be an alternate career. It's not going to happen, of course. But I could be like a female Robin Hood. I could rob bad men and give the money to domestic violence shelters. Victim Support. Rape crisis centres. Reproductive health clinics. Or just to badass women who are out there living their best lives.

I picture that happy prospect for a moment. The dog considers a stick on the ground, remembers who she's with, and carries on sniffing.

Breaking into Simon's house was a whole different proposition. I had to deliberately make it messy, which goes against all my instincts, but I knew the police would be looking for a narrative. Desperate girlfriend jimmies open back door, looking for her kidnapped lover. Though it was very satisfying to get Simon's attention by knocking over that table full of shepherdess figurines. They were awful. A crime in themselves.

Girl examines an empty patch of grass thoroughly before peeing on it.

Anyway, burglary competence aside, the thing that causes me just a *little* trickle of annoyance is that Simon got credit for starting this whole thing off by killing Fanducci. The whole idea is so obviously laughable. Fanducci was a bully, and Simon was a coward. He killed cats and old ladies. He never could have killed Fanducci. Let alone dismembered him, or got his body to Jon's doorstep without being seen, dousing the bin bag in Axe on the way so that Jon could solve another murder, and stitch up someone who thoroughly deserved it.

That's the sort of selfless gift that could only be conceived of and executed by a woman in love. It's too bad that Jon will never fully understand the lengths I will go to, to get his attention and advance his career.

'Still,' I tell Girl. 'Credit or not, it's reassuring that the police are so incompetent. Also, it's nice not to have to worry about what to do with Fanducci's head and hands anymore. They served their purpose.'

A group of young people with a football come into sight, and I check my watch. It's time to get back to the house. Jon and I are having our double date tonight, with Susie and Finlay – at a restaurant that's close enough to mine so that Jon can get there easily on his crutches. It's funny, but I haven't wanted to kill Finlay at all for the past week or two. Maybe it's gratitude because he helped me find Simon, or maybe it's that I'm high on endorphins. I'm loved up as hell, and the world is looking like a much kinder place.

Between Fanducci, Cyril and Simon, there are three fewer bad men walking around in the world – and that's all because of me. Not a bad result at all.

I tug on Girl's lead and we head off home. I smile at the football youths. I smile at the trees and the sky, and even at the dog. Everything, from head to toe, has turned out exactly the way I wanted it to.

I really think that Jonathan Desrosiers and I are going to live happily ever after.

THE END

Acknowledgements

With huge thanks to my agent, Teresa Chris, my film and TV agent, Emily Hayward-Whitlock, and to Ben Willis and the entire Bonnier team. I'd also like to thank my girlfriend, my friends, my teenager, my parents, my dog, my ex-husband and my therapist.